THE TOBACCO GIRLS

LIZZIE LANE

Boldwood

First published in Great Britain in 2020 by Boldwood Books Ltd.

Copyright © Lizzie Lane, 2020

Cover Design by The Brewster Project

Cover Photography: Colin Thomas

A CIP catalogue record for this book is available from the British Library.

Paperback ISBN 978-1-80048-490-0

Large Print ISBN 978-1-80048-486-3

Ebook ISBN 978-1-80048-484-9

Kindle ISBN 978-1-80048-485-6

Audio CD ISBN 978-1-80048-491-7

MP3 CD ISBN 978-1-80048-488-7

Digital audio download ISBN 978-1-80048-489-4

Boldwood Books Ltd
23 Bowerdean Street
London SW6 3TN
www.boldwoodbooks.com

Dedicated to my father who worked in the tobacco bonds, my sister Janet who made cigars at Raleigh Road, and my sister-in-law Jean who made cigarettes in East Street.

1

MAISIE MILES

Slight of stature, dark-haired and dark-eyed, fifteen-year-old Maisie Miles was currently engrossed in a world of her own. Though the newspaper sellers and the wireless shouted warnings of war to come, it meant nothing to her.

The world, her surroundings and everything else, was blanked out by the letter she'd almost snatched from the postman's hand. She'd bobbed out of that front door ten times at least that morning, waiting for him to come so she could grab the letter before he had chance to shove it through the letter box. Hopefully it would be her ticket out of York Street, the Dings and the larger area that was St Phillips' Marsh.

The envelope was blue, the paper of a quality she'd never encountered before. The letter inside matched the envelope both in colour and quality.

Her brown eyes glowed and her creamy complexion burst into pinkness as she read the letter for the third time.

Dear Miss Miles,

In response to the reference I received from your teacher Miss

Smith, and the fact that since leaving school you have experienced some domestic work in the kitchen of the Royal Hotel, in Bristol, I am delighted to offer you the position of kitchen maid at Priory House, Long Ashton, which, as I am sure you know, is just outside the city of Bristol and not far from Ashton Court...

Feeling sublimely happy, Maisie closed her eyes and held the letter to her heart. Bliss. Green fields and trees. She'd never been to Ashton Court, but the redoubtable Miss Smith had told her that the sumptuous mansion had been built with the proceeds of a vast sugar plantation on the island of Jamaica.

The letter had come from the housekeeper who was known personally to Miss Smith.

'A much respected acquaintance,' she had told Maisie. 'It's a private house, so only glimpsed through the gates.'

It was obvious from her tone that Miss Smith herself had never been into the house but would very much like to.

For her part, Maisie wasn't interested in the house. It was the prospect of fresh air far away from the stink of York Street which attracted her.

The house she'd grown up in was situated in the Dings, a subdistrict of St Phillips, a less than salubrious area of Bristol, where the air was thick with the stench of bone yards, soap works and slaughter houses.

Added to the cloying stench was the deafening rattle from the marshalling yards stretching from Midland Road to Lawrence Hill, a sprawling expanse of glistening rails linking the Great Western Railway with the Midland Railway. Like the smell, the railway never ceased: the goods trucks shunting backwards and forwards, chains clanking, metal rails squealing beneath metal wheels. Of late it had been busier and nosier than usual. The old man, the old sod, her father, declared it was all to do with impending war because it said so in the papers. As if he would know! She'd never seen him read anything. It was more likely he'd heard the newspaper vendor shouting out the news from his pitch outside the Kings' Cinema in Old Market.

Maisie didn't care. All she wanted was to get away to something better.

There was nothing attractive about number five, York Street. It had a yard at the back, a patch of dusty dirt between the back of the house and the brick privy that lurched against the far wall. It was a place of mouldy walls and cramped rooms, packed with shabby furniture and a cold hearth that even when lit did little to warm one room, let alone the whole house.

'What you got there?' Suddenly the very air was ripe with menace.

Absorbed in the letter and her future, she hadn't heard her father, Frank Miles, rouse himself from the old cracked sofa in the living room.

Pushing her with one hefty hand, he grabbed the letter with the other.

Maisie did her best to snatch it back, but was brushed so roughly aside that she crashed heavily against the wall and a patch of flaking plaster crumpled into her hair.

Bleary-eyed, he blinked at the letter, mouthing the words as he read each one like a child who cannot quite understand his letters.

'What the bleedin' 'ell's this about then?'

His accent was heavy. His flabby jowls quivered and his bloodshot eyes fixed her with a familiar look, the kind usually followed with a cuff round the ear or a punch to her shoulder. In his youth, he might have been a handsome man, but booze and smoking, plus the advent of age, had blunted all that.

The circumstances of her upbringing and ongoing abuse had

toughened Maisie. She gathered her courage, folded her arms in front of her and held her chin high. He scared her, but to show fear would only make things worse.

'I've got a job in Long Ashton as a kitchen maid. I'll be living in. The job at the Royal was alright, but this is better. You won't have to keep me any longer and you'll have more room.' Pointing out the advantages to him was the only hope she had of getting him to fall in with what she wanted.

For a moment, he stared at her, then burst out laughing.

'You ain't goin' anywhere! Think I've kept you all these bloody years to be a kitchen maid? I want paying back, so you, my girl, is going to work at Wills's. I wants yer wages and I wants the free fags you'll be getting.'

Fear seeped into her defiance, but Maisie still managed to shake her head. 'I ain't working in a factory. I wants to go and live in the country. That's what I'm going to do.'

Frank Miles's fleshy lips sprawled into a cruel grin. His face was greasy with sweat. 'Well, you ain't doing that.' His tone was spiced with the pleasure he derived from being cruel, as there, before her very eyes, he tore the letter into quarters, struck a match and set it alight.

'No!' Maisie sprang forward, stabbing her fingers into the flame but was too late to save a single word. The letter that had promised her a different world fluttered like black feathers to the floor.

In a trice, her father took hold of her by the throat with one meaty hand. His eyes glared into hers. 'You owe me for looking after you. Now I wants me dues.'

She grabbed at his hand, trying to unwind those fingers from her throat before he squeezed the life out of her. Her mouth opened and shut like a fish gasping for air.

'I'm your daughter,' she wanted to shout, but it came out as a faltering gasp.

'Are you?' he snarled. 'Are you?'

For one dreadful moment, she thought he was going to kill her. There was such hatred in his eyes. There had been other times when she'd seen that look, when his hand had cuffed her head and sent her sprawling. This time was worse.

The clanking of beer bottles heralded the arrival of her mother. Her father threw her aside and she rubbed at the soreness of her neck, still gasping for breath.

Her mother, a cigarette hanging from the corner of her mouth, struggled in with a large leather bag.

Frank Miles turned his bad temper on her. 'You bin some time. Should 'ave bin back long before now.'

As usual, her mother pretended nothing was wrong, lifting the bag onto the table as though it was the most important task in the world. In a way, it was. Frank liked his beer and Gwen Miles always did her best to keep on the right side of him. To do otherwise and she'd be the one getting a beating.

'The off-licence was busy. I 'ad to wait and then everybody was looking up at that plane. Did you see it? A Bristol Beaufighter, that's what they said it was called. There's loads of them being made out at Filton in case there's a war, but the one that flew today is the first one. Everyone was dead excited that it was being built 'ere and that there might be a war...'

Frank Miles raised a threatening fist. 'Well, I ain't! You goes on an errand and gets back 'ere. You don't spend yer time gawping up at the bloody sky!'

Gwen Miles flinched and barely glanced in Maisie's direction because she dared not. The bloke she wished she never married had a short temper and liked lashing out. Any sign of sympathy for her daughter would result in her receiving a black eye, a broken finger.

'This stupid cow,' he said, pointing a yellow stained finger at Maisie, 'put 'erself down for a job as a bleedin' kitchen maid at some fancy country 'ouse.'

Her mother blinked, looked at Maisie, then back again at her husband, afraid to say the wrong thing.

'What sort of 'ouse was it then?' she tried.

'That's not the point!' he shouted straight into her face. 'She ain't leavin' 'ere. She's lived under my roof all 'er life and I wants paying back.'

Her mother winced and her face visibly paled. She'd always been paler than Maisie, but of late there was a greyish tinge. The only brighter spots of colour were when she was sporting the blue and yellow of a black eye.

'So what you got in mind?' she asked, her eyes avoiding those of her daughter, her hands trembling with nerves.

'I'll tell you what I've got in mind,' he said, purposely standing between Maisie and the door. 'Tomorrow you take your daughter along to the Labour Exchange and get her taken on at Wills's.'

'Oh, I don't know about that,' she said, frowning as she took off her headscarf. 'I don't know that they're taking anyone on.'

She seemed suddenly diminished in size when Frank Miles pressed his face close to hers.

'Of course they're takin' on, you stupid cow. Wills's are always taking on. Now you take 'er down there tomorrow.

Her chest heaving with anger and disappointment, Maisie took advantage of the situation and dashed for the door.

Her father's angry voice shouted after her. 'Oi! I ain't finished with you.'

But Maisie didn't stop. She headed for the railway bridge in Midland Road, staring down onto the railway lines as she wondered at the hopelessness of her life. The lure of working in the country far away from here had buoyed up her spirits during the weeks before she'd left school.

'It's just a matter of time before you get a reply,' her teacher had said. 'You're intelligent and always do your best and with my help I'm sure you'll get the job.'

Her teacher had been right on one count but had presumed her parents would be pleased. The trouble was Miss Smith was a gentle soul and had no real idea of what they were like, how mean and cruel her father was and how downtrodden her mother.

A pair of arms joined hers in leaning on the bridge parapet. An elbow nudged her arm. 'Ain't gonna throw yerself over, are you?'

'Nobody would care if I did.'

'You're my favourite little sister. I'd be gutted.'

'I'm yer only sister,' she responded.

Alf laughed. 'That's true.'

He was her older brother. He had a wicked grin, a handsome face and his looks were totally the opposite to her own. Whereas she was short with a mass of curly black hair and brown eyes, he was tall with blue eyes and corn-coloured hair. His fingers were long, his nails clean and neatly trimmed. His only flaw was that he followed where his father led, both made a living by stealing, either from commercial premises or from the posh houses in Clifton on the north side of the river overlooking the Avon Gorge. The river ran far below those houses, spanned from one side to the other by the Clifton Suspension Bridge, a wonder of Victorian engineering built by the great engineer, Isambard Kingdom Brunel. The big difference between father and son was that Alf had never been violent towards either her or her mother. He could be tough, but not with his own family.

Maisie turned and looked at her brother's handsome profile, saw his well-combed hair, his tailored double-breasted suit. Her nose twitched at the heady scent of cologne.

'Where you bin then?' she asked.

Her brother flicked the stub of a cigarette down onto the railway line. 'With friends.'

'Lucky you. Wish I 'ad some friends,' she said glumly.

The truth was that she did have friends, though only at school. They'd kept their distance from her and her family. The Miles family had a reputation and she'd heard rumours of her father's wandering hands.

Alf offered her a cigarette. 'It'll calm you down and you can tell me all about it.'

'If I smoke, I'll end up smelling like our dad. He stinks. I hate 'im.'

'Ah!' Alf exclaimed. 'So that's why yer out 'ere. The old bugger's 'ad a go at you. Come on. Tell me all about it.'

Alf was the only bright spark in her life. Maisie's narrow shoulders, stiff with tension up until his arrival, began to relax as she told him why she was out here feeling her life was at an end before it had even started.

'I want to get away from yer, Alf, but that old bugger won't let me.'

Her brother listened patiently and with kindness in his eyes. His little sister was the only female he truly loved. He could remember her as a baby lying in a cot covered by a thin blanket and sucking on an old Camp coffee bottle filled with milk. The funny thing was although he was old enough to do so, he couldn't recall his mother being pregnant – in fact, he couldn't recall those months before her birth at all.

He remained silent for a while once she'd finished what she was saying, then, as though he'd come to a conclusion, he took out a packet of Passing Cloud – one of the best W. D. & H. O. Wills produced and made only from the finest Virginia tobacco. Alf took great pride in smoking something made from tobacco produced in the United States of America. It had come all the way across the Atlantic to Avonmouth, Bristol's larger port that sprawled at the mouth of the river. Ships still did make their way beneath the Clifton Suspension Bridge and up the river, but those who discharged their cargoes at Avonmouth were too large to navigate its treacherous bends and glutinous mudbanks.

Alf liked hearing sailors' tales of where those ships had been – places he'd never heard of that fired his imagination.

'It ain't the end of the world,' Alf finally said. 'You'll be well paid and you'll make good friends at Wills's.' He lowered his head so that his blue eyes were looking directly into her brown ones. 'I'm tellin' you the truth, ar Maisie. You've only just left school, but believe me, you'll find yer feet and make the most of things. You'll make good mates too. I guarantee it. Give it a bit of time and if a war starts there might not be any factory. They reckon they'll be more bombs than the last war. Might see the end of this place too.' He jerked his chin into the night.

As though in response, the lonely screech of a train whistle split the night. The lights were on in the marshalling yards, black shapes moving around in clouds of steam even at this time of night.

Like hell, she thought, and wondered if something much better might replace it.

2

BRIDGET MILLIGAN

Bridget wasn't sure what time it was when her eyes flicked open, but she did know some strange low sound had disturbed her and she had to see what it was.

The first thing she did was to check her two sisters with whom she shared a double bed. They were both sound asleep, their gentle breathing warm and soft against the palm of her hand.

Katy was seven, a rosy cheeked little girl with chubby hands and a rosebud mouth. Ruby was ten, darker haired and like her siblings, Bridget included, possessing the brightest of blue eyes.

Bridget smiled. The family of seven children and two adults were crammed into three bedrooms and the house was always noisy, mealtimes a scramble to grab what you could before it was all gone. Some of their neighbours looked down their noses at the Milligan family. Bridget had heard their comments.

'Typical Irish. 'Im an' 'er should learn to control theirselves.'

For the most part she ignored the remarks, but sometimes, just sometimes, she lashed out.

'Hypocrites! At least our little 'uns aren't hanging around outside pub doors, waiting for their parents to come out!'

Bridget prided herself on her use of words and although she was of a serene disposition, she stuck up for her family and what she believed in.

The sound persisted and it worried her. She remembered another time, something similar, the cries of pain...She shook the memory from her mind. Her mother had been pregnant and she was pregnant again.

Being careful not to disturb them, she swung her legs out of bed and went to check on her two youngest sisters, six-year-old Mary and five-year-old Molly who slept top and tail in a single bed on the far side of the room. One of them murmured for water. Bridget took the mug of water kept on the window ledge for such eventualities and let her sister take a sip before lowering her head back down on the pillow.

Thinking there might be something happening in the street outside, she peered out of the open window. Nothing stirred in any of the unending council houses lining Marksbury Road. There were many such houses built by Bristol City Council to house a growing population that expected more after the carnage of the Great War.

The low murmuring continued, so Bridget decided to check on Sean and Michael, her two brothers, who shared a three-quarter-size bed in the box room.

Taking great care, she opened the bedroom door and stepped out onto the landing. Before she had chance to check the boys, her parents' bedroom door opened and her father appeared. He was in his pyjamas, one leg of which was empty, which meant his false leg was still propped in position at the side of the bed.

Even in the semi-gloom of the landing, she could see the anxious look on his face.

'The babby's coming too early,' he gasped. 'Your mother needs you.'

Nausea prompted by fear formed a knot in Bridget's stomach. 'Dad, I don't know nothing about bringing babies into the world. I'll run for Mrs Knight.'

The truth be told, she would run for anyone who could help. She'd seen her mother give birth to her youngest brother and felt sick at the sight of it. How could any woman go through such pain? And the gore? The stench of a body expelling bloody innards?

Her mother cried out, 'Bridget. Me girl. I need you. I need you, Bridie!'

Bridie was the affectionate term of address her mother kept for special occasions, those when she was doubly proud of her, like when she won the history prize at school – which she seemed to do every year without fail. Being called by that name had always made her feel special, which was why she couldn't ignore it now.

Carefully, so as not to knock over her father, who had lost his leg during the Great War, she eased past him into the room.

Once the door was closed behind them, the main light was switched on.

'Should I get water?' asked her father.

He sounded very panicked for a man who had fathered a family of seven children.

Mary Milligan, Bridget's mother, intervened, 'It's too early, Patrick. Do you hear me? It won't live. Just over six months,' she said to her daughter before her eyes closed and she gritted her teeth against the pain.

Bridget told her father to strap on his leg and fetch up a pile of old newspapers. 'And a bucket of water. Not too hot. Not too cold.'

Same as the last time, she thought. Though she sounded brave, inside she was remembering how it had been before. The prospect of what was about to happen had scared her then and it still scared her now.

Once he was gone, her mother pushed down the bedclothes and told Bridget to pull up her nightgown.

Bridget winced. Her mother's belly was criss-crossed with purple streaks. It was also heaving from side to side and downwards towards her mother's thick bush of pubic hair.

The room seemed hotter than it was, yet the windows were wide open, the early-morning Sunday air gently lifting the curtains.

Bridget clenched her fists and with anxious eyes regarded her mother's face. She looked drained and in dreadful pain, which made Bridget feel doubly helpless and also aware that the heat she was feeling was her own fear.

The sound of clunking from the stairs heralded the return of her father. With great dexterity, he closed the door behind him with his tin foot, one arm tucked around a bundle of newspapers, the other carrying a bucket of warm water. A clean towel was draped over his shoulder.

'Anything happened?' he asked nervously.

Bridget thought how boyish he looked and understood why her mother had fallen for him and allowed him to give her so many children.

Too many, Bridget thought to herself.

Before she could answer, her father had retreated to the door. 'I'd better go, I suppose.'

'You'll do no such thing,' said Bridget. 'I'll lift her hips and you spread the newspaper underneath her.'

Her father's jaw dropped, though only momentarily. It wasn't usually done for a father to be present at a birth – or a miscarriage, but Patrick Milligan was a resilient chap, and besides, this was his wife lying here in pain.

Having a care for her mother's modesty, Bridget pulled the voluminous nightgown down.

'I think I can manage,' her mother whispered.

Nevertheless, Bridget helped her lift her loins whilst her father slid the newspaper beneath her rump.

Almost immediately there was a rush of blood and fluid.

'More newspaper,' Bridget demanded, keeping her voice low so her siblings wouldn't wake up and see their mother in this painful and immodest state.

Her mother groaned through gritted teeth, her jaw so tense it seemed as though it would break under the pressure.

With a final rush of fluid and blood, the baby slid out onto the newspaper.

Mary Milligan's chest heaved, her breath coming in quick rasps as her body sought to regain normality, refresh the energy and blood that she'd lost.

Patrick Milligan went to his wife's side. 'Tis all over, me darlin'. Tis all over.'

Mary's eyes fluttered and a smile that was as much sadness as relief creased her tired lips. 'It's too early for it to live,' said Bridget's mother. She looked directly at her daughter as though expecting an answer.

Bridget hesitated before wrapping the bloodied form in the newspaper. She was no expert, but she could see that something was very wrong. The baby's spine was like a herring bone with the flesh peeled off. It was ill formed, bringing Bridget to the conclusion that even if the pregnancy had gone full term, the baby, a boy, would not have lived.

A slight crying came from one of the other bedrooms.

'It's one of the boys,' she said to her father.

He nodded and went to deal with whatever the problem was.

Bridget wrapped the small corpse in one layer after another before tending to her mother's needs, pulling out the afterbirth, reaching for more newspaper, washing her mother and applying a sanitary dressing.

She felt her mother's eyes looking at her.

'You're a good girl, Bridie. I'll be there for you when your babes are aching to be born.'

Bridget, sweat running down her face, paused in what she was doing. Her mother noticed her pained expression and misinterpreted.

'Don't worry. You're a fair-looking girl and one day you'll find the love of your life, just as I did your father. And you'll have babies for him. Trust me, girl. You will.' Her mother sighed and her eyes closed in welcome sleep.

As she waited for her father to take them for disposal, Bridget stared at the bundle containing a baby, the other the afterbirth. Her mouth felt dry and her stomach heaved with nausea. Just eighteen years of age and this was the second time she'd been present during one of her mother's pregnancies. The first time had disgusted her. This second one had chilled her to the bone and brought her to a determined conclusion.

She would never allow herself to go through this, and if that meant never falling in love and getting married, then so be it.

* * *

A few hours later, the worst was over and her mother was threatening to get up despite the traumatic event she'd just gone through. Bridget insisted she stayed in bed.

'I'll do breakfast then take the kids out somewhere.'

'Oh yes,' sighed her mother and managed a weak smile. 'Take

them to Vicky Park. A bit of fresh air will do them good. Now stop fussing with them pillows and get yourself some breakfast.'

Bridget stopped fussing with the pillows but didn't remark that the last thing she wanted was breakfast. No matter the fresh air doing the kids some good, it would do her good too.

'It's a nice day, so I thought I might take them for a picnic on Brandon Hill. We can get a tram to the centre and walk up from there.'

Her mother's watery smile tugged at her heart. 'Yes,' she said, her voice as weak as her smile. 'That would be nice. There's a lovely view from up there.'

After telling her mother to get some rest and not to worry, Bridget closed the bedroom door.

Her father had already started organising breakfast, though was cutting the bread too quickly. Bridget took the knife from him before he could do more damage. With expert precision, she began to cut the thicker slices into two.

'I need some for sandwiches,' she said to him. 'We're going on a picnic. Do you hear that, kids? We're going on a picnic.'

A mix of hoorays, laughter and excited chatter erupted.

Her father looked at her gratefully, and she had no doubt there were tears in his eyes. 'You're a good girl, Bridget. Whoever marries you is going to get the best woman in the world.'

Bridget looked away, her lips set in a straight line because her father's hope was his and not hers. Never could she envisage becoming a wife but couldn't put the terror she felt into words. Her mother had given birth to one child after another. She'd heard the groans, sometimes the screams, and knew she never wanted to go through that kind of pain. After the rigours of the early hours of this morning, she was doubly sure.

* * *

The fresh air of Brandon Hill went some way to clearing her head though did little to diminish the smells, the sounds and the consequences. Bridget felt great joy watching her brothers and sisters peeling off their shoes and socks and running bare-footed through the grass. It pleased her that they had no knowledge of what had happened earlier. They were children and should stay that way for as long as possible.

She'd brought two bottles of sherbet mixed with water contained in two old Tizer bottles with clip-down lids. Everything was spread out on an old tablecloth and no invitation to eat was needed. Everyone was ravenous.

Once it was all gone, they lay back in the grass, looking up at the blue sky, or sat up and gazing at the city spires.

'There's a lot of churches,' said twelve-year-old Sean, the eldest of her two brothers.

Bridget was a great reader and if funds had allowed would have liked to be a teacher. As it was, she had to stick to reading; any book she came across devoured with great gusto. It was at times like these that she passed on the information she had learned. 'Bristol was called the city of churches. It had so many, and the most beautiful is St Mary Redcliffe.'

'Who said so?' asked Michael, who was nine and beginning to question everything.

'Queen Elizabeth the First back in the sixteenth century.'

Michael jerked his chin at the edifice behind them that dominated Brandon Hill. 'What about this tower? Is that a church?'

'No. I told you before we came that it's called Cabot Tower. It was named after a fifteenth-century explorer who discovered America – not just the islands of the Caribbean like Columbus a couple of years before him, but the continent of America. It's said he landed at a place he christened Newfoundland. You see? New Found Land.'

It was always wise to get in with an answer before Michael could actually ask the question.

It was time to go home and they were packing up, the sun dipping into the skyline when a whole chorus of church bells rang out over the city, inviting the faithful to evensong, but not the Milligan family, or at least not all of them. Her mother was a regular at mass, but her father was not. Neither did he insist on his children going, though her mother usually managed to take the younger ones with her – until they rebelled and followed her father's line: 'Your conscience is your own and for you to answer to.'

A smell of smoke greeted them when they got back to Marksbury Road.

'No roast dinner today,' Bridget said to the kids. 'It's cold meat and bread and dripping and I think there's some blancmange left.'

Too tired to complain, her siblings tucked in.

Presuming her mother was hungry, she spread beef dripping onto a slice of bread and along with a cup of tea took it up to her mother.

'Thought you might need this,' she said with a cheery smile.

It wasn't entirely a surprise to see her mother sitting up in bed, nestled into a knitted bed jacket. She'd bounded back the last time too, her concerns for the family outweighing any personal considerations.

'Put it there,' she said, patting a place on the eiderdown. 'So how was Brandon Hill?'

'We left the grass a bit downtrodden but Cabot Tower's still intact,' she said with a smile. 'Can I get you anything else, Ma?'

'No. This will do fine,' said her mother as she sipped at her tea.

Both ignored the smell of bonfire smoke drifting in through

the open window. Dusk was falling by the time Bridget was going downstairs with the empty cup and plate.

She left them in the kitchen and went out to where her father was prodding at a blazing bonfire, the source of the smoke that was lazily curling upwards.

A lump came to her throat when she looked down at the fire. Together they stood there silently, neither needing to use words to state how they were feeling. As the last of the burning bundles turned to ash, Bridget dared look at her father's face and saw the tears streaming down his cheeks.

3

PHYLLIS MASON

Phyllis had reddish hair, greenish eyes and a heartfelt ambition to go to work in smart clothes rather than an overall.

'Know your place,' her mother had declared when she'd dared mention enrolling on a typing course. 'Stop trying to be better than you are. Working class you were born and working class you'll remain.'

That was the end of the matter as far as her mother was concerned, but no matter how she tried, Phyllis couldn't get the idea out of her mind so she applied anyway.

Her mother, Stella Mason, believed her advice sound; Phyllis had a good job at the tobacco factory and was engaged to Robert who wasn't exciting but was dependable. What more could she want?

With her heart in her mouth she posted off her request for details, though not without letting her best friend Bridget Mulligan in on the secret.

'I don't want it delivered 'ere or me Mum will chuck it in the bin.'

It was arranged for it to be delivered to Bridget's which wasn't that far from where Phyllis lived with her mother.

The letter finally got to her on Sunday morning luckily coinciding with Sunday morning service at the Methodist Chapel. Not that her mother was that religious but as a widow it was one of the few occasions she went out that wasn't for shopping.

'It's a bit of company,' she'd said when squeezing her hair beneath her 'church' hat, a black sombre affair with a bunch of green feathers at the side. 'Now you'll be alright 'til I get back, won't you?'

Of course she would. As luck would have it the brown manila envelope she'd been expecting had arrived second post at the Milligan house on Saturday. It didn't get to her until Sunday morning, the best time it could possibly arrive.

She opened the door to Sean, the eldest of Bridget's two brothers. His hair looked freshly combed and he was wearing his best clothes.

'Hello, Sean. Are you off to mass, then?'

He shivered when he shook his head as though the very idea frightened him to death.

'Not today!' He beamed gratefully. 'Our Bridie can't come. She's gettin' the food ready to take us on a picnic as our mum's not well.'

'Have a good time,' she called after him after taking the envelope.

Then he was gone, his feet kicking out furiously behind him as though that alone would put wings on his feet.

'What's 'e doin' 'ere?' Her mother was back. Another few minutes and she would not have known of the letter's arrival. A few minutes, thought Phyllis as she half closed her eyes. Why couldn't God have kept you at chapel a bit longer? Realising that her good luck had suddenly turned bad, Phyllis's heart beat faster and it was hard not to look guilty.

Her mother frowned at the envelope.

'Are you going to open that or what?' said her mother as she took off her hat before stabbing it with a hat pin.

'It's not that important,' Phyllis said in a nonchalant manner, though in actuality she thought it the most important thing she'd done in her life.

She felt her mother's hard look, eyes as sharp as knives, lips set in a firm pout. Stella Mason liked to know whatever her daughter was up to.

'I'm not interfering. I've just got your best interests at heart, Phyllis. So listen to your mother. Mother knows best!' The same stanza was so frequently repeated that Phyllis could recite it off by heart.

Phyllis felt the full force of those shrew-like eyes dissecting her as sharply and ably as a surgeon's knife.

'If it's anything to do with that business about learning to type, I'd throw it in the bin if I were you. Robert wouldn't like it. Men don't like their wives to work and Robert's no exception, so I'm telling you, my girl, it's too late in the day for you to be thinking about learning anything. Like every other girl, you're going to be a housewife and mother. What's the point of being anything else? You've got your man. Leave it at that.'

She'd guessed right and feeling great shame at being found out, Phyllis turned guiltily away, protectively holding the envelope against her chest.

She took a deep breath and said what she already knew would be a lie. 'You're right. I shouldn't have bothered. I'll throw it in the bin.'

'No. You should not have bothered,' her mother exclaimed. 'Robert's got a good job. He'll never be unemployed. There'll always be a meal on the table married to a bloke like him. He hasn't got a head full of wild ideas. Not like your father. Not like him at all.' The last words were delivered through gritted teeth.

Part of Phyllis wanted to stick up for her father. He'd done his best. How was he to know that labouring on the Canadian wheat prairies would dry up, that the harvest would fail, that the Depression would affect the whole world? Neither was he to know that the Canadian Government would pass a bill effectively deporting the unemployed and others who dared claim public funds.

But he did try to better himself, she wanted to say. He did try, and she too wanted to try.

Gripping the brown manila envelope with both hands, Phyllis went out back to where a zinc ashbin sat next to the door to the coalhouse. At first, she hesitated, lid in one hand, envelope in the other. Then she thought of Celia Ward Bond, a secretary in the offices at W. D. & H. O. Wills, who she'd seen from a distance, notebook in hand, trailing along behind a member of management. She'd looked both efficient and glamorous, in her navy-blue suit, her glossy blonde hair fashioned into an elegant chignon at the nape of her neck.

And I bet she doesn't smell of tobacco, Phyllis thought to herself. Only the girls on the factory floor smelt of tobacco, the dust settling in their hair and on their clothes despite wearing overalls.

At least there was Bridget and all the other girls. At times it felt like one big family, everybody supporting each other. She could see their faces, hear their laughter and giggle at their jokes.

Still, she thought, I'll still see them. Sometimes.

There was Robert to consider, of course. He might not approve, but she was sure she could persuade him to see her point of view. If he loved her, he would, and besides, he worked in an office himself. Surely he would eventually understand and even be proud of her ambition to be something more than a girl stripping tobacco leaves. She wanted to be Celia Ward Bond.

In a moment of instant decision that she might in time regret, Phyllis set down the dustbin lid, folded the envelope and shoved it inside her blouse. Just to make sure it was believed she had disposed of it, she lifted the lid and banged it down onto the bin loudly enough for her mother to hear. She would keep the letter, think about it and perhaps in time she would post it off or resign it to the bin just as her mother advised.

Robert was coming round to take her out at six thirty and Phyllis was almost ready. She was just about to apply lipstick when she sensed her mother eyeing her with a mixture of disapproval and surprise.

'Aren't you forgetting something?' Her tone of voice was as disapproving as her look. 'You know Robert doesn't like you wearing lipstick.'

Her hand paused in mid-action. Robert Harvey didn't like her wearing any kind of make-up.

Phyllis sighed and slid the lipstick into her handbag. He wouldn't know it was there and perhaps might not notice if she put some on during the evening.

The spring on the front gate squeaked, heralding his arrival.

'I'll get it,' said her mother before he had chance to knock at the door.

Her mother's words of welcome drifted into the living room.

'Robert, how nice to see you. Phyllis is nearly ready.'

'Good evening, Mrs Mason. I trust you're keeping well?'

She heard her mother's response, accompanied by a tinkling

laugh, and it almost sounded as though her mother was the one he was courting.

Robert entered the living room, oozing self-assurance and smelling of Brylcreem. He was tall and lean, his back ramrod straight and his sandy-coloured hair was matched by his eyelashes. Large blue eyes scrutinised her hair, her dress and even the shoes she was wearing. He'd never used to do that, not until they'd become engaged. Now he scrutinised her and made comment as though it was his God given right to do so.

With a nervous smile Phyllis waited for him to find some imperfection in her appearance for no matter how good she thought she looked, there always seemed to be something that wasn't right – at least in his eyes. At first, she'd laughed off his comments, but with time found herself half believing that her choice of clothes, hairstyle or make-up was common. The result was that she found herself more diminished and more unsure of herself.

'Your dress is very nice,' Robert said as though he was an expert on women's fashion. Her dress was green and scattered with white daisies, the collar a chaste Peter Pan-style in white, with matching cuffs.

Phyllis was always pleased when he remarked favourably upon her dress and for a moment she was elated – until a frown appeared on his face and he commented on her hair, a coppery glow of colour which tonight bounced loosely on her shoulders.

'It's a bit breezy out. You might want to think about tying your hair back. Putting it up in a bun or something more respectable.'

'I said the same myself,' said Phyllis's mother, rubbing her hands together, her eyes bright with enthusiasm for this young man who she believed was the best offer her daughter would ever get. 'Here. Let me deal with it.'

The tumbling mane that Phyllis had been so proud of was

none too gently fastened up with pins and then bundled into a black snood. The colour didn't go with the dress, but she couldn't find the courage to stand up for herself. That's how it always was. Her mother approved of everything Robert said and did as though being the son of a fellow member of the church congregation made him an expert on everything.

Somehow, Phyllis had slipped into the habit of going out with him and couldn't quite recall the exact circumstances of their first date. She'd looked up to him back then, preened in the comments and envious looks of other girls.

'Such a strong personality,' her mother had said. Only now it seemed something different than strong. It was as though she couldn't get out from beneath a great weight that was becoming heavier and totally inescapable. She was trapped and couldn't get out.

Confused and drained of self-pride, Phyllis felt like an obedient little dog as she followed him down the garden path. As yet he had not told her where they were going. Once they were out on Marksbury Road, she dared ask him.

'Engineers' Arms,' he replied without hesitation He strode along purposefully, eyes straight ahead, her arm held tightly to his side.

Her heart sank. Robert was nothing if not predictable.

'We always go there. Can't we go somewhere else?'

'I like it there. It's a good pint and, anyway, I've got to see Roger about the skittles on Friday and Bill about the cricket match on Saturday. Wouldn't want to miss either of them now, would I.' He said it loftily and as though what he wanted was automatically what she wanted. The world, she thought, seen through his eyes.

'If that's what you want.' The words stuck in her throat.

'Best get used to my timetable now before we're married, then you'll know exactly where I am any night of the week – or weekend come to that – so you can plan meals and suchlike without any problem. Easy for you. Easy for me too, I like to know what I'm eating on any given night when I get home after a hard day's work.'

His words were clipped, rattling inside her head like ricocheting bullets. Her mouth was dry and it was hard to tell him how she wanted things to be.

Any given night? What did that mean? Cold meat and pickles on Monday, meat and onion pie on Tuesday, eggs and chips on Wednesday...

She balked at the thought of being so predictable.

'I could work too,' she said with a sudden burst of courage and her brightest smile. 'Not all women give up work when they get married.'

'Not my wife!' The stridency of his voice made her jump.

She kept reminding herself that he was a good catch. Everybody said so. She imagined how it would be to go to bed with him, the one thing he rarely mentioned, except that he expected her to do her wifely duties.

Duty was the word her mother used too. But what about love, she wanted to ask. What about passion?

She could feel the warmth of his thigh against hers as they walked along, his stride longer than hers. She glanced at his profile, the high forehead, the aquiline nose and fleshy wide mouth. Had she ever thought him handsome? She couldn't remember thinking that. What she did remember were the looks other girls gave him, how they thought him a real dish, a real catch. Would they be so keen once they got to know him, to be told what make-up and clothes to wear?

The manila envelope loomed large in her thoughts. Not wanting her mother to know she hadn't thrown it away she'd hidden it beneath her underwear back in her bedroom. The very thought of achieving a qualification and a better job excited her. On the other hand, perhaps she should be grateful that a man wanted to marry her. It was what every girl dreamed of. Could she really live with Robert for the rest of her life? A set timetable of meals for all eternity?

Am I unnatural? Phyllis wondered. Of late, she really preferred to be with the friendly crowd she worked with rather than with Robert. Was it just him? Was there another man out there who would sweep her off her feet so she would gladly give up her job and her friends?

The thoughts intensified. She fancied the engagement ring he'd given her was making her finger itch and she wondered whether it was some kind of signal that it shouldn't be there.

For the rest of that evening at the Engineer's Arms, she sat with her single drink amongst the others like her, girlfriends, some of whom were on the brink of becoming wives. She flicked her thumb at the offending finger. The itchiness had gone, but not the doubts connected with it.

* * *

Robert kissed her goodbye at the garden gate and waved at the living-room window on the assumption that her mother was looking out, waiting for her to come home.

'Goodnight. I'll see you during the week.'

Phyllis smiled and readily agreed, but her mind was on Friday, payday, when the girls she worked with went out on the town. She badly wanted to be with them and somehow determined that she would.

Her mother was waiting. 'Nice night?' she asked, a look of self-satisfaction on her sharp features.

'Yes,' replied Phyllis. At the same she tried to find any aspect of the night that might be regarded as *nice,* but couldn't. It had been routine. Boring.

Her room overlooked the back garden and the red roofs of many other houses on the council estate. The red brick glistened when wet and the privet hedges were dotted with sweet-smelling flowers.

Beyond the rooftops, Phyllis could see ranks of Victorian terraced houses rising up to Windmill Hill. Lights twinkled from their windows and the glow of sodium lamps splashed patches of orange along the main road. Not that she was really seeing any of it. In her mind, she was wondering at a different future than she'd envisaged that didn't seem as plainly mapped out as she'd once thought.

4

BRIDGET, PHYLLIS AND MAISIE

Despite her despicable home life, it wasn't in Maisie's nature to be nervous, but she was today, her first day of employment at W. D. & H. O. Wills.

The woman who'd filled in the forms and given her an overall also gave her a brochure.

'This is number one factory and only produces cigarettes such as Passing Cloud, Capstan and the very popular Woodbine. Castella and Whiffs are made in the cigar factory at Raleigh Road, Ashton. Your job will be stripping the leaves that go to make our most popular brands. The very best leaves come from Virginia, a state of the United States of America. Other brands used in blends come from Rhodesia and India.'

Maisie was only half listening. Even before entering its grand portals, she'd decided to hate this place and escape just as quickly as she could.

The building resembled a huge temple peopled by many workers, so much noise, so much movement. Even outside, before stepping through the door, she'd watched as big wooden casks of tobacco were rolled into the works by sweating men in dark brown overalls.

The woman, who wore a badge saying her name was Miss Cayford and that she was a supervisor, saw her looking and made further comment. 'W. D. and H. O. Wills employ 13,000 people in this city alone and they're all very well looked after. Your hours will be from seven o'clock in the morning until ten minutes past five at night. There is a twenty minute tea break in the morning and one hour for a cooked lunch which is free for all employees. You will start on a wage of three pounds a week and can earn an extra halfpenny for every extra pound of leaves stripped. There are other factories scattered throughout the country – Swindon, Glasgow, Newcastle. The tobacco comes in to the bonded warehouses down on the Cumberland Basin, where the casks are weighed and the customs tariff applied. There's a tax on tobacco, you see.'

Maisie looked around her with a mixture of amazement and fear. The inside of the tobacco factory was huge and hummed with sound. Not having been brought up in the Bedminster area, she'd never been in such a place before. The factories close to where she lived were tiny in comparison and made her feel tiny, as though she had landed here from a foreign land.

The warm air was thick with dust which tasted and smelt slightly sweet. Fat iron pillars were spaced at regular intervals, holding aloft a fairly low ceiling. Both ceiling and walls were painted a soft cream and the opaque glass in the windows – at least at the front of the building – let in a surprising amount of light from outside.

'Come this way, dear. And don't look so worried. I know you haven't long left school, but nobody's going to eat you.'

Maisie scowled. 'I know that. I'm not a kid. Anyway, I had a job before I came here.'

She didn't add that her father had had a lot to do with her losing that job, arriving outside drunk, demanding his daughter's wages. Bumping into her old teacher, Miss Smith, had been sheer luck. Being offered the job at Priory House had been a wonderful surprise. Unfortunately, her luck had run out.

Miss Cayford raised an eyebrow.

Resentment growing, Maisie searched for a pitying look or the wrinkling of her nose, a sure sign that despite her best efforts she had brought the stink of the bone yards and the soap works with her. There was none. Neither did she get a reprimand in response to her curt comment.

'We take on many of those not long out of school, like you. Some stay with us for years. You'll meet and make many friends around your own age: you just see if you don't.'

Miss Cayford sounded convinced that this would be so.

Maisie pursed her lips. She wanted to say that she had no intention of spending years in a factory breathing in tobacco dust no matter how well paid it was. She'd get out from under her parents' yoke as soon as she could and if she couldn't get a job as a nursemaid, a step up from being the kitchen maid she'd once been, she might get married – or even pregnant. It gave her a degree of satisfaction that her parents would throw her out then.

No matter what the woman said and how kindly she said it, Maisie was disinclined to believe her. School hadn't been particularly kind to her and neither had others of her peer group, because of where she came from. The Dings smelt and so did she, that's what they used to say, so why should a bunch of factory girls be any different? Her expression remained sullen, her attitude less than accommodating. The factory was like a foreign country, a place outside what she was used to. Maisie frowned as she trailed along after Miss Cayford, who was as round as a cottage loaf but possessed an air of authority. She marched rather than walked and despite her short legs covered the ground quickly. Thick plaits of dark hair striped with grey wound like muffs around her ears and she gave off a soft scent – fresh like lemons, certainly not like the cheap perfume coming from dark doorways down Midland Road off Old Market, where the tarts waited for clients.

Thinking of them made Maisie think of what her father had said when she'd voiced her protests about working here too strongly.

'At least I ain't sendin' you out on the game,' he'd said.

Game! How did he have the nerve to call it that? Sometimes those girls came spinning out of doorways, hanging onto the blokes they were with and demanding the money owed them. Sometimes all they got was a good beating, which was far from being a game. Miss Cayford came to a halt outside a pair of double doors that had oval-shaped glass inserts at the top of each one.

'This is the stripping room,' Miss Cayford explained. 'This is where most of our girls start. It's where the leaves are stripped from the plant stems. Your target will be eighty pounds of stripped leaves per day to be placed in a basket you will be provided with. The other girls will show you what to do. They've both been passed to supervise.' She waited for Maisie to make comment, but when none came, pushed open the doors and said, 'Come along then. Let's get you settled.'

* * *

Bridget Milligan was wrapping sticking plaster around Phyllis Mason's fingers. It was something they did at the start of every shift, otherwise stripping left fingers sore and even bleeding.

'You still ain't told me why you sent your kid brother with the envelope. I was counting on you to come.' Phyllis said to her.

'I couldn't.'

'Oh, yeah. Sorry. Your Sean did say yer mother was feeling poorly. Is she all right now?' she asked, her manner a little pensive. Phyllis was sure there was more to this. Normally Bridget had the most serene expression and nothing seemed to faze her.

She eyed Bridget's silky complexion, strands of brandy brown hair peeping out from beneath the bright green turban she was wearing. Bridget was an out-and-out bookworm and seemed to know everything about Bristol, history and a lot of other things besides. She loved talking about the things she'd read, the interesting snippets about the city they lived in that nobody else seemed to know anything about. Everyone in the stripping room agreed it passed the time, but today Bridget was silent.

Phyllis made another attempt to connect with her. Now what was it Sean had said? A picnic. That was it. They'd gone on a picnic. 'So what was the picnic like?' she asked.

'Nice. We went up Cabot Tower. The kids loved it.'

Phyllis screwed her eyes shut, thought of all the tall tales and histories Bridget had told her, and looked as thoughtful as she knew how. 'Now, let me see. That's the bloke who discovered America on a boat called...' She pretended to think extra hard as though she'd forgotten what Bridget had told her. The truth was Bridget was fascinated by Bristol's history and her enthusiasm as she imparted information was infectious. 'The Matthew,' said Bridget in a more distracted way than usual.

'That's just what I thought,' said Phyllis, wriggling her tape tipped fingers.

'That's you done. Now you'd better do my fingers.'

Phyllis began to oblige.

'Whilst you're at it, tell me what your mother thought about you learning to type.'

Phyllis sighed and shook her head. 'She told me to throw it in the bin and I pretended I did,' she said, lowering her voice. 'She said Robert wouldn't like it and that all that mattered was me becoming 'is wife.'

'Dare I ask what Robert might say?' asked Bridget, her eyes following the plasters being applied to her fingertips.

Phyllis bit her bottom lip and giggled. 'Well. Truth is, I ain't told 'im.'

She was about to say more until she saw that Bridget's gentle blue eyes were looking elsewhere.

'Looks like we've got a new girl,' said Bridget.

The girl being led through the aisle of tables by the middle-aged Miss Cayford was slender, young and very pretty. Her dark hair would soon be tied back or hidden beneath a scarf. For now, it sprang in dark tendrils round an elfin face dominated by a pair of brown eyes.

'Poor kid looks scared to death,' murmured Bridget as Phyllis released the last of her fingers.

Phyllis sucked in her breath and whispered, 'Bloody 'ell. Look at them scruffy shoes and laddered tights. Wonder what she's wearing under that overall. Bad as that do you think?'

Bridget didn't answer. Phyllis judged people by what they wore. It hadn't always been like that. She'd always been smart but of late had become fastidious. On reflection, the change had occurred from the time she'd started going steady with Robert. At first, Bridget had thought they suited each other. Now she wasn't so sure.

The stripping room was very large and had a central aisle running down the middle between rows of tables at which the women sat behind piles of tobacco leaves. Porters added to the din, pushing trolleys on small metal wheels that rattled as they trundled past. At each table they brought out a hand-held spring weight, weighed each basket load and entered the weight in the black notebook each kept in his overall pocket. Once that was done, the tobacco leaves were on their way to be processed.

Miss Cayford pulled Maisie to one side before one of the trolleys bumped into her.

Bridget and Phyllis exchanged smiles as the young man pushing it winked at the new arrival and said, 'What's a nice girl like you doing in a place like this?'

Miss Cayford threw him a warning look, then looked pointedly at Maisie. 'Here we are.' She looked straight at Phyllis who had taken a chance on wearing lipstick this morning. She was hoping it wouldn't be noticed. All the girls on this particular table were young. Surprisingly enough, Phyllis, at nineteen, was the oldest.

'Phyllis. This is Maisie Miles and this is her first job. Take care of her, will you luv?'

The bright red lips spread into a smile. 'Course I will, Rosa.'

Miss Cayford was not amused at the casual use of her Christian name. With pursed lips, she said, 'Miss Cayford to you, Phyllis Mason. But before you settle back down, go and wipe that lipstick off your face. You know it's not allowed.'

Phyllis pouted. 'Thought it might cheer everyone up.'

'Cheer everyone up tonight, but not today,' Miss Cayford replied. 'Now go on. Bridget can keep an eye on Maisie whilst you're gone.'

Her cheeks as red as her lipstick, the redhead threw the leaves she'd been stripping onto the table and flounced out.

Miss Cayford pointed at the empty seat beside the one recently vacated. 'Slip in there, Maisie, dear. This is Bridget

Milligan and she will keep an eye. Give her a bundle, Bridget, will you, dear?'

Bridget smiled and tried to ignore the girl's odd smell but linked it with poverty, which would further explain the laddered stockings and worn shoes. It was a safe bet to assume that cardboard inserts covered the holes in the bottom of those shoes. Not that she'd pry unnecessarily, but this was somebody who hadn't asked to be born and hadn't had the best of starts in life.

In that instant, the events of the day before weren't exactly forgotten, but the arrival of this girl was like a healing salve. Somebody in need of tender loving care. Bridget's heart was full of love but needed direction. If there were to be no babies in her life – and she still baulked at the idea – then at least she could adopt a cause. Maisie Miles looked like she might be one.

Bridget's smile was full of warmth and kindness. 'So it's your first job then, Maisie. I take it that means that you've just left school.'

'Yes. But I don't want to be 'ere. This ain't what I wanna do.'

Bridget noted the cocky tilt of her head. This girl might be poor, but she was also proud.

Bridget smiled. 'Why ever not?'

'I don't like cigarettes.'

'Well, don't be worrying about that. Just because you make 'em don't mean to say you 'ave to smoke them. Now come on,' Bridget said, taking out a strip of plaster and a pair of scissors. 'We need to get those finger tips covered or there'll be blood all over the place.'

And I've had enough blood for one weekend, Bridget thought to herself, before pushing the thought to one side and concentrating on what she was doing.

She suddenly became aware of a quizzical look in Maisie's eyes. 'Is something wrong?'

'Before you spoke like me – like any other girl from round 'ere. But just then you were speaking different. You are now. You've got a lovely voice.'

Bridget eyed her with interest. 'Thanks for saying so. It might have something to do with the fact that my name is Bridget Milligan and my mum and dad are Irish, though it's a long time since they lived there. It's affected the way I speak. Clear and only a slight accent – well a mixed one I suppose. They came over here after the war. Before that my dad worked on the pig boats running between Cork and Bristol, though we don't really mention that. Me mum tells everyone he was a merchant seaman; well, nobody would want to be conjoined with pigs, now would they?'

'Conjoined?'

'It means – well – it means joined up with. Anyway, as I was saying, Miss Cayford said she liked my Irish brogue. Reckoned it reminded her of singing. Eggs me on to speak she does, but now and again I take on the local way of speaking just to annoy her. Don't mind that, do you?'

Maisie shook her head.

Bridget prattled on at the same time as ensuring that Maisie was stripping the leaves the right way before throwing them into the basket. She looked up when Phyllis got back. 'You still look our glamorous Phyllis,' she said looking more amused than she had all day

Phyllis grunted a wordless response.

Bridget shook her head. 'You know it's not allowed. Why do you do it?'

Phyllis instantly buried her head in her hands. 'It's the only chance I get.'

For a moment, Bridget stared at her and tried to work out what she meant. She sensed the young girl, Maisie, was peering out from beneath those sooty dark lashes. If only momentarily, she was becoming interested in what was going on around her, though it didn't last. When she thought somebody was watching her, the eyelids came down. Maisie was listening and watching what was going on around her, but in Bridget's opinion the girl probably needed somebody to take an interest in her.

'So where do you live, Maisie?'

Her question seemed to jolt Maisie from wherever she'd been. 'Off Old Market.'

Her response was swift. Her attention went back to her flying fingers.

'You're doing well there,' said Bridget. 'You've got dextrous fingers.'

'That means quick and nimble,' said Phyllis who had learned plenty from Bridget over the years.

Bridget, whose knowledge of Bristol was pretty far reaching, thought she knew where that might be. Not that she'd mention it. Drawing the kid out of herself called for a great deal of delicacy. Feelings could be hurt and instead of opening up Maisie might close more tightly down.

'Have you any brothers and sisters?' asked Bridget.

She tried not to sound prying or make it obvious that she was watching for Maisie's response.

'I've got a brother. His name's Alf.'

Bridget noted a hint of confidence in Maisie's tone.

'Is he older than you?'

She nodded. 'Twenty.'

Bridget pressed on. 'What's he like? Tall, blonde, dark haired, thin or fat?'

Maisie lifted her attention from her work and spoke more than she had all morning.

'He's a kind of light brown, dark blonde colour and 's got blue eyes. Ain't thin or fat but 'e is tall for 'is age. Looks good in a suit too.'

Bridget noted the pride in her voice and knew instantly that she loved her brother just as she loved hers.

'Sounds just my type,' said Phyllis flippantly as she patted down the top of her basket which was close to overflowing with leaves. 'Do you ever go to the pictures, Maisie? I loves the pictures. Or the pub? Do you ever go out with your mates to the pub?'

When Maisie shook her head, Bridget thought how vulnerable she looked and it touched her heart.

'That's it then,' said Phyllis, slamming her hand down on the table. 'You can come with us. How old are you, Maisie?'

Maisie pronounced in a slightly awestruck voice that she was fifteen.

'Too young for the pub,' Bridget reminded Phyllis with a rueful shake of her head.

'She can have a shandy,' offered Phyllis. 'Do you fancy a shandy, Maisie? 'ave you ever 'ad a shandy before?'

Maisie looked quite indignant. 'Of course I 'ave!'

'Then that's it,' said Phyllis. 'You can come out with us. Ain't that right, Bridget?'

'I've got a better idea. How about we do a bit of window shopping in Castle Street? The shops are open 'til ten.'

'And there'll be plenty of people about,' added Phyllis with undisguised enthusiasm.'

'She means chaps,' said Bridget with a laugh. 'And you engaged to be married, Phyllis Mason!'

Phyllis tossed her head. 'Just because I'm engaged don't mean to say I can't study what's available!'

Bridget turned to Maisie. 'What do you think, Maisie? Do you fancy that?'

Maisie took less than a minute to make up her mind. 'That sounds nice. We ain't goin' to buy anyfing are we? I mean, Castle Street is all posh shops ain't it?'

'We promenade,' said Bridget. 'We walk up and down looking into shop windows and saying good evening to passers-by.'

'Especially the fellahs,' laughed Phyllis.

There spoke Phyllis, thought Bridget. She did like looking at what was available. It had crossed her mind more than once that Phyllis was not ready to be married, but there, she'd had the offer and accepted it. Most nights of the week she was out with Robert, but he had other interests: darts, cricket, rugby and football.

'So it's Friday night in Castle Street,' her declaration accompanied by a flurry of tobacco leaves landing in her basket.

Maisie was right about Castle Street being full of shops full of lovely things way beyond their price range. Bridget prided herself on taking the first step to make Maisie feel at home. The girl was like a stray kitten thrown out to fend for itself. Her soft heart wouldn't allow that. She wondered what else she could do to convince Maisie that she was fully accepted.

Bridget wracked her brain how to best do that, then suddenly clicked her fingers so loudly, everybody sat bolt upright.

'Something's just come to me. Your surname's Miles,' she said brightly, pointing at Maisie. 'Phyllis is Mason and I'm a Milligan! Well there's a thing. The three Ms – just like The Three Musketeers – that's what we are. One for all and all for one. That was their motto, you know.' Bridget stood up and shouted it into the room. 'We're The Three Ms. Miles, Mason and Milligan. Just like The Three Musketeers, one for all and all for one!'

Claps and cheers, together with loud guffaws, broke out from the other women in the room.

Phyllis leaned in to Bridget. 'Who did you say these musketeers were?'

Bridget explained that they were three French friends who fought for the king.

'Oh, I see,' declared Phyllis brightly. 'We're the three Ms who fight through piles of tobacco leaves every day.'

The rumbling of a trolley heralded the arrival of the cheeky young man who had winked at Maisie earlier. This time he was wheeling an empty trolley. The stripped leaves were weighed on a hand held measuring device before being tipped from the women's baskets and into its depths. The discarded plant stems had been tipped into the basket Maisie was sitting next to. Thinking he was about to take that one, she eased herself to one side in her chair, but he put her right.

'I'll be back for that one. Just the leaves for now.' He winked at her again. 'So what's your name then?'

She glared at him but said nothing.

Phyllis told him to leave her alone. 'She's our mate,' she said. 'She's coming out with us on Friday night.'

'Is that right, Phyllis? You ain't gonna lead 'er astray are you?'

'No odds to you,' said a cocky Phyllis.

He turned back to Maisie. 'You should tell me now, you know, whilst I'm still 'ere. If this bloke Hitler goes on the march in this direction, then I'll be off. Ready to fight for my king and country, then you'll be sorry you didn't tell me.'

'So you're going to die a hero, are you, Bert?' Bridget said laughingly.

'No. That's what the enemy is goin' to do when he runs into me.'

There was laughter all round, along with the sweet smell of fresh tobacco as yet another shredded mass was tumbled into the trolley.

5

MAISIE

For nights after, Maisie dreamed of Castle Street. The lights, the shops, the mannequins standing in eccentric poses in shop windows, the crowds and the laughter had transported her to another world.

Phyllis, cigarette in hand, had posed in front of a shop window mimicking the pose of one of the mannequins. It had made her laugh.

Bridget had pointed at some of the old buildings, relating bits of their history and seemingly ignoring the interested glances and comments of young men who obviously found her very attractive.

'Have you got a boyfriend?' Maisie asked her.

'She's saving herself for Cary Grant,' said Phyllis. 'He's from Bristol you know.'

Maisie looked at Bridget. 'You haven't got a boyfriend?'

Bridget shook her head. 'It's not compulsory is it?'

Her mouth clamped shut. She turned away and it was obvious to Maisie that the subject was closed. Still, she thought, that's her business and who can blame her?

There were other nights out with her new friends; the pictures and even a sneaked shandy in one of the girls' favourite pubs, The Bear and Rugged Staff adjacent to the thrilling shops of Castle Street.

She found she was surprisingly happy, far more so than she'd ever expected to be, yet couldn't help being apprehensive that something would happen to shatter these new friendships.

The fly in the ointment came within two weeks of her beginning work in the tobacco factory. The fly was Frank Miles, her father.

Maisie had wondered whether there had to be more about her father forcing her to work at Wills's besides the free fags and good wages. The first inkling she had that something was amiss was when her mother beckoned to her from the end of the passage that led into the scullery.

Maisie frowned but before she could respond, she was dragged into the living room by her father's beefy hand.

'I wants you in 'ere.'

The living-room door was slammed shut behind her.

There were two other men in the room besides her father. One of them was sitting in the middle of the sofa as though it was a throne and nobody but him had any right to sitting on it.

'This is my daughter, Maisie, Eddie. Maisie, this is Eddie Bridgeman, a business acquaintance.'

The third man standing behind the sofa remained silent and was not referred to. The only thing noticeable about him was that his shoulders were as wide as a wardrobe.

'Pleased to meet you, sweet'eart.' Eddie Bridgeman glanced at her father. 'She's a pretty girl, Frank. Don't take after you, that's for sure.'

Her father laughed nervously. 'Well 'er mother was a bit of a looker when she was young.'

'And ended up with you?' Eddie Bridgeman threw back his head and laughed. At no point did his eyes leave her face. 'Enjoying yer new job then?' he asked.

She shrugged. The way he looked at her made her squirm. Everything about him made her feel uncomfortable and his asking about her job, apprehensive.

'I 'ear it's good money,' he went on.

Maisie glanced at her father. 'It would be if I got to keep a bit of it.'

Eddie Bridgeman eyed her father with disapproval. 'Now, now, Frank. The girl earns 'er dough. Let 'er keep a good bit of it. The kid wants to live a bit before she settles down. Get 'er some nice clothes too. Everybody should be rewarded for putting in the graft.'

It surprised her when she heard her father agreeing. The thought of having new clothes made her heart leap with joy. On nights out with her new friends, she'd had to wear her one and only good dress, given to her by her brother not her father who stole to make a profit not to clothe Maisie.

'P'raps after you've got yer first pay packet and can afford some nice new clothes,' Bridget had said.

She'd known what they were hinting at. She looked like a ragamuffin and if her father had his way, he'd take every last penny she earned, but maybe not if Eddie Bridgeman had anything to do with it.

'That would be nice,' Maisie said. 'I'd like working there more if I could go dancing and stuff now and again.' She didn't mention window shopping which cost nothing and might not gain her the new clothes she desired.

Eddie's black eyes bore into her as he leaned forward, elbows resting on his knees, thick fingers interlaced. She noticed his clothes were as sharp and well-tailored as her brother's clothes and came to the conclusion that Eddie Bridgeman was a far more successful criminal than her father. And a criminal he had to be. He looked like one and acted like one. But why was he interested in her? The fact that he was made her feel nervous.

Frank Miles was only a small-time criminal and fence. Some of the stuff he'd stolen was piled into an upstairs bedroom, mostly jewellery, silverware and clothes. He'd always bragged about branching out and getting into the big time. There was no doubt in her mind, though, that in this room at present, Eddie Bridgeman was the one in charge.

'The workers at the fag factory are well paid. Bonuses too, so I hear. There's not many in Bristol or anywhere else for that matter, paying like they do,' he said.

Maisie shrugged. 'I suppose not.'

Eddie leaned back and studied her with narrowed eyes. 'Thing is, Maisie, I'm interested in what you earn. I'm interested in the factory and what goes on there. I likes to keep me finger on the pulse, if you like. I did 'ave somebody on the inside who kept me informed.' He exchanged a swift glance with her father. 'But he turned out to be a silly bugger. Got caught with 'is fingers in the till. Heard about 'im, 'ave you? A bloke named Simons.'

She shook her head, fearing where this might lead. Her stomach fluttered with nerves. 'No.'

Eddie waved his hand as though he was brushing away a fly. 'That's neither 'ere nor there. Fact is, are you going to be my girl on the inside? Are you going to find out a bit of information when I need it?'

A growing fear gnawed at her stomach and her mouth had gone dry. For a moment words would not come. 'I work in the factory. I don't know nothing.'

'You probably know more than you think,' said Eddie, spreading his hands. 'Any bit of gossip you can get 'old of, and in return, you get nice clothes and go out and enjoy yourself. I insist.' He looked directly at her father. 'See the girl all right, Frank. She's an asset, working where she does. Good move, me old mate. Good move.'

He turned back to Maisie, his tight-lipped smile barely enough to conceal a gold tooth at one side of his mouth.

'That's it, sweetheart. Me and yer old man will hammer out the details and let you know what we want you to do.'

She felt confused as she left that room, wondering what was going on and also feeling discouraged that nobody had asked whether she was willing to do whatever it was. In other words, she'd been given no choice.

As Maisie came out of the living room, her mother beckoned from the end of the narrow passage that led into the kitchen.

'Maisie,' she whispered. 'What does yer dad want you to do?'

Maisie studied her mother's greying hair, the dark lines beneath her eyes. The nose that had once been straight was now slightly off-centre, the blow landed by Frank Miles breaking her nose.

'I ain't too sure,' said Maisie. 'It's all to do with Wills's.'

Her mother tossed her head. 'Ah. They want fags.'

Maisie shrugged. 'I don't know fer sure.'

She'd spoken the truth. It didn't seem as though they were asking her to do anything criminal, just to listen to gossip, she presumed amongst the girls. Was that it? She feared there was more, but so far preferred not to make guesses. There was one thing above all in this that appealed to her.

'Eddie told dad to give me some new clothes and make sure I've got enough money to go out and enjoy myself.'

Her mother looked startled. 'Did 'e now.'

Maisie couldn't recall ever receiving much in the way of affection from her mother. It had always fallen to her brother to pat her shoulder or kiss her on the top of her head, hug her and swing her off her feet. Only rarely did she come close to showing anything close to that, but only when Maisie's father was not around or he'd accuse her of being soft, of spoiling her daughter – as if that were ever likely! She'd never been spoilt, always kicked into the corner like an unwanted dog.

Her mother glanced at the living room door, saw it was still closed and leaned in closer. 'That Eddie ain't offering to take you out, is 'e?'

'No,' Maisie replied. 'Nothin' like that.'

Her mother looked relieved. 'So it's about fags and tobacco,' she said and looked relieved. It was a statement not a question. 'Well, that's all right then. Want some supper, do you?'

* * *

'Pretty little girl, your daughter.'

Eddie Bridgeman sipped at the whisky Frank had poured for him. He'd been impressed by her slender figure, the budding breasts and the long legs. There was also her elfin face that even as she got older would remain childlike, the velvet brown eyes shining like pools in moonlight.

He was close to forty and married with kids, but his family life was strictly separate from his business: the shady deals, the extortion and his little gem, the Flamingo nightclub. The club was his pride and joy. People came there to drink, gamble and dance to some pretty good bands. He did like a good band and good singers too, preferably a female singer wearing a tight, low-cut dress; singers like that brought the punters in. So did having a smattering of hostesses – girls employed to get male punters to part with their money.

Men of his age went to the club to escape the drudgery of

family life and the familiarity of wives who'd run to fat with age. They wanted to relive their youth, the excitement of sexual arousal. They saw their wives as over the hill, but when they looked in the mirror saw themselves as they had been. That's why he employed very young hostesses, some of them not long out of school, and all pretty and fresh-faced. The punters loved them, and so did he.

Eddie could see Frank was impressed with his comment about his daughter and although he was willing to do business with this two-bit crook, he couldn't say he liked him.

Eddie disliked people who drank too quickly. The whisky was good and should be savoured, but types like Frank swigged it back like water and ended up drunk.

Time and time again, Frank Miles had come to him with ideas for jobs – all thieving jobs of course. He'd been lukewarm about most of them until Frank had outlined his scheme for nicking fags from the tobacco factory; not just a few measly packets but a whole lorry load – perhaps more than one. He'd agreed with him about getting inside information on delivery procedures, but getting hold of the right information wasn't easy from outside – but to have somebody inside...Eddie had given him the green light. Maisie was to be their conduit. Her eyes and ears would tell them enough then it was up to them to plan accordingly.

'Let's see how things go, shall we. In time, I might give 'er a job at my club, you know, as an hostess. How would that sit with you Frank? You up for that?'

He eyed Frank with narrowed eyes as he waited for his response. Any decent father wouldn't let his daughter anywhere near his club, but Frank wasn't decent. Neither was he. He'd taken a shine to that girl, imagined her beneath the sheets, trembling and virginal. He'd like that most of all. For him to be the first to bed her.

'Alright by me, Eddie, alright by me,' said Frank.

Eddie watched more whisky being poured.

'Still got some,' said Eddie, putting his hand over his glass. 'Now I'd better be off.'

Eddie's broad-shouldered companion led the way back to the front door followed by Eddie, Frank bringing up the rear.

He wasn't the only one who watched the car pull away. The heads of women gossiping on front steps came together, commenting on who it was and what Frank Miles might be up to. Curtains twitched.

Frank, his face florid from an overindulgence in whisky, saw them. 'Had yer eyeful,' he shouted.

Heads turned away; women disappeared inside their dingy houses. Some of them who'd borrowed money from Frank, couldn't afford to upset him. Their husbands boozed away the wages so the women borrowed on a regular basis to pay the rent and put a meal on the table.

Frank chuckled to himself. He'd get no hassle from them in future when they claimed they couldn't pay. The more hardened non-payers would receive a visit from one of Eddie's heavies. On top of that he'd seen the way Eddie had looked at Maisie. Well that too was an advantage, one he'd make use of.

6

Maisie lay in bed tossing and turning haunted by the way Eddie Bridgeman had looked at her. Each time she closed her eyes he was there, undressing her with his eyes. It had made her feel sick and she didn't really understand whatever it was she was supposed to do: keep an eye on things, tell them what was going on, report back details. The only thing that appealed to her was that she'd keep more of her wages so she could go out with her new-found friends. She'd almost choked when Eddie had urged her father to supply her with decent clothes.

Sleep continued to prove elusive. Eventually, she kicked off the bedclothes, flung on a dress and cardigan and left the house. The night air smelt of cinders and factory effluent. Her footsteps took her to stare at the trains passing under Midland Bridge. It didn't matter that a fog of smoke and steam puffed like dragons' breath up into her face. She was thinking of her new friends and smiled on recalling the name Bridget had applied to them: The Three Ms. Thinking of them helped soothe her troubled mind.

Cupping her heart-shaped face in one hand, elbows on parapet, she continued to stare down at the trains and the railways lines. A distant church clock sounded the midnight hour. The other sound that came to her ears was that of male footsteps heading her way.

'What you doin' out 'yer?'

A gas street light caught the sheen on her brother's hair. As usual, he was smartly dressed, most of it stolen property, though occasionally bought with the proceeds of his ill gotten gains. Alf was meticulous about his appearance and also about his cleanliness, going to the local public or Turkish baths nearly every day and studiously avoiding the zinc bath hanging out back.

'We've 'ad a visitor,' she said to her brother.

Alf lit up a cigarette, inhaled and then exhaled, a circle of smoke rising into the air. 'Go on.'

After taking a deep breath she went on to tell him about Eddie Bridgeman wanting her to be his ears and eyes in the factory. 'Now why would 'e want that?' she asked. 'Dad nearly choked when 'e told 'im to reward me with new clothes.'

Alf grinned. 'I bet 'e did. Tight old sod!'

She waited for Alf to say more, tell her everything would be all right and not to worry. Whatever Alf said was absolute wisdom in her eyes. He was one of the few people whose opinion she valued. He was also in tune with local criminals and their methods.

Alf narrowed his eyes into the night. 'What else did 'e say?'

'That I was well paid and should go out and enjoy myself.'

A knowing look came to his face that made her realise that Alf had been present at conversations between his father and Eddie Bridgeman. 'And I bet our old man didn't argue. Not with Eddie. If Eddie asked 'im to lick 'is boots, 'e would. Took 'im a long while to get Eddie's attention. Cigarettes sell well. That's what this is all about.'

Hands resting on the rough stone of the bridge parapet,

Maisie tangled and untangled her fingers then shook her head. 'What's that got to do with me? All I do is strip leaves.'

Alf took a few more puffs before replying. 'Have you met any of the warehouse or lorry drivers?'

Maisie frowned at the thought of Bert who pushed the trolleys that supplied them with tobacco leaves and took away the stripped leaves and discarded stems. 'Only Bert, but all 'e does is deliver leaves for stripping and takes them away when they're done.'

'Ah,' said Alf. He flicked the spent ash from his cigarette. 'Early days, ar Maisie. Early days.'

By the light from a railway lamp hanging on a gantry beneath them, she saw his expression darken.

'Surprised Eddie would bother involving you – unless there's something bigger 'e's got planned. A lorry load rather than a few packets of fags.'

Maisie frowned. 'I'd lose my job if I got found out.'

'I didn't think you wanted to work there.'

Now she was the one who fell to silence surprised at her sudden change in attitude. She'd so wanted to escape York Street and live in a grand house in the country. It had sounded such an idyllic life. Losing the job at Wills's might give her the opportunity to follow her dream. Yet inside, she found herself confronting the fact that leaving the tobacco factory would also mean leaving her new friends behind. Who's to say how she might feel a few months down the line? She might want to go or she might want to stay. Either way, she would have the option.

She chose to keep her thoughts to herself and took a deep breath. 'That's true.'

'So you'll go along with it?' Alf asked.

She shrugged her narrow shoulders, felt the fug from the

funnel of a shunting engine puff into her face. 'Don't 'ave much choice, do I?'

She heard her brother sigh audibly. 'Did Eddie suggest anything else?'

There was a slight catch in his voice that hadn't been there before.

'No. But I didn't like the way 'e looked at me. Like the big bad wolf.'

Alf sucked in his breath. 'That's just about it, sis. He *is* the big bad wolf! If I could get you out of this, I would, but, well, you know 'ow it is. I'll point out to you now; Eddie Bridgeman is bad news. Very bad news. But the old man wants to be one of the big boys and will do all 'e can to get up that ladder – even if it means using you. Be careful, Maisie. Be really careful. It ain't only money Bridgeman likes. Likes girls too and the younger the better. You're exactly 'ow 'e likes 'em. Young and fresh.'

Maisie shuddered at what he was suggesting. She didn't want to believe it, wanted him to tell her he'd only been joking, but although Alf had a sense of humour, she knew this wasn't one of those occasions.

She didn't get the chance to ask him anything else because he suddenly stalked off. She followed behind him, confused and full of questions she feared to ask. She adored her brother, the only person who made living at 5 York Street bearable. If anyone else had warned her about Eddie Bridgeman she would have said they were jealous. But Alf wasn't any other person. He was her brother and knew how bad the world could be.

Two weeks following Maisie joining the workforce, the monthly Tobacco Thrift Club took place in the canteen. It had nothing whatsoever to do with tobacco, except that everyone participating was an employee and the majority female.

The idea was that things no longer of use to one person were brought into the factory to be passed on to somebody who could make use of them. There was no charge. Everything from clothes, shoes, blankets, curtains and kitchen utensils were picked over and doled out at lunchtime. There was always somebody in need, especially those with children. It was agreed by everyone that children grew too fast.

Phyllis and Bridget had brought clothes in they thought would fit Maisie, although both noticed that her stockings didn't seem so laddered and her shoes seemed almost new. They could tell nothing about her clothes, which were hidden under her overall but couldn't help thinking that something had changed. Most of the girls wore their overalls to and from work and were issued with two, which easily lasted a week.

Aggie Hill, a senior worker, was in charge of the Thrift Club and claimed it to have been her idea. Nobody could prove otherwise, though some said it had been in existence long before she took it as her own.

The canteen was always noisy, but picking through the piled-up items generated even more chattering and laughter than usual.

'I don't need anything,' said Maisie.

Bridget and Phyllis exchanged looks. They'd purposely brought in a couple of dresses that no longer fitted them, thinking they'd suit Maisie.

'No need to push and shove,' shouted Aggie, her meaty arms throwing aside those who hogged the goods on offer. 'There's loads for everybody. Stock up while you can. If this bloody war starts and we 'ave rationing, you'll be hard-pushed to find a decent pair of knickers!'

A lot of laughter ensued.

As Maisie was one of the few who held back, Aggie targeted her to take her pick. 'No need to be proud, love. We're all the same in 'ere. Most of us got the tastes of a toff and the purse of a pauper.'

Maisie refrained from saying that she wasn't being proud, that she had some very nice new clothes, thank you very much. Following Eddie Bridgeman's urging, her father had honoured his word and let her have a look through the haul in the back room. Most of the clothes were from dress shops like Bon Marche on East Street, a shop owned by people who lived out at Long Ashton. At one point, and with Alf's help, he'd burgled a smart clothing store in Castle Street which was how come Alf got to wear a smart suit, crisp white shirt and silk tie. At Eddie Bridgeman's insistence, she did now get to keep more of her wages so wasn't completely dependent on her father's ill-gotten gains stashed up in the spare room.

She eyed the flurry of women and girls sorting through the clothes, chattering avidly and laughing as they tried things on. She wanted to join in with them, but although the women working there had accepted her as one of their own, she couldn't shake the feeling that she didn't belong, that they were only being nice. As Alf had said to her, it was early days. The fact was that she'd been brought up to accept that being on the wrong side of the law was a way of life, not that she'd ever stolen anything herself. The truth was she resented her father's dishonesty and couldn't see it in herself

'You didn't choose anything,' Bridget said to her once the scrum was over and smiled pleasantly.

'I don't need anyfin',' said Maisie. 'I got some new stuff.'

'Spent yer wages already then?'

'Not all of it.'

Phyllis, who was holding up a satin slip in front of her eyes, giggled. 'Not enough to buy anyfin' in Castle Street, I bet!'

'Might do,' Maisie declared with a toss of her head.

Her thoughts were elsewhere, recalling when her father had told her to get the lay of the land, to nose around a bit.

'What the bloody 'ell am I lookin' for?'

Her hasty response had earned her a slap round the head.

'Make yer way to where they load the trucks. Say you got lost if you like, but take a gander there and let me know what you find. Get one of the despatchers on yer side if you can. They're the ones who know the delivery times with the lorries, when they're goin' out and suchlike.'

She rubbed her cheek as she turned on her heel away from the canteen and headed back towards the stripping room. Once out of sight, she headed in the opposite direction, past the production halls where cigarettes rolled along conveyor belts to be sorted and packed. Sorting and packing were jobs for women on the grounds that they were thought to be more dextrous and keen-sighted than male workers. The double doors of the production line, where Woodbines the most popular cigarette ever were made, swung open as she went past and Bert came out. As always, he was pushing his trolley.

"Ello,' he said and beamed at the sight of her. 'What you doin' out 'ere then? Fancy a job in production already?'

'I might do.' She glanced over his shoulder. 'Do you deliver tobacco in there?'

He nodded. 'Yep. At the other end where the tobacco's fed into the machines. This ends the packin' line. Come on. Take a look.' Opening the door just a few inches, he invited her to join him. 'See? They're dead nifty with their 'ands them girls. Once you've bin 'ere a while, you can apply for a job in there. The end of the line, where I deliver the stripped leaves to the machines, is right down the end, out of sight. Usually I get to it from the other corridor, but it's blocked off today on account of the casks being delivered.'

The task her father had set her lay heavy on Maisie's mind and he was getting impatient, although she had explained to him that it wasn't easy for her to get to the loading bays. And, anyway, why couldn't he go direct to one of the drivers? Their lorries were always out on the road.

'We wants the schedule. Try and get yer 'ands on a delivery schedule. We want all the trucks, not just one.'

Her father scared her, and although she still had that dream of getting away from Bristol, it wasn't as strong as it had been. Her life had changed. She had friends and really felt like one of the girls.

'So what's down the end 'ere?' She nodded down the corridor, which although well lit was not as bright as the daylight she could see coming in at the end.

Bert seemed pleased to oblige. 'That's where the lorries get loaded with fags and tobacco. Then they're off to deliver to the shops.'

What he said was joy to Maisie's ears. The girlish smile she gave him brimmed with innocence. 'Can I go down there and take a look?'

At first he frowned. 'Well... I don't know...'

Her brown eyes were full of pleading and her dark lashes fluttered. 'I'd love to. There I am stripping off those leaves all day. It would be lovely to see the end result – the results of my work being loaded onto a lorry.'

Bert eyed her thoughtfully.

She waited to be rebuffed, though prayed otherwise.

His friendly face, all pinkish cheeks, merry eyes and dark eyebrows, broke with pleasure. 'Why not? Can't do no 'arm, can it?' His expression suddenly changed and became more serious. 'On one condition. Will you tell Bridget that I'm still on for taking 'er out? I keep asking 'er, but... well, 'er bein' a good-looking girl and all that...'

'I'll tell her,' she said. 'Now can we go and take a look?'

Bert parked up his trolley and bid her follow.

The far end of the corridor was indeed opened to daylight. A large platform thronged with men loading the merchandise onto three distinct lorries.

Bert bid her to keep out of sight and whispered to her: 'There's sometimes as many as ten or twelve lorries all waiting to be loaded. A bit quieter at the end of the week. There's no deliveries on weekends, the shops being shut or on 'alf-day. It'll pick up again on Monday.'

'Oi! What you doin' 'ere?'

The man who shouted wore a brown overall and a flat cap. His face was bright red and he seemed ancient – at least forty.

Bert was sheer bravado, acting as though nothing was wrong. 'All right, Reg?'

The man's double chins flopped one on top of the other when he glared down at Maisie.

'What's goin' on, I said! You don't work 'ere and neither do she!'

'She got lost. I followed 'er along. I'll take 'er back.'

The man's frown deepened, his bushy brows like a caterpillar wandering across his brow. 'Get out of 'ere. Now.'

Out of the corner of her eye, Maisie saw one of the men pause from loading the lorry, look directly at her and wink. He had a gypsy look about him, dark curly hair and a red neckerchief.

She blushed and turned away but somehow knew that the man loading the truck had singled her out. She couldn't place him at first, then recalled seeing him in the Duke of York, though not that often.

To her left was a huge noticeboard with a sign saying 'Delivery Schedules'. Beneath each one, dates were listed in bold letters, and beneath these were the schedules, each attached to a clipboard. It was one of these that her father and Eddie were after.

They'd coin it, she thought. Not just steal from one lorry on one specific delivery but over a period of time, one delivery after another. It suddenly occurred to her that they wouldn't just be stealing from W. D. & H. O. Wills, they'd be stealing from her and every other person who worked in the factory. It wasn't unknown for blood to spurt from the sore fingers of the girls in the stripping room.

The sudden guilt got the better of her.

'Can we go now,' she whispered to Bert.

She was scared – scared of being caught and scared of her father. How could she do what she had to do without being caught? The delivery schedules were hanging in a row from metal hooks. The closest was within arm's length. All she needed was a diversion and she could grab one. Just one. That's all she could grab. It wouldn't be enough. What Eddie and her father were after was access to one schedule after another. They needed somebody who worked in the loading bay. *The man who'd winked?*

Reg spread his arms and ushered them back into the factory. 'Get on back where you belong. This is a restricted area. Go on. Get!'

She saved to memory the features of the man who had winked at her – especially the red neckerchief which was particularly familiar. If he was someone she recognised there was a distinct possibility that her father would know who he was.

Heart thudding against her ribs, Maisie headed back into the factory. Bert reminded her of her promise to tell Bridget that he still wanted to take her out. She promised she would, but by the time she got back to the stripping room, it had gone from her head. All that remained was convincing herself that she had a future away from the tobacco factory and the camaraderie of the other girls.

Then you can leave here, she thought to herself. *Once you've done what they want, you can go after the job you really want.* On the one hand, it excited her. On the other it scared her witless. On top of that a job in a country mansion didn't appeal so much as it once had. Things had changed and so had she.

Bridget and Phyllis both lived in Marksbury Road, so it had always been their habit to walk home together. The Milligan household was reached first, an end terraced council house that differed little from all the others in the road.

Its big drawback was being positioned right opposite the gasometer that sat like a fat green monster on a piece of wasteland known as *The Cut* or *The Malago*. The huge green tank stunk pretty high when coke was being processed from coal, a by-product of coal gas which fed into every gas stove hereabouts. Phyllis lived a bit further along, where the remains of Clancy's farm skirted the main road. At one time, it had all been farmland until the building of the council houses had commenced following the Great War.

The creaking of the front gate was the signal to the Milligan kids to fall out of the front door to welcome their eldest sister home. Like a gaggle of excited ducklings, they flocked around her. As usual, she had brought them a bag of bullseyes to share. Their excitement was instantly transferred to the minty hard-boiled sweets.

'They're the best money can buy,' Bridget said to them. 'The man in the shop told me they're boiled in a copper pan for better flavour.'

Unimpressed by the information and their cheeks round with sweets, they sat on the grass at the front of the house, competing as to who would finish first and grab the next sweet.

Bridget's and the children's mother, Mary Milligan waved from the door. 'And how are you, Phyllis?'

'Fine, Mrs Milligan.'

'So when are you going to walk down the aisle?'

'I'm not sure.' Mrs Milligan, insensitive to her doubts and a great believer in the romantic idyll, carried on.

'You've missed your chance to be a June bride this year. Still, I suppose any month is good for a wedding.'

'Sorry about me Mam,' Bridget whispered to her once her mother had gone indoors. 'She does like a wedding. It's the romantic in her.'

Phyllis came out of her dark moment and laughed. 'That means she'll be fifty times more romantic when you tie the knot.'

'No doubt,' returned Bridget and smiled as though she knew it to be true. It was true on her mother's part, but for her it was a truth she couldn't face, one soured by the thought of a bonfire and two hastily wrapped bundles.

* * *

'Had a good day at work, me darling?'

'Fine, ma. Do you need help with the dinner?' Bridget asked.

'No, me darling. You go on out back. Yer dad's out there in the garden reading the paper.'

Mary Milligan's movements were quick, and her figure had not become overblown following the birth of so many children.

Bridget wondered at her powers of endurance. She was sure she could never go through what was, to some women, the very heart of their existence.

Neither did her mother refer back to the event two weeks previously. As far as she was concerned, childbirth was something a woman had to endure.

'All forgotten,' she declared when Bridget had asked. 'Anyway,' she'd added with a smile. 'I had great pain with you all and don't regret giving birth to any one of you.'

Despite the fact that her eyes were blue, her skin soft and pale and her hair luxuriant and still as dark as the day she'd married, she never referred to that either. All in all, she did not possess any vanity, only a great deal of love for her family.

'I'll take him a cup of tea,' Bridget offered.

'That'll be three he's had.'

They joined in a wry chuckle. It was a well-known fact that her father consumed more tea than the rest of the family combined.

Her brothers and sisters, having now finished their sweets, were full of questions, gathered tightly round her as she made a fresh pot of tea.

'Our dad 'as a lot of sugar in his tea,' remarked Sean on seeing Bridget spooning three helpings into tea that was far too strong for most people. The colour was that of a piece of tanned leather, the colour of satchels and handbags.

'He also likes it strong,' returned Bridget. 'Now let me take it out to him.'

She knew even as she made a path through her siblings, cup and saucer balanced carefully above their heads, that they'd follow her out.

Patrick Milligan looked up from the old green and orange striped deckchair he was sitting in, put down his newspaper and lay it flat across his lap. The smile on his mouth was matched in his eyes. He loved all his children but perhaps had a special spot for his eldest, for she'd been born of first love when he and Mary had been very young.

'Bridie, you're a good girl and that's for sure, bringing yer old dad a cup of tea, and you only just got back from work.'

Only the family ever called her Bridie, a term of affection towards a well-loved daughter.

After handing him the cup of tea, she squatted down in the grass. It was uncut, long and dry, for her father had never been much good at gardening and his gammy leg didn't help. Occasionally he had flirted with the idea of growing vegetables, but after a few weeks of digging and planting, nothing growing and his leg aching, he'd decided his energies might be better used elsewhere.

Bridget's brothers and sisters also squatted in the grass, forming a rough semicircle around their eldest sister and their father, their faces bright with interest.

'So have you had a good day, daughter?'

She gave him an outline of what had happened: a cask had fallen off the back of a lorry and onto a man's foot; somebody had set up a netball team with a view to keeping fit during lunchtimes; the athletics club was looking for new members to train at the Imperial Ground in Knowle West, just a couple of miles from the factory.

'I hear they have a fine cricket pitch,' he said after some thought. ''Tis an English game, but I do like the intricacies of cricket. It taxes the mind,' he said and tapped his forehead.

'And how about you, Pa? Have you had a good day?'

Her father took a sip of his tea before replying. 'Father Francis brought his father's pocket watch for me to mend. Father's father – sounds funny, don't it? Though one is a priest of course, and the other a natural father.' He chuckled at his joke before the further telling of his story. 'It crashed to the ground when he knelt before the altar and he hurt his knee. That was when he realised he was kneeling on the watch.' He laughed. 'No good praying for it to be made better; he had to bring it to me. Oh, and that Mrs Furze from along the road brought me a clock to mend. It wasn't for her; it was from the shop down in East Street. Their usual mender is off sick, so I was second choice. Still might bode well for more work in the future. I'm getting a good bit of work nowadays, and that's for sure. Happy I am, oh yes, happy I am.'

Bridget smiled. The fact was that on losing his leg in the Great War, work had been hard to come by. Thousands of returning servicemen, able-bodied as well as injured, had come back hoping for a better life than they'd had before the war. As it turned out, unemployment had been their reward for serving their country. The little invalidity pension her father received was not enough to live on and he'd turned to mending watches and clocks. It was intricate work and he enjoyed it, though it did crowd up a house with bits and pieces, which was difficult when it was already packed with people.

He eyed her speculatively as her expression turned thoughtful. He was good at reading her mind, though there was nothing magical about it. He loved and knew his daughter that well. He also had a heart of gold.

'How about you keep all your wages this week and go and buy yerself something dandy: a new frock, a pair of shoes or ribbons for that bonny hair of yours? Or go to the pictures? P'raps find some young man to go with, though I'd want to know if he was a sound proposition, mark you.'

Bridget laughed into eyes that were as blue as hers and just as kind. 'I'd expect a young man to do the paying, not you, Da.'

Her father sighed and gave the newspaper a purposeful flick

as though in preparation to return to reading it. 'Some young man will come along some day and whisk you away from me.' He looked saddened at the prospect.

'Oh, go on with you, Da. How can anyone measure up to Cary Grant? It's him I'm waiting for.' This was her big joke. Not that she was particularly keen on the Bristol-born Hollywood star, it's just that he was well known in the city.

Her father threw back his head and laughed heartily. 'That's my girl. Aim high. I always said that if you aim for the sky, you might end up sat on the roof – just don't fall down the chimney pot. Are you going out tonight?'

'Phyllis said she might drop by. She wants to borrow one of the magazines Mum bought with some books at the jumble sale the other week.'

'Don't tell me. The magazines are all about film stars.'

'They are that. I said she could have them. I'll keep the books.'

Sean piped up, 'Is there a picture of Roy Rogers in there?'

Bridget tousled his hair. 'There might be. You'll have to have a look through.'

'Does Phyllis like Roy Rogers?' asked, Katy.

Bridget made a so-so face. 'I'm not sure. I think she prefers Clark Gable.'

Kathy frowned. 'Who's he?'

'Bet he don't shoot the baddies like Roy Rogers do,' said Sean with an air of knowledgeable confidence.

Bridget brushed off her skirt as she got up from the grass. 'I think you'll find he does sometimes. It depends what films he's in.'

Her father brushed a few insects from his newspaper, his expression one of concern. 'Enough talk of shooting and killing. There's plenty of that in the newspapers as it is and a sorry concern it should be for us all.' Realising what he'd said and not wanting to lay unnecessary worry on his children's shoulders, he ordered them to go in and get ready for their evening meal. 'While you wait for supper, do a bit of reading, any homework you have, then after you've eaten, bed.'

The kids went off, their high-pitched voices questioning what story Bridget would read tonight and what was homework anyway? Seldom did they get any. Once the school gates were closed, that seemed to be it for both pupils and teachers.

Bridget folded her arms and squinted at the sky. A slight breeze disturbed dust from where the bonfire had burned to ash some weeks before. Her father had attempted to flatten the area, but a few scorched twigs remained.

The kids went inside leaving a hollow silence behind them. She looked to her father, noticed that he too was eyeing the fire. Suddenly their eyes met in mutual understanding and she felt his pain, just as surely as she knew he felt hers.

Neither father nor daughter wished to dwell on the fire and what had burned to ashes on there. The talk returned to the gathering storm of a war that seemed to be coming closer though nobody really wanted it.

'Do you think there'll be a war, Pa? I mean, now there's this pact between Russia and Germany?'

He grunted what sounded like a reluctant yes.

Bridget lowered her eyes and looked at him. He was still a relatively strong man, but how much stronger had he been when young and sailed the seven seas? And what if there had been no war back then? At least he'd still have his leg.

She caught a glimpse of the newspaper headlines, something about the Prime Minister, Neville Chamberlain, something else about the King inspecting a Royal Navy dockyard. Everything that was happening seemed to shout the word 'war'.

An odd chill took hold of her. Up until recently, war had been only a word. It had now darkened to something else entirely.

'Bristol's buzzing with talk of war,' she said, wrapping her arms around herself. 'It's on the wireless, at the pictures and even on the trams and buses, all I could hear was people giving their opinions.'

'Opinions don't hurt anyone.' He looked up.

Bridget winced.

Patrick Milligan saw her fear and thought perhaps he'd said too much. The last thing he wanted was to upset his children. He wanted them all to have a happy life, untainted by war, and cursed the likes of the German Chancellor, Adolf Hitler, for his militaristic ambitions.

'Now listen, sweetheart,' he said, his voice softer and gentler than it had been. 'Don't worry about war. Tell you what, how about you take all your wages this Saturday and go shopping for a new dress. It's my job to put the meals on the table, not yours.' He spoke with the same soft Irish brogue he'd always had. Bridget's accent was similar though tainted by the local one. To make herself more easily understood, she tended to articulate her vowels and consonants very carefully.

Bridget kissed him on top of the head, grateful for his generosity and excited at the prospect of shopping with her friends. 'I'm excited already. The whole of Saturday would be nice. I'll have to check whether I'm needed. It'll make a change from just window shopping.'

The factory worked five and a half days a week, sometimes six for those who wanted overtime.

Crossing her fingers, she closed her eyes and made a wish. *The whole of Saturday please.*

The thought of shopping in Castle Street was very attractive, though of course she wouldn't go alone. Phyllis would love the opportunity and perhaps even little Maisie who had thoroughly enjoyed the window shopping and might be persuaded to shop for real – perhaps in the cheaper shops and stalls of St Nicholas Market, a series of narrow alleys where the sky was a mere strip between the overhanging gables of ancient buildings. Perhaps they could go for a tea and bun or even – a really naughty thing at lunchtime – they could indulge in a small sherry at the Llandoger Trow in King Street, just down and across from the Old Vic. The theatre was said to be the oldest in the country, and the Llandoger Trow, named after the long barges that brought whole tree trunks from the Forest of Dean via the village of Llandogo on the banks of the Wye, was a huge old black-and-white half-timbered place. In the book *Treasure Island*, Robert Louis Stevenson had based the dockside pub owned by Long John Silver on the Trow.

She smiled at the thought of going in there and surprising the exuberant Aggie, who had chosen to work in the tobacco factory rather than put up twenty-four hours a day with her husband, the landlord of this famous hostelry.

'Thanks, Pa. No doubt Phyllis will come with me. So will Maisie,' said Bridget as she helped her father up from his chair, his tin leg an encumbrance to doing it by himself. 'The Three Musketeers will be on the loose,' she added in a jolly manner.

'Maisie. Is that the new girl?'

'It is.'

Bridget had told him about Maisie some weeks earlier.

'Funny little thing. Don't seem to have any friends. I've adopted her – so to speak.'

Patrick Milligan beamed at his daughter. 'You're a kind girl, Bridie that you are. Where does this girl live?'

'York Street. It's in a place called The Dings. Can't say I've ever heard of it before.'

Her father stopped folding up his newspaper into four equal

pieces and looked at her. 'The Dings! That's in St Phillips.' He frowned. 'I've heard tale it's run-down and best avoided. Poverty-stricken and full of ne'er-do-wells and criminals.'

'There are poor people everywhere, Pa.'

His frown deepened. 'You're right, child. Nobody can help being poor. There's many that fall on hard times through no fault of their own. It's the undesirables that worry me, and from what I hear, The Dings, like most of St Phillips, has more than its fair share of them too.'

'I can't help it, Pa. She needs a friend.'

Her father's eyes were moist. 'You'll make a good mother one day, me girl.'

'I'd have to find a good man first, Pa.'

'You'll be snapped up,' he said with conviction. 'You're too gorgeous to ignore, me girl. Too gorgeous by half.'

'I'm your daughter. You would say that.'

He laughed and she smiled without betraying the turmoil she was feeling inside. Other young women looked forward to marriage and motherhood, but she did not. Why didn't they fear it like she did? Was she really that much of a coward? She thought of Bert at work, how he was always asking her out. She'd always said no. Every other young man who'd asked her had got the same response. She couldn't find it in herself to take that first step on the road almost every woman took and couldn't see it ever happening.

Ready to go indoors now, her father took her arm in his, though the truth was it was him leaning on her rather than the other way round. The garden path was a bit uneven, though for the most part he managed well, even negotiating the three steps at the end that led to the back door.

'Do you think the Great War had a hand in making people poor?' Bridget asked.

He grunted before answering. 'We were told things would be better and those of us wounded given a bit of a pension. Not enough. Proud men brought low by lack of limbs and lack of support.' He bent forward slightly and slammed his hand against his false leg. 'I swore it wouldn't stop me from supporting my family.'

'It didn't. You're famous for mending watches and clocks.'

Sadness clouded his eyes as he nodded his agreement. 'At least I didn't end up like some, selling matches on street corners.'

'Or turning to crime.'

They'd reached the back door. A huge sigh heaved in his chest before he said, 'You're right, Bridie. I shouldn't assume and neither should I condemn.'

Back inside the house, the children had already demolished most of the monstrous pile of bread and butter from a blue-edged meat platter in the centre of the table. The bread was meant to fill them up before the cooked meal. With hungry eyes and sniffing appreciatively they regarded the steam rising from a cast-iron cooking pot containing potatoes, more from another containing mutton stew.

Bridget's siblings watched wide-eyed as a portion of each was ladled onto a selection of mismatched dinner plates.

It didn't take too long for the plates to be cleared and packed onto the wooden draining board, the small fry heading for the garden for more play before bedtime.

Mary Milligan sat down at the kitchen table and picked up some darning.

Bridget finished the washing-up and asked, 'Cup of tea anyone?'

At first, her parents seemed not to have heard her, understandable for her father who was absorbed in whatever he was reading. Her mother would have answered more readily, but on this occasion she was peering over the top of her darning mushroom, reading the newspaper headlines.

Bridget noticed that her gaze skimmed the words more than once.

'Do you think it will happen, Patrick? After all that carnage the last time? You'd have thought they'd have learned by now.'

Bridget heard the fear in her mother's voice.

Her father's concerned eyes met those of her mother. A sudden greyness had come to his face and a tightness round his mouth as though he'd tasted something bitter. He took a deep breath as he closed the paper, turning it so the headlines his wife had been reading were face down on the table.

'That depends on the politicians, though if they're anything like the last lot...' He paused and looked down at the back of the paper, as if the advertisements for cough linctus and women's foundation wear might provide a clue. He shook his head. 'Mary, all we can do is hope that we hold onto this peace we've enjoyed now for these twenty odd years. Nobody wants anything but peace, not if they've got any sense that is.'

As planned, Phyllis came to borrow a magazine, a welcome relief from the talk of war. They settled themselves on the front step, a solid concrete affair that still held the warmth of the sun. As usual, Phyllis, flipped through it commenting on the stars and their dresses.

'You can take it with you if you like,' Bridget said cheerfully.

Phyllis nodded and gave a wan smile but said nothing. Bridget immediately perceived that something was wrong. Phyllis wasn't usually lost for words.

Bridget peered over her shoulder at the opened magazine. 'I

think I might see if I can buy some material and make a dress like that,' she said, fingering a picture of Hedy Lamarr.

'Best do it whilst there's material in the shops. Everythin' will be on ration if we 'ave this war,' said Phyllis. Her gaze wandered off to somewhere beyond the privet hedge.

Bridget sighed. 'My dad's worried.'

Phyllis pulled a face, her brow creased in thought. 'I wonder where our lives will go if there is a war? We don't really know, do we?'

Bridget hugged her bent legs and rested her chin on her knees. 'It's best there's not one. All those young chaps we know ending up in uniform.'

'I do like a man in uniform,' Phyllis declared with obvious enthusiasm. 'Just imagine, streets of young men in uniform.' The tip of her tongue slid along her lower lip as though savouring the prospect.

Bridget frowned. She was thinking of her father's lost leg, part of it blasted, the rest cut off. 'Didn't your father fight in the Great War?' she said to Phyllis.

'Sort of. He died.' She said no more but left the words hanging in the air between them.

Bridget didn't ask how he'd died, though had heard it whispered that his mind was unbalanced, a fact that was talked about as though it was an ugly item and a coward's way out. Many men had come back from that war suffering from shell shock. Unable to cope with the aftermath, many had taken their own lives.

'The thing is...' Phyllis began. She sucked her red lips inwards and her pencilled eyebrows dived in a frown. 'I don't like my life much. Oh, I like nice clothes and make-up and all that, but not much else, yet I feels there should be summut else.'

'What about your job? Your friends?'

'Well, yes. I do like me job. And my mates,' she said, throwing

Bridget a faintly apologetic smile. 'That's about all I'm sure about. It's just that at times my life seems a bit empty, as though there's summut out there that I ain't discovered yet.'

'Sounds exciting. Let me know when you find out what it is.' Bridget's comment was accompanied by a light-hearted laugh. She had known Phyllis for years. They'd both gone to primary and secondary school together. Even back then, Phyllis had been flamboyant, laughing, singing, dancing her way from childhood to adulthood. She'd never seemed to take anything very seriously. Unlike Bridget, she'd never been that keen on books and learning. All she'd ever wanted was to leave school and start earning money. 'And then I'll get married,' she'd proclaimed. 'When the right chap comes along.'

'At least you've got something to look forward to,' said Bridget. 'Well, two things come to that. Marrying Robert and beginning your typing lessons. Are you still going to do it?'

Phyllis was hesitant at first but finally nodded. 'Yes. I want to do it. I want to better meself, Bridget, though Robert...'

'You haven't told him yet.'

Phyllis bit her bottom lip. 'No. I haven't.'

Bridget had her own thoughts on Robert. He was not her idea of Prince Charming, in fact she got the impression the first time she'd met him that he was uncompromising and stubborn. He would be master in his house. She only hoped Phyllis realised that.

'You don't have to get married,' she finally said.

As her words sank in, Phyllis seemed to snap out of her deep thinking.

'Oh, don't take any notice of me. It's all this talk of war. That's what's getting to me. Let's just forget all I said.'

* * *

The house in darkness, Patrick Milligan stood outside the back door watching smoke from his pipe curl in a slow spiral to a night full of stars. There was a smell of freshly cut privet hedges in the air; all the gardens were divided from their neighbours with the same hedge, planted at the same time as the houses had been constructed. As an ex-serviceman and recipient of an army disablement pension, he'd been lucky enough to get one almost as soon as the plaster had dried.

After the carnage he'd fought through, he'd felt unimaginable joy at the prospect of raising a family in the hard-won peace.

The war to end all wars. That's what the Great War was supposed to have been.

It was with a frozen look that he eyed those stars. They were the same stars that had shone down on him when all around was mud, blood and desecration. He could still smell the filthy mud, the cries of pain and the hint of oncoming gangrene. When he'd first smelt it, he'd thought it was coming from somebody else. He'd been convinced that his wound was clean, straight through his flesh and out the other side. As the days passed and the fever began, the smell intensified. He was being eaten alive, not just by the fleas and lice, even the occasional rat, but his own body was feeding upon itself.

His eyes turned watery staring at the stars above, not so much because of their gleam, but because of the dark memories they revived.

A patch of light fell out from the back door.

'Pat. It's late. Are you coming to bed?' Mary still had the soft-spoken voice of the girl he'd fallen in love with all those years ago.

'Just having a smoke, darling.'

Not wishing her to see the moisture in his eyes, he turned and tapped the remains in his pipe against the drainpipe.

'And looking up at the stars,' he added.

'Aye. They're a constant in this topsy-turvy world that's for sure.'

'I think I'll just get the chicken feed up together for the morning,' he said. The truth was he sought composure before he went inside. The chickens were as good an excuse as any, a dozen of them, mostly cockerels which would be fattened up and sold at Christmas.

Like us in that war, he thought to himself as he scattered a bit of evening feed. He knew what people thought of him, always the chap with the cheery smile.

They knew nothing of the night sweats, the lashing out as he fought to beat back the enemy, the one supposedly vanquished many years before. The enemy was still with him, living in his mind, the sound of the guns still in his head, death all around him and there 'till the end of his days.

9

MAISIE

Maisie described both the situation in the loading bay and the man with the dark features who wore a bright red neckerchief. Her father recognised him at once and was overjoyed.

'You done well, me girl. He's called Red on account of that red neckerchief. Always wears that.' A vaguely malignant look came to his eyes. 'Covers something nasty, I bet. A right bit of luck though. Now this is what I want you to do.'

For what must be the first time ever, he put his arm around her shoulders and tugged her close. His breath was stale and damp against her ear and his thigh rubbed against hers.

He began scribbling on a piece of scrap paper. 'You take this message to 'im. Got that?'

It was a tall order. She tried to tell her father that, but he reminded her about the nice new clothes he'd given her.

His stout fingers tightened, digging into her flesh as he growled a threat. 'I'll rip 'em off yer back if you don't do something to earn them.'

'You don't want to meet 'im at the Duke of York?'

She rubbed at her shoulder once his hand had dropped away.

'Course not. Anyway, it won't be me meetin' 'im, it'll be Eddie. The London Inn's convenient for the factory, seein' as it ain't too far away and that bloke will be going straight there after work.'

The London Inn was situated at the top end of East Street in Bedminster. The red-brick Gothic-style building that was W. D. & H. O. Wills was about halfway along.

He thrust the piece of paper into her hand and pointed a threatening finger only an inch or so from her face. 'Don't let me down, girl.'

In a week's time, she would be fifteen. Not that it warranted a celebration. Nothing much was celebrated in her house. His intimidation brought home to her just how young she still was, how vulnerable, how afraid. He still had the power to make her stomach churn.

His eyes narrowed on seeing the look on her face. 'Now, now,' he said, taking her chin between thumb and index finger. 'Don't you fret. Just do as yer old dad says and he'll see you all right.' He shook her chin, then kissed her on the nose, then paused. 'Eddie Bridgeman likes you. Finks you're pretty.' He eyed her as she'd never seen him look at her before, as though he was seeing her through Eddie Bridgeman's eyes. 'Yeah. You're a pretty little thing. Just like yer mother used to be. Now thur's a thing!'

The following day, it was raining and in order to build up her courage and plan a course of action, Maisie walked to work all the way along the Feeder Canal until both she and the canal reached the River Avon. The river was tidal and the same colour as gravy browning. It looked better at night, the street lights making it sparkle.

Puddles had gathered at the side of the road and she got

splashed by the passing traffic, especially the new dark green buses that were slowly replacing the trams.

At East Street, she went round the back of the factory to where a pair of double gates lay wide open to allow the factory's lorries to go in and out.

'Here goes,' she muttered and stood as close as she could to a puddle. A lorry splashed through it and she was soaked from head to toe.

As she dashed through the gates, sopping wet and apparently breathless, a security guard stepped out.

'Excuse me, Miss, but where do you think you're going?'

She came to a halt, hair clamped to her skull and still showing all the signs of being breathless. 'I'm late. Could I nip through 'ere? I'll get stopped if I'm late. And just look at the state of me. One of your lorries did this.' She looked and sounded as though she was about to burst into tears. She'd also moderated her voice in order to earn his pity.

The truth was that she wasn't that late, but if she didn't get the note delivered this way, it meant following the route Bert had shown her and getting stopped by the man with the red face and bushy eyebrows.

The security guard smiled at her. 'Blimey, you look like a drowned rat. Well go on with you. Go on through.'

There were a number of men already busy on the loading bay. She sought the one she now knew was called Red. He still wore a red neckerchief and she couldn't help but wonder what was hidden beneath it. She found him holding a clipboard in one hand and a cigarette in the other.

'Good morning,' she said, and suddenly dropped her handbag. The note was tucked in her hand.

'Let me,' said Red, flashing her a thin-lipped smile, his complexion sallow and dark hair dripping beneath a battered hat. As he handed her the bag, without another word she slipped the note from her palm into his.

That's it, she thought, her heart pounding in her chest as she shot off, not daring to look back.

After she'd dipped her card into the slot beneath the clock, she headed with the rest of the girls for her table in the stripping room. Somebody reported that the production department was being required to fill tins with tobacco and papers for the army.

'Piles of them there are.'

Aggie shouted out for the wireless to be turned on. 'Let's listen to the news.'

Maisie was only vaguely aware of the comments about the Prime Minister and also the news that a large number of Bristol Beaufighters were rolling off the production line and that numerous air forces around the world were buying them.

A great cheer went up. It was a Bristol plane and apparently its success was way above expectation, especially once it was fitted with a Rolls-Royce engine.

There followed another news item about the plan for all men of twenty and twenty-one to be called up before the end of the month.

A deep sigh of silence descended. Every woman was thinking of all the young men likely to end up in uniform, except for Maisie. She was thinking of that note she'd delivered and what it would lead to.

She looked around at her work colleagues: Phyllis who owned an exuberant personality and never seemed to stop laughing, Bridget with her serene expression, informative comments and wisdom far beyond her years.

In the background, there was Aggie Hill, shouting out her commands and keeping everyone in order. The slightest sign of discord or bullying, and Aggie sorted it out.

Wracked with guilt Maisie bent her head to her work, wishing as she did so that her father wasn't a thief and that she hadn't fallen in with his plans. It wasn't fair on the people who made the cigarettes and this made her feel bad.

Once she'd carried out what her father and Eddie Bridgeman wanted, she could leave York Street for that fine house in the country, where she would live far away from the stink of her home. Only she wasn't so sure it was what she wanted, but in the circumstances, she might have a choice.

10

BRIDGET

It was the following day when Maisie remembered to pass on Bert's message to Bridget. 'He still wants to take you out.'

Bridget sighed and rolled her eyes. 'He just doesn't give up. He came along here this morning and asked me. He asks me every day.' If he was hoping to wear her down, it wasn't working. The more he asked, the more she dug in. Going out with him might be the first step to a future she wanted no part of.

'Why don't you go out with 'im?' said Phyllis. 'You're a good-looking girl and 'e ain't a bad bloke.'

Bridget sighed. 'I just don't want to.'

She tried not to appear irritated by her friend's urging and never, ever would she admit anything about her fear of child-birth. Phyllis had never witnessed what she had. She just didn't think she would understand.

'You're gonna get left on the shelf going on like this,' said Phyllis with the air of authority of somebody twice her age. 'When was the last time you went out on a date with the same bloke more than once?'

Bridget was no fool. It seemed that Phyllis wanted everyone to be married, as though it was the ideal situation for all women. Although Phyllis's badgering did get her down at times, she tried to sound nonchalant, as though it was of no great consequence. 'Not long ago.'

'Who was that with then?' asked Phyllis.

'I don't remember.'

'I do. A policeman, though only once. I remember it clearly. You met 'im up by the bowling green in Vicky Park.'

Bridget didn't want to be reminded of that particular date. Her parents had introduced them. They too had expected her to go out with him more than once.

'He's such a lovely chap,' they'd said, almost in unison, their faces wreathed in smiles of expectation.

They weren't to know that they'd hardly been out an hour when he'd guided her down a dark alley, lit only by an ancient wall-mounted gas light, and slid one hand up her skirt and began unbuttoning his flies with the other. The gas light had brought satanic shadow to his gaunt face, his salacious leer.

'Do you like my truncheon?' he'd sneered.

'You're disgusting,' she'd shouted and ran off.

Her parents had asked her why she was home so early. She'd said she had a headache. Again, there'd been that look between them, only this time far darker than before.

Her father was a wise man. He also defended his own. She had no doubt that he'd had a word and wondered whether the confrontation had come to blows, but wouldn't ask and her father never offered the information.

Bridget picked off a plaster from one of her fingers before rewinding it again. It was usual to refresh the plasters every so often, but there were none left in the box that sat in the middle of the table.

Phyllis was like a dog with a bone. 'But that's it, Bridget, you only go out with a bloke for one night. I can't remember you ever going steady with anyone.'

Bridget tucked a brandy-brown wisp of hair back beneath her turban. 'I just haven't met Mr Right.'

It was true what Phyllis was saying. Discounting the policeman, she'd gone out with some really nice blokes, even managed a second or third date, but once they got serious, she got cold feet.

Engrossed in thought, Bridget was careless stripping a golden Virginia stalk from its leaf. A spot of blood broke out on her finger where the plaster had broken away and the bead of redness trickled down her finger.

'That's a nasty cut,' said Aggie, who was hovering nearby. She picked up the empty plaster box and flicked it back onto the table. 'Somebody better go and fetch a fresh box from matron,' she said.

Besides overseeing the running of the medical unit, the matron also gave out the plasters they used to wind around their fingers. Every employee was entitled to treatment in the unit and those with problems were monitored and put on less strident duties. They also kept an eye on expectant mothers until they left when they reached the sixth month of their confinement.

'I'll go,' said Bridget when nobody else offered. 'Matron can dab a bit of iodine on my finger whilst I'm there. The truth was she wanted to get away from Phyllis and her continuous harping on about boyfriends.

The medical unit was on the first floor above the main production areas of the factory. Besides matron, there was a doctor in residence and two nurses on duty at any one time. Matron carried out her duties with great efficiency and the minimum of conversation. Just as expected, she dabbed a little iodine on the wound and applied another plaster. Beyond her, the two nurses currently on duty resembled statues. They certainly didn't seem to be doing much beyond tidying rows of bottles that seemed already tidy. After each small task, they smoothed their aprons and flicked at their triangular headdresses that fell in points to the nape of their necks. It all seemed very odd, almost as though they were looking for things to occupy their time. She'd been here before when it was much busier than this.

'There you are,' matron said, handing her another box from her ample storeroom. 'Sign here please.'

Her manner was as stiff as her starched headdress and crisp white apron. Bridget thought what fun it would be to break through matron's brittleness and make her laugh, or at least smile.

'We're so lucky to have you here.' It was a benign comment accompanied by Bridget's pretty smile.

People usually responded to her dancing eyes and warm smile. Matron seemed impervious. But Bridget wasn't giving up that easily. She tried another tack.

She looked round at the folded screens tucked back at the side of three examination couches and three proper hospital-style beds. The chairs in the waiting-room area were all empty and the air was heavy with the smell of carbolic, so strong it caught in her throat.

Bridget maintained her smile. 'You're very quiet in here today, matron. Not a sick person in sight.'

'Visitors,' snapped matron. 'We don't see anyone when there are visitors.' She glared at Bridget, lips pursed. The message was clear. Bridget had upset her best laid plans.

Bridget was just about to ask what visitors, when the door marked 'Doctor Meredith' jerked open. A bald-headed bespectacled man appeared wearing a white coat. A stethoscope dangled from his neck and his whole demeanour was one of agitation.

'Ah, matron. I've been having second thoughts...' He stopped when he saw Bridget. 'Ah. A patient. That's exactly what we need.'

Suddenly, matron's manner changed. She looked totally amazed. 'But, doctor, I was given to believe our visitors wanted to inspect the unit, not the patients. Everything is in order and indeed quite a credit to you and your staff – you especially,' she added, with simpering flattery

Bridget's jaw dropped at the sudden change in matron's manner, which had swung 360 degrees and all because she was addressing a doctor.

'What's your name?' the doctor addressed Bridget.

'Bridget Milligan.'

She was aware that the two duty nurses who were also present had refrained from realigning items that didn't need realigning and were watching with interest.

The doctor was also regarding her with interest.

'And what are you here for? Have you had an accident? Are you ill?'

Bridget held up her finger. 'I cut my finger and needed more plasters.'

'Oh.' He frowned and looked a bit disappointed, then brightened. 'Never mind. You'll have to do. Lay down on the couch please.' Before she had chance to protest, he guided her over to one of the examination couches. 'Now don't worry. Just get up on here.'

He ordered one of the nurses to place a screen round her.

'Right,' he said, his pale eyes blinking rapidly behind his large spectacles. 'You cut your finger and fainted. We're just making sure you didn't concuss yourself when you became dizzy and fell. Make a note of that, matron.'

Bridget attempted to raise herself. 'But I...'

Doctor on one side and a nurse on the other pressed her back down. Her turban slipped off and her hair fell over the pillow in silky skeins.

'You've beautiful hair,' said the nurse, stroking it as though to calm her. 'Beautiful eyes too.'

The doctor took note of her comments and regarded her accordingly before telling her what he wanted her to do.

'Now listen. We have a very important visitor taking a tour of the factory today. His name is Lyndon O'Neill the Third and he owns one of the largest tobacco plantations in Virginia.'

Matron's voice piped up from the foot of the bed. 'Doctor, everything is spick and span. The nurses and I have made sure it is. Do we really need to show this man that we treat patients? Surely he already knows that?'

The doctor's hairless scalp gleamed as he turned and fixed her with a superior look. 'I think we should show something of what we do here, how well we treat our employees.' He turned back and placed his palm on Bridget's forehead. 'Probably better than he treats his workers.' He added the last sentence softly so only Bridget could hear it.

'They're here,' matron hissed.

The doctor's parting shot was to tell her to rest. In a flurry of whiteness, doctor, matron and the two nurses disappeared and Bridget was all alone behind the screen.

She heard the introductions, the doctor's perfectly rounded English vowels as he detailed everything the medical facility had to offer.

In a more casual drawl, the Virginian plantation owner responded. 'It's very impressive. In fact, my son Lyndon, named after me of course, and I have both been impressed by what we've seen of England. My son intends carrying on with a further tour of this country and Europe.'

'You're not worried about the current situation in Europe?'

asked another voice, not the doctor but possibly one of the directors.

'We're Americans and so far, neutral. I don't think we should have any problems.'

Another plummy voice asked him what his son was most interested in seeing in England, or Europe if he could get there.

Bridget gulped. These were very important visitors and were being shown round by equally important people and here she was just a few feet away.

'I kind of like history.'

She heard it suggested he took a look round the city.

'There's a lot of history here in Bristol if you're interested, some of it very well known and concerning America.'

'I sure would like to see that.'

'I'm sure we can arrange for you to be shown round the more interesting spots. No doubt we can find some knowledgeable person to accompany you.'

'That would be welcome.'

'I must say this factory is very well run and I dare say you have a contented workforce.' Bridget thought this was the father, heard footsteps and guessed he was walking about, surveying the length and breadth of the medical unit.

She held her breath. His footsteps were coming closer. Suddenly she didn't want to be discovered like this, lying here like a fool when there was nothing wrong with her. She decided to take control. She sat up, determined to do something. 'Doctor? Doctor? Do you think I can go back to work now?'

At first, there was silence, then a single folding panel of the screen was swung back and matron appeared and raised a finger in front of her mouth in a bid to get her to be quiet.

'I'm fine. I want to go. I've work to do.'

'Hey,' said an American voice. 'I like the sound of this girl. Never stop a willing horse, that's what I say.'

'I'm not a horse,' Bridget retorted.

'Hey. Is that a slight Irish accent? Come on. Let's see this willing worker.' He sounded intrigued and suddenly there were a sea of faces staring at her open-mouthed.

Bridget was sat up. 'Can I go now?'

The doctor glanced at the note passed to him by matron before offering an explanation. 'Miss Milligan had a dizzy spell and hit her head. She's purely here for observation.'

The most youthful of the group grinned. 'Well, she's certainly being observed.'

Especially by you, she thought and felt her face warming.

'Milligan you say?' said an older man with the same accent, presumably his father. 'What part of Ireland did your family come from?'

'Cork.'

'So you're an alien planted here.' His comment drew smiles from those of his own age. Only his son seemed immune to the remark, his interest fixed on Bridget.

Bridget was indignant. 'I don't count myself an alien. I love this city. It's where John Cabot set sail to America two years after Columbus, where Robert Louis Stevenson set *Treasure Island* and Daniel Defoe met Alexander Selkirk and, based on the story he told, wrote *Robinson Crusoe*.' She stopped.

Father and son were regarding her with dropped jaws until the son finally said, 'You're well read.'

'For an Irish girl who strips the leaves that make you enough money to travel the world,' she replied.

She saw the father give a sidelong look at his son, the embarrassment on the directors' faces. It could be that she'd gone too far and might get the sack. *Oh well*, she thought, *I said it as it is.*

Resigned to her fate, she swung her legs down from the bed.

The nurses had disappeared to the far side of the room. Matron stood some distance off, her eyes flickering nervously over everyone except the doctor. For him, she reserved a look that bordered on love, or at least huge respect.

One of the directors declared that time was running short and they'd better move on. 'There's so much more to show you. Best make use of the time we have left,' he said jovially, his thick neck fighting against his shirt collar.

Humming with conversation, the party proceeded towards the double doors, the older men first, the young American bringing up the rear. Just before he followed the rest, he paused, one hand on the open door.

'You're a mine of information, Bridget Milligan. Perhaps we could meet up some time and you could tell me more about this city of Bristol.'

Her jaw dropped. He had the most amazingly blue eyes. For a moment they were all she could see, then he was gone and she became aware that her cheeks were on fire.

'Well, that's that. Back to work,' said the doctor once the doors closed behind the band of visitors.

'You could thank me for helping out,' said Bridget as she tucked her hair inside her turban before waving her hand in front of her hot cheeks.

'How dare you say that to Doctor Meredith,' hissed a sour-faced matron.

'You're right,' said the doctor, poised outside the door that showed his name in black letters on white. His eyes twinkled. 'I think you put him in his place, my dear. He is now aware that the working class is not necessarily the ignorant class. I'm a great believer in education, Miss Milligan, and hope that one day it isn't only the rich who benefit from it. Good day, Miss Milligan, and thank you again. Oh, and if your supervisor asks why you're late, refer them to the company chairman.'

Bridget was left looking at the closed door, aware that matron was huffing and puffing in the background and the nurses were keeping well out of the way.

It didn't hurt to leave on a high note, she thought, so gave everyone a smile before departing. Once outside the medical unit she was still smiling, but it had nothing to do with the nurses, the matron or the doctor. She was still returning the smile the young American had given her, still blushing at the thought of his sky-blue eyes.

She was halfway along the corridor outside, her feet tapping on the shiny brown linoleum, when somebody called her.

'Miss Milligan.'

She recognised the voice and immediately stopped in her tracks. Alone now, the young man she'd heard referred to as Lyndon O'Neill covered the ground in long strides. He was wearing a navy-blue double-breasted suit, a pale grey silk tie against his white shirt. His trilby was light in colour with a black band. He swept it off as he got close to her and she saw the merriment in his eyes, the gold streaks in his brown hair. His shoulders were broad and he was taller than her father. She guessed that the double-breasted suit jacket hid slim hips and strong legs.

It was rare indeed for her to note anyone in such detail, especially a man. The sudden realisation that she'd reacted in such an uncharacteristic manner brought a fresh flush to her face.

She was transfixed by eyes as blue as her own and his smile was enough to make her want to hear what he had to say.

He glanced at her turban. 'Your lovely hair's covered. What a shame.'

Gathering up her reeling senses, she held her head at a cocked angle and told him in no uncertain words that rules were rules. Nobody wanted to go home with hair stinking of tobacco dust.

'And it gets in the way,' she added.

He rested his elbow on the wall, his head against his hand – a nonchalant gesture yet at the same time full of confidence.

'So you don't wear a turban outside of work.'

The merriment was still there and his voice and accent had a musical ring to it – a bit like her own, a mixture of where her family was from and where they were now. At home, the accent was stronger. In the world outside, it was modified.

'What are you doing here? I thought you were off to Europe before it closed down or traipsing around the city with a tour guide. I believe they exist.'

He smiled, though looked taken aback, even a little bashful. He began feeding the brim of his hat through his fingers. 'Truth is, I think my visit of Europe won't happen. Things are getting a bit too hot over there, but I would like to see more of this city, and I wondered whether, as a local girl, you would consent to showing me round?'

Up until now she'd held on to a small vestige of hostility. He was the favoured son of a very rich man and she'd fully expected not to respond to those laughing eyes and that honest, handsome face. What was it that made him seem familiar, that beat down any barrier she put up to ward off his effect on her? A sudden rush of realisation gave her the answer. In a strange way, he reminded her of her father.

'Well,' he said, a thoughtful look appearing when she failed to answer. 'I can get you time off. The chairman's my godfather. It wouldn't be a big deal to arrange some time off beginning Saturday morning?'

She eyed him speculatively. The thought of telling him all she knew about Bristol thrilled her. It was almost a feeling of power and as if she'd climbed and reached some kind of pinnacle in her life. Somebody wanted the benefit of her knowledge. What was more, she wanted to give him that knowledge.

She was struck again by his golden looks, the sparkle in his eyes, the way his lips curved in an almost secretive smile. She took a deep breath. 'How long have you got?'

He shrugged. 'I guess, two days, three at the most, then we're back to London. Will that be long enough?'

She smiled. Two days. Long enough to enjoy but not long enough to get involved.

'Two days should do it.'

'OK. Tomorrow's Friday. Shall we say Saturday morning? Give me your address and I'll send a car.'

'A car?' Her eyes almost popped out of her head. Few cars were seen in Marksbury Road and when one was spotted, it usually belonged to the doctor. The only other motorised vehicle that turned up on a regular basis was the coal lorry. Tradesmen mostly still used a horse-drawn vehicle, including the milkman.

'Shall we say ten o'clock?' he suggested.

Too excited to utter a word, she nodded and went weak at the knees when he smiled at her.

'What kept you so long?' asked Phyllis when she got back.

'I'm starving,' said Maisie as the one o'clock bell rang for lunch. For the moment at least, Bridget would not be pressed further.

She maintained her silence all the way to the canteen, feeling as though she was walking on air.

11

PHYLLIS

On their way to work, long shadows followed Phyllis and Bridget across the patch of waste ground locally known as the tip. Even in the full brightness of the day, the gasometer threw a dense shadow that held back the daylight.

'Well,' exclaimed Phyllis after Bridget had told her about Lyndon O'Neill. 'Fancy that! You takin' a millionaire American around Bristol, and me startin' my typing course.'

Bridget had sworn her to secrecy. 'There's a lot that ties Bristol with America, you know. And that's all it's about, but I don't want everyone to know.'

'Me neither,' said Phyllis, as though her own secret was just as exciting. Laughter gurgled in her throat. 'Robert will kill me when he finds out that I'm going to learn how to type. But there, a girl has to try and better herself. I'm looking forward to getting a job in the office. But I won't forget me mates though, you do know that don't you, Bridget?'

The truth was she'd felt a notch above her workmates since enrolling for the typing course, the twelve pounds it cost saved from her wages, and was looking forward to September. Her mother needn't know and neither did Robert. Working in an office had something glamorous about it. She'd be smartly dressed all the time and not wearing an overall.

That feeling that she was going to better herself had been diminished. A posh car was going to pull up outside Bridget's house.

'He was going to travel on to Europe, but it's getting dangerous even though America is neutral,' Bridget explained.

Bridget wasn't crowing. She wasn't the type, but all the same Phyllis couldn't help feeling resentful.

'So they won't get involved.' Phyllis tried to sound knowledge-able on current affairs, though she'd never read a newspaper or a book. Magazines that dealt with fashion or film stars were more her cup of tea.

'They're keeping out of it,' returned Bridget, 'though they started out the same in the Great War.'

'Still,' said Phyllis, determined to look on the bright side, 'we're not at war yet and I 'ope we never will be.'

She turned her attention to where single-storey concrete buildings were beginning to rise in front of the green gas tank that so dominated the tip. Suddenly the sound of a concrete mixer starting up drowned their ongoing conversation.

'Air-raid shelters,' Bridget shouted over the noise.

Phyllis eyed them silently. Once the shattering sound was behind them, they resumed their conversation. Phyllis tried to invite herself round on Saturday morning so she could take a peek at the glamorous American.

Bridget told her not to, but Phyllis had made up her mind. She wanted to take a look, to see what she was missing being engaged to be married and all that.

The truth was that the news had hit her head on and got her questioning whether there was somebody out there better than

Robert. What if she ditched him and bade her time? Perhaps getting married at twenty-five?

A few other girls also heading for the factory joined them. There was laughter and conversation, and although Phyllis badly wanted to crow about Bridget's meeting on Saturday, she kept her mouth firmly shut.

The rumbling of the concrete mixer was replaced with the sound of a different kind of machine assaulting their eardrums, causing all eyes to turn skywards.

'An aeroplane!'

Hands were pressed against foreheads, everyone awestruck by the course of the modern marvel slicing through the summer sky.

'First one I've ever seen,' said Phyllis, her voice full of amazement. 'Makes you wonder how they manage to stay up there.'

'Aerodynamics,' said Bridget. 'That's what it's called.'

'Get you, clever clogs,' said one of the others.

Bridget remarked that her father had seen them during the Great War and had told her all about dog fights between the old string bags – officially known as Bristol Bulldogs – and the German air force.

Gradually, it faded into the distance. Everyone sighed to see it go but instantly reminded themselves that they were on their way to work and at this rate they'd be late getting there. Footsteps quickened. Stopping to stare had robbed them of valuable minutes.

'Oi. Fancy going out tonight,' shouted one of the men building the air-raid shelters.

Unfortunately for the would-be Lotharios, young women were not the only ones taking a shortcut.

'Love to,' shouted back Mrs Delaney, who was pushing forty and had ankles like milk bottles that overhung her shoes. 'Where you taking me?'

Everyone laughed until someone remarked about the connec-tion with the plane flying overhead and the air-raid shelters and the hope that they were never needed.

'Fingers crossed,' said Phyllis. 'Let's forget about it and go out and enjoy ourselves tonight. I fancy going to the pictures. There's a comedy on at the Town Hall.'

The Town Hall was the name of the small local cinema just off East Street. It had been there since the twenties so its seating was a bit battered and it didn't have quite the glamour of newer establishments. The locals referred to it as the Fleapit.

Inside, the tobacco-filled air in the corridor grew warmer and noisier with the sound of the tobacco processing machines as they walked.

Phyllis had to shout to make herself heard. 'How about we meet outside the London Inn first?'

'All right by me,' said Bridget.

The doors of the stripping room opened to the sound of chat-tering women, a cacophony of voices, scraping chairs and a little light music from the factory wireless. The wireless kept them going for most of the day. Whilst there was music, the sound was turned up. When the God hour or the news was broadcast, it was mostly turned down, the women filling the gap with their own singing.

The wireless interrupted: 'Here is the news.'

'Let's turn it off until there's music.'

One of the younger women climbed up onto a table to turn it down but met a hail of protest. Nobody would normally have said a word, but this time, a number of the older women protested.

Aggie almost dragged her back down. 'We wants to know what that old bugger Hitler is up to.'

One of the other older women chimed in, 'These knows what

'e's up to, but do that Neville Chamberlain know? Leave it on. Let's 'ear what the silly old sod is up to now.'

A strange silence fell over the whole room. The stripping still went on, hands working as methodically as the machines that chewed the leaves into tobacco. Everyone was listening.

The underlying message in the BBC newscast was that give Herr Hitler an inch and he'd take a mile. Aggie confirmed the fact in a loud voice.

'I don't fink there's going to be a war,' said a peroxide blonde called Muriel, who, rumour had it, was having an affair with George Benson, one of the foremen.

'All a load of fuss about nothing, if you ask me,' piped up a younger girl.

Aggie slapped her round the head with a palm, made coarse and hard from years of stripping tobacco leaves.

'Ouch! That 'urt.' The girl rubbed at the spot where the blow had landed.

'You won't be saying that when Hitler's throwing people off Clifton suspension bridge,' growled the older woman, a chain smoker with a gravelly voice that struggled to come up her throat.

Bridget and Phyllis exchanged wry smiles at the thought of Adolf Hitler strutting along the length of the Victorian bridge. It seemed comical more so than possible.

From that point on, the subject of conversation barely strayed from what might happen. Everyone had their own concerns.

Aggie broke the stalemate.

'My brother's already at sea on the banana boats. So careful what you says. We gets a lot of seamen in the bar of the Llandoger. They got a lot to say about what's goin' to 'appen. Shortages of food for a start. We import a lot. It's got to come in by ship, and if the Germans do like they did in the last war, we'll be lucky if 'alf of the ships get in. The rest will get sunk. As I said, my brother's on the banana boats, so no more bananas once war breaks out.'

Another woman, Florence Brown piped up. 'My boy was called up back in May. Twenty - to twenty-two-year-olds for the reserves and now they reckon it won't be too long before they're called up again. A lot of the fellahs in 'ere got made reservists as well. It seemed kind of part-time at first. Even gave those that finished the training a suit.' Her big bosoms pushed against the buttons of her overall in a big sigh. 'I thought it was a nice suit 'til I realised what it meant – if there's a war my boy'll be one of the first to go.' The woman's voice trembled.

As a tear rolled down her cheek, one of the other women patted her fat arm. 'He'll be all right, Flo. After all, 'e's only a reserve. It might not come to anything, and then he'll be 'ome with you. But there you are. All the young men will be in uniform before very long whether they want to be or not.'

At all this talk of war, Phyllis turned thoughtful. The minuscule diamonds on her engagement ring flashed and twinkled. The captured light drew her attention and gave form to her thoughts. She no longer listened to the banter going on around her. She was thinking of Robert, when he was likely to be called up and how it might affect their relationship. Everyone said they were a well-matched couple and would be downright surprised if she called it off. Doubts had set in, but she turned cold at the thought of telling him to his face that she didn't want to marry him. If he got called up, she might not need the courage to raise those doubts. The war might make the decision for her.

* * *

The weekend was coming and thoughts of Robert were pushed to the back of her mind, replaced by enthusiasm at the thought of going to the pictures with Bridget and Maisie.

'I'm wearing my blue dress,' trilled Phyllis. 'The one with the sweetheart neckline.'

Her high spirits dropped like a stone when she saw Robert outside the factory waiting for her.

Bridget and Maisie came to a halt but were close enough to hear what was said.

Phyllis tried not to sound ungrateful when she asked, 'What you doin' ere?'

'I've got these,' he said, waving tickets of some kind. 'A mate's got a dog running up at Whitchurch tonight. Had a couple of spare tickets. Thought I'd better meet you so you could know to get ready. I'll be round for you after you've 'ad your tea.'

'Well, actually, I did have something planned,' she said as he took hold of her elbow. 'I was going to the pictures with the girls. We've already made arrangements.'

He was totally dismissive. 'Well, you ain't now. You're going out with me.'

Phyllis winced at the tightness of his hand on her arm and the quickness of his steps as he marched her off up East Street. He totally ignored Bridget and Maisie. Neither did he give her chance to say goodbye. Their arrangements were nowhere near as important as his.

Phyllis did her best to get out of it. 'Robert, I don't much like greyhound racing. For a start I'm allergic to dog hair.'

'You won't be that close to them, so it don't matter.' He gave her arm a squeeze. 'Gather the rosebuds, Phyllis. Let's enjoy ourselves whilst we still can. Who knows where we'll all be this time next year. You could be married to a man in uniform. A bit of the right training and I could be a second officer on a ship – perhaps even a first officer.'

Sheene Road that led into East Street was crowded with more factory girls, some of whom worked at the Robinson paper bag factory. Phyllis smiled and nodded at those she knew, though only briefly. Robert wasn't giving her chance to linger.

She tried another tack. 'You're right, Robert. We should make the most of it. That's why I wanted to go out with the girls.'

His expression soured. 'You work with them all day. It'll do you good to have a change. You can see them tomorrow. Anyways, you better get used to not seeing them. I'll not 'ave any wife of mine out working. Once we're married, that's it. Your job is to run a house and look after me.'

Phyllis immediately thought of the typing course. It seemed to her it was now or never so briskly told him all about it. 'I know you've always tried to better yourself, Robert, and I thought I would do the same. So once we're married, I might not be working in the factory. I might be working in the office – in the typing pool.'

The very thought of her ambition filled her with excitement. To think that at some point in the future, she, Phyllis Mason, would be going to work wearing smart clothes and not an overall. Surely Robert too would be thrilled at the idea. They'd be climbing the social ladder, both working in offices rather than on the factory floor.

Robert's response was brusque and his look condemning. 'I don't care where it is. No wife of mine is going out to work, no matter where it is.'

She struggled to plead her case, hoping against hope that she could persuade him to let her do what she wanted.

'But what if there is a war? I might have to go to work.'

He stopped, took hold of her roughly by the shoulders and gave her a shake.

'Now stop all that stupid talk. I'm telling you, Phyllis. You're going to be my wife and that's it.'

Phyllis gulped. Robert had always been controlling, but he'd never laid down the law so vehemently and neither had he gripped her shoulders so tightly.

'There's not going to be any war.' The words tripped reluctantly off her tongue.

He looked pleased, loosened his grip on her shoulders and patted them instead. 'That's my girl. Me and you will live in our own little world. We'll keep all the troubles on the other side of the door.'

Her face felt frozen, too frozen to return his smile. His suggestion filled her with foreboding. It seemed they would live in isolation, in a home chosen by him, somewhere she wouldn't be able to see her friends, perhaps not even her relatives. The idea alarmed her, and yet she'd not told him so. Why hadn't she stood up to him? Why did she always compromise and take the easy way out, Phyllis Mason who was always the life and soul of the party?

His expression was one of pure satisfaction as he took her right hand in his and marched her along beside him, looking very pleased with himself.

More visions of their married life popped into her mind: her waving him off to work in the morning, making sure his dinner was set on the table by six on the dot. He'd already told her that he expected his dinner to be waiting for him. His mother did that. Robert had hardly got through the door and hung his coat up when there it was, hot and steaming, ready for him to eat.

Only lately had it come to her that Robert lived to a timetable. Could she live like that and totally conform to what he wanted? She was beginning to think not. In a strange way she wanted this war to happen, for lives to be altered, hers especially. At some point, Robert would be called up. It was only fair to tell him long before that happened, but truth be told, she lacked the courage and truly hoped the war would do it for her. In her case, parting wouldn't be sweet sorrow, it would be damned welcome!

She sighed, resigned to seeing him tonight rather than her friends. For now, she would let sleeping dogs lie, but in time, one way or another, she had to break off their engagement. It was just a question of when.

12

MAISIE

Before going out, Maisie had had a strip-down wash; she preferred to get the tin bath in front of the fire for a proper bath on a night when she knew her father was out, usually on a Saturday.

The scullery she'd washed in was little more than a lean-to at the back of the house, a structure streaked with green mould on the outside and black mould inside. The hot water from the kettle provided just about enough water to wash in and she'd made sure to shut the door behind her and jam a chair against the handle for extra privacy.

Despite it only being late August, the draught coming in through the gaps beneath the door and around the lopsided windows kept it cool.

Maisie shivered as she took off her clothes until she was standing there in knickers and a camisole top. She piled her dark hair on top of her head and regarded herself in the old chipped mirror hanging above the sink. The mirror was speckled but had just enough clear surface to see herself in. A pair of velvet brown eyes set in an elfin face looked out at her. Her lips were girlish, dark pink and well-shaped. She used only the most minimal make-up – a little face powder on her cheekbones, some shading on her eyelids. Her lashes and eyebrows were all her own, black, bushy and neat.

The clothes she'd chosen to wear were hanging on a hook on the back of the door. The dress was red, a colour which complemented her dark hair and complexion, one of a number of dresses chosen by her from a suitcase in the front bedroom. She'd eyed the sales ticket before putting it on. At least he'd stolen it from a shop not from some woman's wardrobe. It still wasn't right but she could hardly take it back.

It had been a few days since her father's visit to the London Inn and she'd heard nothing about it. Hopefully she was no longer needed and consequently felt more relaxed and optimistic there would be no other demands for her to betray her employer – and her friends. But then, she was going to leave all that behind, wasn't she? Once her father agreed to let her leave home and go into service. All she had to do was choose the right time to ask his permission.

The sound of voices came from the other room. For a moment, she thought they were coming her way and grabbed a towel to cover herself.

People were always coming and going to the house in York Street. Her father traded from here, selling on stolen goods and buying in things he thought he might get a profit for. On top of that was his new business of lending money to impoverished families at extortionate interest rates. For the most part she kept out of the way of his transactions and the people he dealt with, but sometimes they were unavoidable – like last night, when she'd come home in time to see Eddie Bridgeman getting into the back seat of his car, his driver installing his bulky frame in the front. She had tried to duck into the house before he saw her, but didn't quite manage it.

His voice had rung out between the rows of terraced houses lining each side of the street. 'Maisie, isn't it? Care to come for a ride?'

She'd spotted her mother coming in the opposite direction from the off-licence loaded down with a shopping bag full of beer. One shoulder was sagging with the weight of it and she'd seemed much slower than usual, coughing and spluttering as she went, cigarette hanging from the side of her mouth.

Completely ignoring Eddie Bridgeman, Maisie had headed for her mother and suggested they carry the bag between them.

A bout of coughing dispelled any attempt by her mother to dissuade her. Maisie had grabbed one of the handles. Thankfully, Eddie had driven off.

As she washed, Maisie thought of Eddie Bridgeman. He was visiting York Street more and more often, but was it all on account of cigarettes or was there something else he was after?

She recalled her brother's words about Eddie liking young girls and the younger the better. Disgusting for a married man, she thought.

There was more shouting on the other side of the door and then a silence, broken only by the clumping of heavy footsteps. This was followed by a voice – the one she least wanted to hear.

'What's the matter with this bloody door?'

Suddenly the door flew open and the chair she'd wedged beneath the doorknob crashed to the ground.

Her father stood there, not attempting to apologise or retreat, but staring at her with dropped jaw and bulging eyes.

She clutched the towel more tightly, shoulders hunched

forward, hands grappling to spread the towel over as much of her body as possible.

For a man who considered he had improved his lot in the world, he was as scruffy as ever. She firmly believed that even if he became a millionaire – which was about as likely as the train to Weston Super Mare diverting and flying to the moon – he would always look a mess, always be scruffy, always be disinclined to wash or take a bath.

She threw him as indignant a look as she could and shouted as loudly as possible, 'Dad, I'm washing.'

He ignored her, rested an arm against the door frame and looked to have no intention of going.

'Got our first consignment today,' he said to her, his slimy tongue flicking along his equally slimy bottom lip. 'And all fanks to you, me little darlin'. We'll be getting a despatch note whenever we want – thanks to you and my mate Red.'

Maisie held her head at a cocky angle, her expression full of contempt. 'Your mate? Since when did 'e become that?'

He took a step closer to her, a sleazy smile curling his wet lips, his eyes glistening with a look she instantly disliked. 'Since you renewed our acquaintance. Lucky thing for 'im 'e never bin nicked. That's good,' he said, wagging his index finger as if to reaffirm how important this was. 'You did well, me little darlin'. Very well.'

There was something about the look and smell of him that turned her stomach. The intent in his eyes was frightening. She took a step back, her heart thudding against her ribs, the ragged towel tightly held against her chest. She was vulnerable, but so in a way was he. There was something he wanted that she wasn't prepared to give but what she also sensed was his weakness. She instantly decided that this was a now-or-never moment.

'Seein' as I done so good, do this mean I can get that job I want at the big 'ouse in Long Ashton?'

In all probability the job in Long Ashton was long gone, but there were plenty more. She'd heard big houses were always looking for competent maids, that there were shortages of good staff thanks to the changes that occurred after the Great War.

Her father looked astounded, with eyes bulging and a gurgling coming from his throat that became mocking laughter. 'Big 'ouse? You ain't goin' to no big 'ouse, my girl. There's no money in that.'

'I don't want to work at the tobacco factory forever.'

In all truth, that wasn't quite the way she felt nowadays thanks to the friendships she'd made, so what her father said next took her by surprise.

'You ain't gonna work there forever. I got plans fer you, me girl. You're too pretty to be wasted in that place.' He looked her up and down in a way no father should look at his daughter.

'What do you mean?' Her voice trembled and she clutched the towel even tighter.

'Me an' Eddie's got plans fer you...' His fingers got as far as hooking into the towel before she screamed. Suddenly he was jerked backwards.

'Shouldn't you be somewhere else, Dad?'

Alf looked angry and his father looked diminished. There had been times in the past when Alf had taken beatings from his father, but no more. The son was now bigger and stronger than the father. He could fight back and had done, but never before had Maisie seen him display such anger, grasping the old man's shirt collar tight enough to choke him.

Her father was spluttering to say something and his hands were grappling with those that were almost squeezing the life out of him. but Alf was young and definitely stronger.

Her brother spun his father round in a circle, then shoved him out into the passageway and slammed the door behind him.

'You all right, sis?' he said, his face full of concern and his hands rubbing her shoulders.

She nodded. 'Yeah. I'm fine.'

Alf glanced at the dress hanging behind the door and forced a smile. 'Goin' somewhere nice, are you?'

'Yeah. The pictures with me mates.'

Saying she was going out with her mates brought a smile to her face, not just because she was going out, but that thinking of Bridget and Phyllis pleased her. The girls she'd gone to school with had been tough. They'd also given her a wide berth on account of her obnoxious father, who was known for being a thief, a drunk and a bully.

'Well, you go out and enjoy yourself. Forget about the old man. He can't do anything to hurt you while I'm around.'

The thought of him not being around filled her with alarm. 'What if you get called up, Alf? What do I do then?'

He grimaced. 'We'll cross that bridge when we come to it. Now come on. I'll hang around until you're ready to go out.'

* * *

Maisie waited for Bridget close to the London Inn where the barrow boys were clearing up after a long day selling fruit and veg. Crowds of boys and girls trooped past, all determined to enjoy themselves, and the buses going by were pretty full.

The pub door opened and a figure she recognised came out. He was wearing a red neckerchief and his hair was curly and longer than it should be.

Instinctively, she sank back behind the carts of fruit and

vegetables. A man selling from one of them asked her if she'd like to buy a pound of bananas. 'Whilst you still can before all the bloody boats get sunk,' he added.

Maisie shook her head, her gaze remaining on the man she knew as Red.

He set off towards North Street, his long thin legs covering the ground quickly as he headed towards the Town Hall. How long, she wondered, before the first consignment of cigarettes was stolen?

She shook the thought from her head. She didn't want to think about it. She didn't want to face her part in it.

Bridget was late and was puffing and panting by the time she got there, apologised, then commented on Maisie's dress. 'That colour really suits you, and your hair looks lovely.'

'It's too curly,' Maisie said bashfully, pulling at her springy curls, but Bridget's comment had pleased her no end.

Bridget was dressed in a red spotted navy-blue dress, the skirt skimming her slim figure. A small gold crucifix gleamed at her throat and gold studs graced her ears.

'We'd better get going then,' said Bridget.

They stepped briskly along, but their steps slowed once the picture house was in sight. The queue snaked quite a way along the frontage, past the billboards advertising the film and along in front of the shops.

'Oh no.' Bridget's face was a picture of disappointment. 'We'll be lucky to get in. What shall we do?'

As she scanned the queue a sharp whistle split the air. 'Hey Bridget. You're late. Come on, we've bin waitin' for you, ages. Thought you'd 'ave got 'ere earlier seeing as I'm paying.'

Bert Redmond from work was waving at them as though they really had arranged to meet up.

'Come on,' he said.

The girls exchanged relieved smiles. Despite a few disbelieving looks and grumbles from those in the queue, they were let into the space Bert and his friend had made.

He put his arm around Bridget. 'I didn't think you were coming. Glad you're here though.'

Bridget's first thought was to shrug his arm off until a few sour looks and muted grumbles in the queue behind them changed her mind.

'Cheeky bugger,' she whispered.

Maisie was getting the same treatment and was immediately on her guard, though decided that dealing with the man next to her would be a piece of cake compared with dealing with her father's unwelcome advances.

'My name's Sid,' said her companion in a hushed voice, his breath warm against her ear. 'What's yours?'

'Maisie,' she whispered back.

He had red hair, freckles over his nose and a slight gap between his front teeth. She judged him to be about nineteen or twenty.

'Where do you work?' she asked.

'Mardons. We make cigarette packets and cards.'

'Playing cards?'

She knew her father was a sucker for playing cards. 'Me dad plays cards.'

Sid laughed. 'Not them kind of cards. The ones Wills's put inside cigarette packets for people to collect. Ain't 'alf nice of them. I likes the football and cricket cards. I got the complete set of each – you know, Dixie Dean and Stanley Matthews. Don Bradman...'

'Do they all play football?'

He shook his head and maintained a wide grin. 'Don Bradman's an Australian. 'E plays cricket.'

For a moment, his hazel eyes held hers and it seemed he might kiss her. Her look hardened.

'Don't even think about it,' she growled softly.

* * *

The darkened interior of the Town Hall Picture House had tempted Sid to take advantage. A quick whack in the groin with her handbag and he swiftly got the message.

Once the film was over and they were outside, the boys offered the girls cigarettes. Bridget took one, but Maisie declined.

'No thanks.'

Sid looked at her in surprise. 'You works in a fag factory and don't smoke? Why's that then?'

'Me dad makes up for it. Smokes like a bloody chimney. Stinks the 'ouse out. I can't stand the stink of 'im 'cause of that and I don't want to stink like 'im either.'

They sauntered off away from the Town Hall Picture House, the boys all bravado and cigarette smoke, the girls walking slightly behind talking about work mostly and what they were doing over the weekend.

Maisie sensed Bridget was a bit less forthcoming than usual. In the past, she'd always shared what lay ahead, but tonight she seemed to be holding back. It made Maisie wonder whether Bridget had a date with somebody who wasn't from the tobacco factory, someone they didn't know. If anyone knew whether she was or no, it would be Phyllis. Maisie made a mental note to ask Phyllis when she saw her.

Bert was talking to Bridget about his plans to join the RAF.

Maisie asked Sid about his plans when he was called up.

He drew long and hard on his cigarette before exhaling a whitish fug that whirled like a dancer up and away into the night.

'I already 'ave. Got called up to the reserves back in April. If war does 'appen, I'll be first to go.'

His tone was sombre. Maisie felt for him. His answer surprised her and somehow softened her attitude towards him. He looked too young now to be called up, let alone back in April.

'How old are you?' she asked.

'Twenty. All us that were called up for the reserves back in April were around the same age. Trained us, gave us a suit and sent us 'ome again.'

She thought about his age; five or six years older than her, but still young.

'Where do you live?

'Same as Bert. Southville. Do you know it?' he asked.

'I've heard of it.'

'I lives in Beauley Road, not far from the cigar factory in Raleigh Road. How about you?'

She badly wanted to lie, but Bridget answered before she could.

'Maisie lives in St Phillips, so don't even think about walking her home.'

'Yer right. That is a bit far.'

'Then, if you're a gentleman, you'll get on the bus with her,' Bridget added laughingly.

'That's no problem. Be glad to in fact,' answered Sid.

Maisie felt her face reddening. Its reputation brought a certain look to people's faces, well known as one of the shabbiest and smelliest places in the city, an old Bristol working-class area and a hotbed of poverty and crime. Most of it was still gas-lit, not just the streets, but the miserable little houses as well. Rats and mice lived cheek by jowl with people.

She became aware of Sid being a bit closer, heard his breathing, felt the warmth of his body despite the space between them.

'I don't mind coming on the bus with you, Maisie.'

'You don't need to,' she snapped, her earlier softening hardening again.

He grabbed her arm, forced her to stop and look at him. 'I'm trying to be nice.'

She stuck out her chin defiantly. 'You don't 'ave to be.'

He swore, shook his head and looked away.

There was something innocent in his expression she hadn't noticed before. His eyes were hazel but gentle; like the puppy dog she'd once found. Her father had played hell when she'd brought it home, grabbed it and threw it out onto the street. The puppy had yelped and so had she when her father had clipped her round the head.

Her feelings were complex; on the one hand, she very much wanted Sid to come with her. On the other hand she'd didn't want him to see where she lived.

She decided to let him come with her on the bus, but not to get off with her and walk her home.

Finally, having made up her mind, she said, 'As long as you promise to keep yer hands to yerself.'

'Scouts' honour,' he said cheerfully, and saluted her – not like a scout, but as a soldier would.

After Bridget and Bert had walked off in the opposite direction, Sid continued to puff on a cigarette until the bus came. Swearing under his breath, he stubbed out the end and slid it behind his ear.

'Didn't expect it to come that quick and seeing as you don't like smoking,' he said almost apologetically.

'Don't mind me,' she said in an offhand fashion, grabbed the upright bar on the bus platform and swung herself up. 'You don't belong to me and I don't belong to you,' she said in as aloof a manner as she could manage.

The bus was packed and Sid suggested they go upstairs.

The conductor stopped them. 'Sorry. No room on top. Inside only. You'll 'ave to stand. And no smoking inside. Just remember that, lad.'

'Did you 'ear that,' Sid said to Maisie. 'Called me lad. Well 'e won't be calling me that once I'm in uniform and fighting for my country.'

Maisie laughed. Sid was growing on her. She couldn't imagine him going off to kill anybody. Just like that puppy she'd found; he was too soft.

The inside turned out to be cramped and stuffy, so Maisie was glad when they finally got to her stop at the top of Old Market.

'Goodnight,' she called out, breaking into a run the moment her feet hit the pavement. 'Thanks for everything.'

She was desperate Sid wouldn't follow, wouldn't see where she lived or come face to face with any member of her family – especially her father.

'Hey! I can't let you walk the rest of the way by yerself,' he shouted out from some way behind her.

She shouted over her shoulder, 'I don't want you to take me home. I can get there by meself, thanks very much.'

Clutching her handbag, head down, she dare not slow down and allow him to catch up.

His voice echoed against the blank walls and dark houses as he shouted out if he could see her again.

'Might do,' she shouted back.

She didn't know whether he heard. Her footsteps were heading for home and nothing could stop her now from getting there, though, if she could live anywhere else, she would.

The sound of her footsteps echoed against the cramped

houses, the blank factories and high walled yards. Before very long, that's all she heard, the sound of her footsteps alone.

A patch of golden light fell out from the door of the Duke of York, the pub on the corner of the street. The sweetly acrid stink of cider and the yeasty smell of beer came out from the open door. Whoever had come out was no more than a silhouette against the bright light. She heard his voice.

'Hey, girlie.'

She tried to hurry on by, but a strong hand grabbed her.

He smelled of Brylcreem and good clothes. The top of her head was level with his chin.

Two more figures came out from the pub behind him and brought some of the inside light out with them. That was when she saw who had grabbed her.

Eddie Bridgeman half turned to the two other men. 'Carry on without me for the moment, gents. I've got a bit of business to attend to with this little girl here.' He turned back to her, his eyes like black pits, a mixture of shadow and light demonising his features. 'You've done your little bit for us,' he began. She knew he was referring to her finding out about the delivery sheets and finding somebody willing to pass them on. 'I'm grateful, though I could be even more grateful if you let me.'

She held herself stiffly. 'I don't want you to be grateful. I don't want to know anythin' about it.'

'You're bound to 'ear, what with working with all them women.' A gold tooth flashed in his mouth when he smiled. 'Right load of gossips, I bet.'

The guilt she felt was only vaguely tolerable, as was the yearning to escape her life. He was right about one thing; she would hear of any cigarettes being pinched – especially a whole lorryload. News travelled fast in the factory.

As he leaned in close, the smell of his cologne was like spice on her tongue. The breath that fell on her was minty and sharp. His voice was low and had a hint of menace about it. 'Never mind,' he whispered, his lips close to her ear. 'You'll be out of there soon.'

'I don't know what you mean.'

She felt the colour draining from her face and winced at the tightness of his fingers on her arm.

'I think you do, sweetheart. I got plans for you. You could do alright by me, darling.'

'Let go of my arm.' She said the words as though each was well considered before being uttered. Her chin was firm, her eyes big and round looking back up at him.

His eyes glittered in the flickering light of a streetlamp.

'What Eddie wants, Eddie gets.'

'Not me!'

Her knee connected with his groin. She was smaller and slighter than him, younger and much quicker.

He howled to the heavens, and bent double. Both hands left her arm and went to his groin. She was free.

One of his mates made a lunge for her but missed.

She ran off down the street, her heels drumming the pavement in double quick time.

Somebody shouted. 'Oi! Come back 'ere.'

But Maisie didn't stop running until she was inside the house that was home, the one she'd been so keen to escape from. Tonight, she needed it, sanctuary against a man and a world that she wanted no part of.

* * *

One of Eddie's minders bent over so his face was level with Eddie's. 'You all right, boss?'

Eddie glared at him. 'No! Of course I'm bloody not!'

'Shall we go after 'er, then?'

Eddie shook his head. His gaze took in the whole length of York Street, the small Victorian terraced houses lining the cobbled street. 'Nah! I know where she lives. Can get 'er any time I like.'

13

BRIDGET

When the chauffeur-driven car pulled up outside the house for Bridget, her father was there to see this rich young man she was taking around the city.

Lyndon got out of the car at the rear, leaving the door open. He smiled at her as she came down the garden path, her mother standing at the front door looking pensive. Both parents had questioned her in depth about this young man's motives.

'The big bosses at Wills's wanted somebody to show him round. I opened my mouth and they thought I'd swallowed an encyclopaedia so was well suited for the job.'

The truth was, everything had been arranged between her and Lyndon that day in the corridor following the VIP visit but she'd kept it to herself just in case it never happened. She'd heard nothing from him since and had half wondered whether a car would really come to fetch her. Perhaps he'd been joking, but on the off chance that he really was telling the truth, she'd got up that morning, washed and chose a dress to wear. The dress she chose had been made by her mother. It was as blue as her eyes and she wore a white bolero top with it and, as the weather was still fine, white sandals.

Her heart was racing as she made her way to the car now, her eyes sparkling, her hair glossy and falling to her shoulders.

'All set?' he said to her.

She smiled and nodded before replying that she was indeed ready to go with him.

In the last few days, she had asked herself whether he would stir her again the way he had done when they'd first met. Her doubts were firmly dismissed. That smile, those blue eyes and that mane of dark gold hair were exactly as she remembered and thrilled her through and through.

Lyndon flicked a finger at the brim of his hat as he invited her to get into the car.

Never in her whole life had she travelled in a motor car and the prospect was thrilling. She slid slowly across the seat, taking in everything about it, the smell of warm leather and its softness beneath her inquisitive fingers.

Lyndon slid in after her. He was dressed in a light-coloured suit, striped shirt and dark blue tie. She'd never seen an Englishman dressed like that, especially the shirt. It had never occurred to her that men's shirts were anything but white.

Neighbours gathered round. A group of children stood in front of the bonnet, pensively reaching out to touch the figure-head of the handsome car and tracing the maker's symbol just beneath it. Rolls-Royce. She saw her parents watching from the front door of the house.

Unsure what to say, Bridget stared straight ahead, aware that her dashing companion was doing the same. So was their chauffeur.

One minute after another went by and they hadn't moved. Eventually it was the driver who broke the silence. 'Where to, sir?'

Lyndon looked at Bridget. 'Where are we going?'

'Oh my word,' she said and laughed. 'I'm a fool, that I am. You're a stranger here and there's me sitting here as though you know exactly where to go. I'm sorry,' she added. 'I'm supposed to be your guide and I'm just sitting here—'

'Don't fret yourself.' His laugh rang out and his teeth flashed a brilliant white. 'Henry knows where to go. He drives for the management at Wills.'

Bridget took deep breaths to calm herself. 'Right,' she said, fanning her hand in front of a face that was pink with embarrassment. 'Right. Let's begin in the city centre. Can we head for King Street, please?'

She almost fainted when Lyndon patted her hand. 'We can do anything you want. Can't we, Henry?'

The chauffeur replied that indeed they could.

Lyndon did most of the talking on the journey, relating details of the plantation, the vast fields of tobacco, the curing rooms, the drying rooms, the cold Virginian winters and the languid summers.

She noted he spoke little of his family except to say that his father had already left for London where his mother was doing a grand tour of the most upmarket shops and stores.

Bridget heard the pride in his voice for both his family's achievements in America and the country itself. As a consequence, she found herself wondering how best to impress him that this country and this city were also part of his heritage.

The spire of St Mary Redcliffe church came into view and she immediately knew this was the answer.

'Stop,' Bridget shouted. 'Can we stop?'

'Are we going into the church?' asked Lyndon, sounding just a little surprised.

Bridget confirmed that they were. 'Can we park the car in the road at the side of the church?'

'My thoughts exactly, madam,' said Henry. 'Otherwise the doors will scrape.'

The pavements in Redcliffe Hill were three steps high from the road. The side road was flatter and quieter, the entrance to the church through an avenue of yew trees and close-cropped grass.

Lyndon helped her out of the car and cupped her elbow as they took the shady path.

'I get it, this is an old church,' he said to her. 'What's in here to interest me?'

She smiled to herself. 'Quite a lot.' She started off by telling him that the church had been visited by Queen Elizabeth the First.

'I can see it would be of her time,' he said, once their footsteps were echoing to the vaulted ceiling.

She sensed he was spending more time looking at her rather than his surroundings, but soon that would change. Soon she would really impress him.

Three quarters of the way down the south aisle, she stopped.

'I don't think you're showing enough respect for this place.' She nodded at his hat, which he had failed to remove.

'Right,' he said, and promptly removed it. 'Is that OK, now?'

She threw him a reproving look. 'Don't look at me. Look at the church.'

'Yes, ma'am.' He glanced around a bit before his gaze went back to her. There was no doubt he was being casual about the whole thing.

Bridget held her own amusement in check. She jerked her chin to the tomb of a man whose son had helped shape the American constitution. 'Do you see that tomb?'

Lyndon glanced at the imposing monument. 'It's pretty big.'

'I suggest you inspect it more closely – by yourself.'

He looked contrite. 'Is there any chance we go get a meal somewhere?'

Bridget was adamant. 'Go and look at the inscription on the tomb.'

Creases of amusement circled his eyes. He raised his hand and saluted her. 'Yes, ma'am.' He did as she said.

At first, he maintained the nonchalant amusement that seemed to define his character. He strolled up to the tomb as though he was about to shake hands with somebody in front of it. He stilled once he had come to a halt and read the inscription.

For a moment after reading it, he stood with his head bowed, almost as though he was saying a short prayer. Finally, he turned slowly on his heel and came back to her.

A stunned look on his face turned into one that touched on humility.

Bridget was pleased with herself. Up until this moment, she'd half believed he was more interested in her than in history and culture. Now he looked visibly moved.

He thanked her and there was a serious look in his eyes that hadn't been there before.

'Admiral Sir William Penn: The father of William Penn? Founder of Pennsylvania?' His words echoed off the ancient stone.

'Yes,' said Bridget. Other places of interest followed in close succession, including the burial place of the daughter of Richard Ameryk. Legend had it that John Cabot had named America after him.

They got back to the car where he looked at her in disbelief.

'I didn't expect that,' he said and sounded genuinely moved.

'Part of your history,' she said to him. 'There's more to interest you.'

'OK. Where next?'

'King Street. How about we eat as we walk when we get there?'

It was only a short journey to King Street where yet again the car was parked and they got out and walked. All the time she told him little snippets of information, how tobacco was said to be smoked by sailors on the Bristol quay way back in the sixteenth century, how James the First, who hated smoking, had ordered the tobacco fields of Gloucestershire to be burnt. How, when smokers had protested, he'd also gone on to allow tobacco imports through Bristol and London and slapped on a hefty import tax.

Lyndon seemed fascinated.

'I'm so pleased you're interested,' she said to him.

'Yeah,' he said. 'I'm very interested.'

She guessed from the look he gave her that he wasn't just referring to the history lesson she'd given him. He was also referring to her.

Together, they strolled over the uneven cobbles of King Street, where they shared a hot pie bought from a street trader. Mouth full of crumbs and succulent steak and kidney, Bridget managed to tell him about the Theatre Royal, also known as The Old Vic. Further along, they stopped outside The Llandoger Trow, its diamond panes twinkling from his windows set high in a series of seven gables frowning like old men over the street.

'Have you read *Treasure Island*?'

'Indeed I have,' he managed to say beneath meaty mouthfuls of pie.

Bridget swallowed. She was in full flow and thoroughly enjoying the day. 'Legend has it that Robert Louis Stephenson based The Spyglass on this pub. The Benbow, where Jim Hawkins lived, was supposed to be some miles from the city. It's also said that this was the watering hole of Blackbeard, Captain Teach. He was from Bristol too.'

'There seem to be a lot of famous people from Bristol.'

'Including Cary Grant,' she said proudly. She noticed a smudge of gravy had landed on his tie. 'Let me get that or it'll stain.' She got out her handkerchief, wetted it with her tongue and did her best to eradicate it.

'There's some nice ordinary people from Bristol too,' he said softly.

That look again. She tried not to raise her eyes to meet his, but failed miserably. They both remained silent whilst that look held until it came to her that they were standing too closely. Her mouth felt dry, but somehow, she suddenly gathered her senses and took a step away.

The distance between them was narrowed again when Lyndon suddenly took a step towards her.

'Can I kiss you?'

Bridget's breath caught in her throat. She swallowed an imaginary lump and before she had chance to answer, he kissed her.

It was a gentle kiss on the mouth, but long enough and sweet enough to make her not want it to stop.

When he did, he smoothed a stray wisp of hair back from her face. 'Can we go and watch the sunset somewhere?'

She nodded. 'I know just the place.'

She took him up to Brandon Hill and Cabot Tower. Standing at the base of the monument to the man who had discovered mainland America, they silently watched the glow of the sunset.

Bridget didn't object when he wound his arm around her. His hand was warm on her arm and she was aware that he was no longer looking at her but at the sunset.

'Amazing,' he said. 'My dad's folks sailed all the way from Ireland to America and I've sailed all this way from America here and met up with a girl whose folks came from Ireland. How special is that?'

'Very special,' she said softly, and knew that she meant it.

* * *

The car that had taken her away from Marksbury Road now took her back.

As the sleek vehicle pulled up outside her house, the neighbours gathered just as they had on their way out. It wasn't often they saw a private motorcar drive along, and certainly not a Rolls-Royce.

'Looks like an official welcome,' said Lyndon.

'Makes me feel like royalty,' she responded and managed a light laugh.

Suddenly he took hold of her hand. 'I'm going to try to get down here again before we go back to the states. I'd like another day like today – if you don't mind.'

She looked shyly down at his hand. The sound of his voice earlier had reminded her of her father. It still did.

She nodded. 'That would be nice.'

* * *

Her mother joined her at the garden gate as the car swept away. Her hand gently touched her daughter's shoulder. 'Had a nice day?'

'It was lovely,' Bridget replied and wished she was at the beginning of their day together, not seeing him drive away.

'Oh well,' said her mother. 'A lovely memory. You're never

likely to see him again and that's for sure.'

'He said he'd be back before sailing for the states.'

Her mother's fingers gently brushed her hair back from her face. 'Don't count on it, darling. This moment in time might be all there is.'

14

PHYLLIS

Phyllis paid no attention to the newspapers nor the latest news on the wireless. Even if she had, she would have just shrugged it off as acceptable – just like Mr Chamberlain had thought it acceptable to hand over a country that wasn't his to Herr Hitler.

Tonight was Phyllis's first attendance at the typing course and she could barely eat her tea. The butterflies were still whirling around in her stomach.

She felt her mother's eyes on her.

'Go on. Eat up. It's egg and chips.'

Phyllis put down her fork. 'I'm not really hungry. Think I ate too much at lunchtime.'

'You can at least manage the egg.'

'I can manage that.'

She ate slowly and methodically though had made up her mind to throw it in the bin once her mother's back was turned.

'Is Robert not calling for you? Surely you've got time to eat before you goes out?'

'I've eaten the egg and some chips. I don't want any bread and butter.'

Her mother stopped hacking a slice from the loaf and rewrapped the whole thing in greaseproof paper. 'It'll do toasted tomorrow morning.'

'I said I would meet Robert at half past six. It's the first house at the Broadway and I daren't miss the bus.'

'Number two three two, is it?'

'That's right.'

The truth was that she wasn't catching the two three two – at least not the one going to Filwood Broadway.

'I won't be late,' she called and left as quickly as she could.

In order to keep up the pretence that she was off to the Broadway Picture House in Knowle West and heading for the bus that would take her there, she turned left and marched off along the road. When she came to a convenient side turning, she took it and got on the bus heading in the other direction.

The course was being held in Redcross Street, Old Market, and the bus seemed to be taking forever. Her fingers tapped nervously against her handbag. She wished the bus would go faster. Looking out of the window at shops that were still open and shoppers still shopping did little to ease her apprehension. She wondered what the teacher would be like; probably some old spinster with thick spectacles and iron-grey hair scooped into a hairnet. And she would be wearing brogues and thick lisle stockings.

Phyllis drew an image of what this woman might look like in the condensation that misted the windows. Grim and faintly comical like some of the spinster teachers she'd come across at school, she thought and smiled at the result.

The bus conductor rang the bell and shouted that they'd arrived in Old Market, so-called because back in the Middle Ages it had indeed been a market. People had come in from the surrounding countryside to sell their animals or their goods.

There had also been a market court to settle disputes, which had doubled as an inn. Now named The Stag and Hounds, the plaque above the door evidenced what it had once been: Pied Poudres – interpreted as dusty feet, or, as Bristolians called it, The Pied Powder Court. It was Bridget, of course, who had told her that it was French and what it meant.

The lane she required was on the other side of the street to The Stag and Hounds and took her from the wide expanse that was Old Market, with all its many bus and tram stops, into Redcross Street. The building she headed for was built of grey stone and had a sombre look. Next door was a small park where the breeze whispered through summer leaves.

Her heart was in her mouth. She had hurried, yet still thought she was late.

Once inside, her footsteps echoing round a central assembly hall, she was directed to the correct room, which was on the ground floor. Her heart sank when she peered through the top half of the door and saw she was indeed a little late. A number of people, mostly women, though sprinkled with a few men, sat behind typewriters. As yet, they were not clattering in unison, fingers flying over the keys and she was very grateful for that. Such a thing would be too intimidating and she'd hate to be the least experienced in the class.

Heads turned as she pushed open the door but looked neither surprised nor particularly interested.

One voice made comment.

'You're late.' The voice was male.

She looked to the front of the class, where she'd expected to see somebody similar to the drawing, she'd left in the misted bus window. There was a desk and a blackboard, but no sign of a person.

'Well don't just stand there, find yourself a seat. There's a few to choose from.'

Her jaw dropped when she saw him. He was nothing like she'd imagined, and most definitely male. Neither did he present himself as being anything like an average teacher, but he was quirky in his look, with his attire and the fact that he was sitting on the sill, his legs spread across the full width of the window.

His appearance was as different as his behaviour. He had long hair that reminded her of a film about old-time knights and princes. She vaguely recalled the main character being played by Laurence Olivier. His hair had been just as long and the timbre of his voice had made her toes curl – just like the voice of this man. He had a casual air about him and a defiant look in his eyes.

'You've not been here before, so I need to tell you that my name is Alan Stalybridge and I don't stand on ceremony. As we are going to be thrown together for some time, you may call me Alan.'

'My name's Phyllis,' she blurted, not sounding at all like her usual bubbly self.

'Pleased to meet you, Phyllis.' He pointed a finger. 'Just there, girl. Sit. I can't start the lesson until you do.'

That voice again. Her jaw dropped and she fancied she saw amusement in his eyes, along with a forthright gaze as though he knew that she'd left something of herself the moment she'd faced him.

The table she sat at held a typewriter with the word 'Imperial' emblazoned above the keys. To one side was a piece of card replicating the order of letters and numbers on the keyboard.

'The keyboard layout is printed on the card beside you. Use that card to feel your way over the keys. Do not look at the keyboard. Master the art of feeling your way and you will in time become a touch-typist.'

He lectured the class from his perch before swinging his long legs down and winding up a gramophone. The music had a perennial thud to it that made Phyllis want to bash the keys. She was no expert on music, but it seemed the notes played were identical distances apart, just like the space between striking the keys.

Once they were all engrossed in hitting the keys in time with the music, Alan walked between the rows of tables and clattering typewriters, stopping to check how each individual was doing.

It might have been her imagination, but she couldn't help feeling that he stood by her table a bit longer than he did everyone else. She felt the intensity of his eyes scrutinising her progress. Her cheeks warmed, but her fingers kept up the same unfailing rhythm.

'Good,' he said. 'Carry on regardless.'

By the end of the session, her fingertips, already sore from her job at W. D. & H. O. Wills, were sorer still and her fingers ached.

She prided herself that she'd kept up with the music and the rhythmic clattering around her.

Smiles and small comments were exchanged between those attending.

Inspired and happier than she'd been in a long while, she lingered, wanting to share her feelings and thank Alan Stalybridge for his part. As it turned out, he too was lingering, assisting a very pretty lady with blonde hair and wearing dark glasses from her desk at the front of the class. Phyllis couldn't hear what was being said but saw the blonde girl smile, nod and turn slightly red.

His hand lay gently on her arm, a hand covering hers. 'Now, Jessica, what shall we do? Shall we dance or would you prefer to go home?'

The golden-haired beauty laughed coquettishly. 'I would

much prefer to go dancing, but as I can't see one foot moving in front of the other, I'd better go home.'

Mr Stalybridge laughed and patted the girl's arm. 'But you have rhythm, Jessica. Move in time with the music and you will never fall flat on your face.'

The girl laughed. As they came level with Phyllis, she saw the white stick and instantly understood. Jessica was blind and was training to be a touch-typist, just as she was.

Alan's eyes glanced at her over Jessica's head and spoke directly to her. 'Here endeth the first lesson. I trust you enjoyed it.'

'Yes. I did.' Phyllis nodded, taken aback that he'd deigned to single her out.

Another girl, one she remembered as named Susan, giggled and paired up with her to follow them out. 'Well, he's a right card. Did you ever see a teacher like him before? Sitting up in the window ledge. Strange bloke. Nice-looking though. Could do with a haircut. But he's an arty type. They do wear their hair long.'

'Yes,' said Phyllis, just a little too wistfully. 'Yes, he is different. Kind too.'

They watched as he helped Jessica into the passenger seat of his old Ford, little more than a box on wheels, though no doubt envied by those who didn't own a car and were never likely to.

On the bus going home, Phyllis thought about what Susan had said and why Alan Stalybridge had intrigued her. His voice and his looks were so contrary to any other man she'd ever known and his assisting the blind girl, Jessica, had impressed her deeply.

By the end of the journey, she had worked out why she was so impressed, why she couldn't shift him from her thoughts. In appearance and behaviour, he was the exact opposite of Robert Harvey and it made her smile.

15

THE OUTING

It was the last weekend in August and Aggie Hill had arranged a trip to the seaside.

'Roll up, roll up,' she shouted from a high vantage point on a chair in the middle of the canteen. Her loud voice was accompanied by the jarring clatter of a football rattle that she spun above her head. 'Get 'ere and buy yer tickets. This might be our last chance to 'ave a bit of fun before the bombs start falling.'

Her urgings had the desired effect and the demand for tickets surprised even her. She'd arranged initially for one charabanc to take them on the annual trip, which this year was to Weston-super-Mare. By the time the numbers were counted against deposits paid, there were three coaches going.

The Three Ms queued up for tickets with everyone else, their money at the ready.

Maisie was more excited than anyone. 'I ain't never been to Weston before.'

Although the resort was properly called Weston-super-Mare all the locals – that is most of Bristol and Somerset – shortened the name to Weston.

'Hope it stays fine the weekend,' said Bridget.

'And that the tide's in,' added Phyllis.

'It's the second highest tide in the world,' declared Bridget. 'Forty feet difference between high and low water.'

'So, what's the highest?' asked Maisie, who had started taking an interest in Bridget's many pearls of wisdom.

'It's in Canada,' Bridget replied.

Phyllis smiled and winked. 'Not Virginia?'

Realising what was implied, Bridget felt her face reddening. 'No. Of course not. Keep your voice down, will you?' she hissed, warily looking round to see if anyone had heard. 'I told you to keep it a secret.'

She'd told Phyllis most of the details of her day out with Lyndon and that he was planning to come to Bristol shortly and see her before he sailed for America.

On their way back to the stripping room, Phyllis leaned in close to her and whispered. 'Did he try anything?'

'No,' snapped Bridget.

A short silence ensued before Phyllis whispered, 'I've got a new man in my life.' She went on to describe her typing teacher: his long hair, his admiration that she'd mastered the typewriter so quickly. 'He's like a prince in a fairy tale,' Phyllis said with a sigh.

Phyllis was evasive when Bridget enquired if he'd asked her out.

'Not yet. But he will, and then we'll go somewhere really posh and smashing. He's got a car, you know. He drives it himself.' Dots of pink appeared on the alabaster complexion.

'And what about Robert? You are engaged you know.'

Phyllis fidgeted with her plaid turban. A stray lock of coppery brightness fell against her cheek before being tucked back in.

'I'm getting fed up with all this overtime 'e's doing. And even when we're going for a night out, it's the pub, the pub, the pub – with 'is mates. Or the bloody dog track! His mates were there too! Honest, I'm gettin' fed up with it.'

'Then tackle him. Tell him how you feel.' It seemed simple enough to Bridget, but she knew Phyllis was more complex than at first sight; exuberant on the outside but not so on the inside.

Phyllis attacked a tobacco leaf with renewed vigour giving it her undivided attention. Her eyes were downcast.

Finally, she said, 'You don't know what 'e's like.'

'You mean he doesn't listen?'

Phyllis shook her head.

Bridget carefully considered what to say next. 'Then should you be marrying him?'

'Oh, he'll make a good husband,' said Phyllis, her hazel eyes bright as she attempted to reassure Bridget – or herself – that all was well and she'd be a fool to call it off. 'Everything will be fine once we're married.'

Bridget couldn't help feeling a sense of foreboding. She so wanted Phyllis to make the right decision, in fact any kind of decision, but knew her well. Strangely enough it wasn't part of her makeup. She was open to suggestion, vulnerable to the opinion and wishes of others. Bridget eyed the red and rust coloured scarf wound round Phyllis's copper hair.

'That's not your usual scarf.'

'Mum put the other in the wash. Said it was too silky for work anyway.'

Bridget guessed that Stella Mason had chosen the scarf.

'I've never seen that one before,' she said in a tactful manner.

'Mum bought it for me. It's good quality.'

But the wrong colour, thought Bridget. Phyllis was trying to convince herself that if her mother said it was right, then it must be. She allowed herself to be dominated and that, thought Bridget, was a recipe for disaster.

* * *

It was a far more cheerful Maisie who boarded the charabanc than the girl who had first walked through the mahogany double doors of W. D. & H. O. Wills and into the stripping room. Unlike everyone else, she had not brought a packed lunch.

'I'll buy fish and chips. I really fancy eating fish and chips on the sea front. I can, can't I?'

It was agreed that she could.

'Nothing like eating fish and chips out of newspaper along the seafront,' stated a smartly dressed Aggie.

Just for once her hair was out of curlers and she was wearing a big dress that on anyone of normal size would have looked like a tent. She was also wearing face powder; no lipstick or mascara, just face powder which made the bristles on her upper lip look thicker than they really were.

Whooping with joy, Phyllis led Bridget and Maisie to the five-seater row at the back of the coach.

Bert squeezed in along with his mate Sid, who, despite not working for Wills, had wangled his way aboard.

'Room for two little 'uns?'

Maisie whispered to Phyllis her surprise that her fiancé wasn't coming. 'Why is that?' she asked.

Phyllis whispered back, 'Because I didn't tell 'im.'

The charabanc's gears crunched and it nudged forward. A big cheer went up. Then the charabanc stalled, restarted and shunted forward again.

Another cheer.

'I'm learning to drive,' said Sid, shouting above the noise of the engine.

'Well I 'ope you do better than this bloke,' chortled Aggie Hill and everyone laughed along with her.

All the girls and women were wearing their best bib and tucker: smart white sandals, striped or flowered dresses and white cardigans. Some of the men were wearing suits, the younger and more fashionable gaberdine trousers and blazers.

Taking the opportunity to be her flamboyant self, Phyllis was wearing wide-legged trousers in a striped green and blue fabric with a matching top that tied at the front which drew everyone's attention. She looked sultry and glamorous, just as much as any film star. Maisie wore a blue skirt, a short-sleeved white blouse and a blue checked cardigan. Bridget had on a green dress with a cinched-in waist in a material that accentuated her slender figure. Out of all of them, she was the one with the most faraway expression in her eyes, who didn't seem to be getting into the spirit of the trip like everyone else.

The boys were now chatting war.

'I'm still gonna get in the RAF,' said Bert and nudged Bridget's arm. 'No crunching of gears up there. You won't 'ardly recognise me. Dead smart, I'll be.'

'Let's laugh today, shall we, and make it a day full of fun. That means no more talk of war,' said Bridget. she turned her head and looked out of the window. They'd been picked up in North Street, Bedminster, far enough away from the factory and close enough to the road south out of the city.

Although there was much merriment and laughter going on around her, Bridget was distracted. Her eyes were studying the passing scenery, first the shops and factories, then, as the road widened, more humble houses gave way first to suburban semis, then to those safely ensconced behind high hedges with double gates and garages at the end of driveways.

A big house was a dream for a family like hers. On this particular occasion, she wasn't really seeing those houses, though. Her thoughts were elsewhere. There'd been no word from Lyndon and yet she'd been so convinced he would come back or at least write and say he was on his way back to America.

Forget it, her mother had said and she was right. What was the point in hanging onto a hope for something that might never happen?

Pushing all thoughts of him from her mind, she made the effort to concentrate on her friends. Bert and Sid were still going on about the prospect of war and their part in it. She could stand it no more and lost her temper.

'Oh will you please shut up about war! We're off for a day out and we're all going to enjoy ourselves. Right?' They looked at her in amusement until encountering her serious expression and set of her jaw, when they realised amusement had nothing to do with it.

Sid opened his mouth to say something, but before he had chance, Bridget sprang to her feet, gripped the back of a seat on each side of the aisle and addressed the whole charabanc.

'Are we all agreed we don't want any talk of war?' her voice rang out loud and clear. Inside, she felt slightly irritated. It felt as though they were not just in a charabanc on their way to the seaside but careering at an alarming rate to something much more terrible. She determined to put aside the worries – at least for today. 'Are we here to enjoy ourselves or what?'

'To enjoy ourselves,' everyone shouted back.

Bert grinned at her sheepishly, then shrugged his shoulders. 'You're a woman who knows what she wants.'

Song after song was sung and a couple of men were playing cards. In the absence of a table, they'd placed a beer crate in the aisle. It was usual for any good outing to load the boot of the coach with crates of beer. This trip to Weston-super-Mare was no exception.

Throats dry from all that singing necessitated thermos flasks appearing from striped straw shopping bags and cups of tea being passed round. A few of the men took advantage of the single crate that had not been consigned to the boot, though the form was that indulgence in alcohol was confined to the journey home.

Remarks were made about the countryside, shorn golden fields, the harvest being gathered, the hedges, fields of cows and sheep, lots of trees and houses encircling a church.

Maisie let Sid hold her hand, though did throw him a look, warning him not to go any further. She'd been out with him since, only for a drink at The Shakespeare in Victoria Street, which was a bit closer to where she lived in St Philips than where he lived in Southville, an area in Bedminster.

The atmosphere in the pub had been congenial enough, though she'd still cast her eyes over the clientele, looking to see if the sallow-skinned Eddie Brightman, with his black hair and thick eyebrows, was there too. If so, she'd been ready to make a sharp exit, but there wasn't a sign of him. All she'd seen were the faces of strangers. Perhaps he'd lost interest in her. She certainly hoped so.

She looked across at Sid. He posed no threat and she liked being with him.

The tide was on its way out when the three charabancs got to Weston, lining up along the front to disgorge their eager passengers, who tumbled out like baby ducklings about to swim for the first time.

The sun shone and a warm breeze blew in from the sea,

cooling the land. The smell of fried food – fish and chips – fresh cockles and the sticky sweet smell of candy floss mixed with the salty air.

Some of the group took their sandwiches and flasks to the Winter Gardens, where goldfish slid through the dark green water and late-blooming roses climbed up the pillars that formed a colonnade on either side of the pond.

The smell of food, that mix of grease and sweetness, lured a hungry Maisie to the pier.

'Roll up, roll up,' cried a man at the entrance.

Sid shared a portion of fish and chips with Maisie. The chips were golden and tasty, the batter crisp and juicy.

Just as Sid suggested they walk to the end of the pier, a plane appeared in the sky. Faces were upturned, some looking worried, as though half expecting to be bombed.

The closer it approached, the more obvious it became that it was not a war plane but an old-style biplane, its spindly under-carriage looking like a pair of bicycle wheels. Behind it fluttered a long banner on which were the words 'PEACE IN OUR TIME. NO TO WAR.'

There were mutterings of both agreement and disagreement, but Maisie also sensed confusion, as though people were not sure what to think or what to expect.

Up until now she hadn't thought much about the war, but today, despite Bridget's encouragement to have fun, there existed an undercurrent. It was as though people were waking up to the fact that although at present this war was only being talked about, it was very likely that it would become real.

'I don't think flying around with a few words fluttering is gonna stop anything,' said Sid, his eyes following the progress of the plane before it disappeared towards Sand Bay, a less built-up resort some way further round the bay. 'How do you fancy wearing a uniform, Maisie? I reckon you'd look good in one, meself.'

She was that surprised, the chip that was on its way to her mouth paused midway. 'Women will be able to join up?'

'Yeah. Course they will. More so than last time. My,' he said, breaking off another piece of battered cod. 'This is bloody tasty.'

The group from the tobacco factory strolled along, laughing, chatting and posing for the professional cameraman who had a monkey perched on his left shoulder.

Deckchairs were hired, handkerchiefs were knotted at each corner and perched on heads for those unused to excessive sunlight. Those that wanted to paddle did so. Others paid twopence for deck chairs and another penny for windbreaks, bagging a place where the sun was strongest and the sand not festooned with donkey droppings.

Sid kept close to Maisie. She refused his offer of a donkey or carriage ride. Instead, they found a seat at the end of the pier where they could eat their meal properly.

Phyllis and Bridget sat on the next bench along with Bert. Packed lunch already eaten they too had bought fish and chips.

'This sea air makes you 'ungry,' remarked Phyllis.

'Lovely day for it,' shouted Bert.

'Lovely day for what, Bert?' Sid shouted back. At one time Maisie wouldn't have felt inclined to laugh. Their ribaldry would have washed over her, but she was used to them now and part of their gang.

There was an iron saltiness to the air. She took a deep swallow of it and turned her gaze skywards. I'll remember this day for the rest of my life, she said to herself.

Seagulls wheeled around in the hazy sky, which was almost blue, though a little undecided.

Maisie watched them soaring and diving with a look of outright wonder.

Sid threw them a piece of batter. A gull dived on it.

Maisie laughed. Sid laughed with her.

'Do you know they've got no stomach? It goes right through them.'

'Are you making that up?'

'No. Honest. I 'eard it from somewhere.'

'Don't mean it's true.'

The chips were deep-fried and soaked in salt and vinegar. Maisie reckoned it the best meal she'd ever had.

Sid was squinting at the sea, looking thoughtful as his jaw chomped away. 'We'll 'ave to do more of these, Maisie. Days out, I mean. Away from Bristol. Out in the countryside. We can get a bus out to Hanham. There's a walk out there. Or we can go over the suspension bridge to Leigh Woods. You can hear all different sorts of birds up there.'

'Why not? Beats York Street and the noise from the marshalling yards.' She couldn't help sounding cynical, not that Sid seemed to notice.

He looked at her and she looked back, decided she liked his brown eyes and cheeky smile.

'You've got nice eyes,' he said, almost as though he'd been reading her thoughts. 'No problem with us going out together, is there? I mean, I'll ask yer old man's permission if I 'ave to.'

Maisie nearly fell off her seat. 'You bloody well won't! I can make me own mind up. No need for you to go asking that old bugger!'

'Crikey! No need to blow yer top. I only thought I should do things right – you know – seeing as yer only fifteen.'

'Nearly sixteen.'

She thought of the scenery on the way here and Sid's offer to take her on the bus on excursions to the city outskirts. She wanted to see those places he talked of. All that fresh air. All those open fields.

She eyed his profile and was tempted to run her fingers through his silky hair. The deep brown colour matched his eyes.

The boys went on talking about the aeroplane and whether there was going to be a war or not.

'That's two planes we've seen this year,' said Phyllis with a hint of wonder. 'One flew over the gasometer down the Malago.'

Bridget was noticeably silent. If her father was right, they'd be seeing a lot more. She'd taken on much of what her father said, that, like it or not, the matter was beyond their control.

They left the bench on the pier and strolled along the promenade eventually sitting on a low stone wall. The tide was coming in and the sun shining on it made it glisten. On a dull day, it would be a muddy colour thanks to the huge amount of sediment brought down into the Bristol Channel by the River Severn.

Bert sat down beside them.

'Dying for a sandwich,' he said as he dipped into the canvas shoulder tote containing his tea and sandwiches.

'You've already scoffed fish and chips,' stated Bridget, disbelieving as he bit into a fish paste sandwich.

The wind was blowing on shore and tossing the sand with it. Bridget narrowed her eyes. In the far distance, she could see the outline of a ship. Closer to the shore, the incoming tide heaving around the cast-iron legs of the pier. The whitewashed building at its far end which housed the theatre looked like an iced wedding cake against the blueness of the sky.

Bert suddenly pointed to a scene closer at hand. 'That's cruelty to animals,' he chortled.

Down on the beach, Aggie Hill was having a donkey ride. Her

skirt was thigh-high and Bridget did indeed pity the donkey, though he trudged stoically on despite the bulk he carried.

Bridget's laughter was short-lived.

Bert asked her what was wrong.

'Nothing,' she said brightly enough.

Bert eyed her quizzically before saying, 'You wanna take a leaf out yer own book.'

His comment dragged her back from where she'd been – deep in thoughts – somewhere else – with someone else.

'I don't know what you mean.' Rarely did she sound so truculent, but she did now.

'You told everyone to shut up about war and enjoy themselves. But you certainly ain't yer merry self. Somethin' on yer mind?'

She threw what was left of one of Bert's uneaten sandwiches at a seagull. Too big a piece for one to handle, its feast was suddenly the centre of attention for many more of the greedy birds.

As they made their way back to the charabanc, they all agreed it had been a good outing.

'Same time, same place next year,' shouted the ebullient Aggie.

'She's got 'igh 'opes,' Bert muttered to Sid. 'Might be at war by then.'

Bridget overheard. At the same time the sun finally disappeared behind a bank of black cloud. The world suddenly seemed much darker.

* * *

Shadows were growing long by the time they climbed aboard the charabanc for the journey back to Bristol.

The same question went around the charabanc once everyone was on board.

'Did you see the aeroplane?'

Aeroplanes were rarely seen and never failed to excite anyone who saw one, especially if it was for the first time.

Arguments ensued as to whether the sentiments portrayed on the banner were the right ones. The comments and points of view only went on until the beer was passed out, and then it was singing all the way home – except for Bridget, who frowned at her reflection in the glass, her thoughts far away with Lyndon, who had probably already embarked for his home on the other side of the Atlantic.

He hadn't fulfilled his promise to return to Bristol and she'd received no letter. At least he could have written even if only to thank her for showing him around.

She pouted at the window and the encroaching darkness beyond. Why had she allowed herself to be so taken in? A foolish moment, she told herself. But never mind, you'll get over it. Falling in love is overrated and only leads to pain, both of the heart and also of the body. No falling in love, no getting married, no children and no bringing them forth in pain. Her heart was sealed. Her future affirmed.

16

Lyndon O'Neill had his mother's good looks but not her heart or the ruthless look in her eyes. Neither did he possess her calculating mind and unshakeable belief that although their family was already rich there were steps to be taken that would make the family that much richer.

Mrs Betty Jane O'Neill was a Southern belle of a wealthy family who, following The Civil War, had bowed to the inevitable and turned covetous eyes northwards and a marriage of convenience, though at the time she'd professed love when being courted by his father.

The moment he'd got back to London, his mother had insisted she tell him everything about his stay in Bristol.

'I understand it's a kind of provincial place, hardly a city at all,' she'd declared, whilst surveying each of her London purchases being hung on hangers by her ladies' maid, a black girl from Georgia who she'd brought over with her. Factories were far below her favourite places to visit. Harrods, Selfridges and tea at the Savoy were not.

'Hardly provincial,' he'd said to her. 'Quite a fine historical city. Full of American connections and a great literary tradition.'

He went on to tell her about the places he'd seen and the girl lent by W. D. & H. O. Wills to show him around.

'Not only was she pretty, a real Irish rose, but she showed me the tomb of William Penn's father. Can you believe that? I'm thinking of going back for a second look before we leave,' he continued.

His mother's eyes widened. 'A second look at the city or the girl?'

'Both of course.'

He pretended to look out of the window at the London traffic in a bid to hide his amusement. His mother was so entrenched in old values and bigotries, ones that should have died with the century.

His mother's irritation was short lived. 'We're leaving tomorrow,' she declared almost triumphantly. 'We need to go back before things in Europe escalate. Your father insists.'

So your son won't be contaminated with folk you want nothing to do with, thought Lyndon, *even though it's their labour that put the clothes on your back and the jewels at your throat.*

'It's of no great consequence,' he said, though of course it was. He wanted to see Bridget again, he wanted to hear her lyrical voice and share her enthusiasm for everything historical.

Before leaving the hotel, he wrote a letter:

My dear Bridget, the memory of our day together will live forever in my mind and my heart. I will return.

He wrote down everything he was feeling, placed it in an envelope and instructed, Bella, his mother's maid, to make sure it was taken down to hotel reception with instructions for it to catch the earliest possible post.

When tackled by his wife, his father laughed at what he called just a youthful infatuation.

'It will pass. It did for me. Did for all of us.'

Betty Jane, who matched her husband in wealth but exceeded him in breeding, was less tolerant. 'I think you should lay down the law.'

Her husband looked at the clear-skinned beauty of his wife, remembered the coquettish girl she'd been, and wondered why he'd never seen the harder side.

'Leave the boy alone,' he said at last. 'It's a trivial dalliance that he'll forget in due course.'

Betty Jane knew deep in her bones that her son would never forget. She'd visited this country once before when she was young, when heiresses with great wealth sought husbands with titles. A whole army of well-bred young women had come over in the nineteenth and early twentieth centuries to seek a duke, earl, knight or baron. One of the most famous was Jenny Jerome who had bagged Lord Randolph Churchill, father of the First Lord of the Admiralty, Winston Churchill.

Betty Jane too had found and fallen in love with the younger brother of a baron – the one who hadn't inherited a title. In response to her parents' objections, they'd planned to run away but been caught. How different her life might have been if they'd got away with it. But in the absence of any other suitable aristocrat, her parents had dragged her back to Georgia.

Her eyes clouded when she thought of him. She could still see him now. But she was content with her life. Her marriage had worked out well. She had everything she wanted and now firmly believed that the emotions of youth were not to be trusted. Her dream was for her son to marry a girl from a suitable family with a magnificent fortune.

She was fully prepared that Lyndon would write a letter to this girl in Bristol and she knew who would take it down to reception for him.

'Bella?' She snapped her fingers. 'My son's letter.'

Bella knew better than to disobey. The letter was snatched from her hand and torn into pieces.

'You will not tell my son that it wasn't posted. Is that clear?'

Perhaps before leaving London Lyndon might have asked Bella to confirm she had carried out his instructions if his attention hadn't been overtaken by the frenetic comings and goings in London and then in Southampton. Following the news that war had been declared it seemed the whole population of England were buzzing around like bees whose nest has been disturbed.

The Prime Minister had broadcast that very morning from the cabinet office in 10 Downing Street:

> ...I regret to inform you that no such undertaking has been received and consequently...

It was the consequently that really bit. After months, even years, of procrastination, the war Neville Chamberlain had tried so hard to avoid had come.

Lyndon watched as the tugs pushed the transatlantic liner away from the quay and out into the Solent and then Southampton Water.

Although it was September, the wind coming off the sea seemed far colder than usual. He watched the land drift by, then the dying of the light. Like the world, he thought. The light had gone out in England and he wondered how long it would be before the darkness of war encompassed the world – even the United States of America.

* * *

Maisie's mother was almost crying as she set about picking up the last bits of the smashed wireless set. Frank had come home drunk, decided he hated the music and smashed it to bits. 'Look at it. All in bits. I do like listening to that Andy MacPherson bashing out a tune on the organ. Now I won't be able to.'

'P'raps me dad will get you another one,' Maisie suggested. She was going to add, 'if you ask him nicely,' but asking him nicely or otherwise could well result in the same answer, so it wasn't worth trying.

'Might do.'

The fact that it would have to be stolen first went unsaid.

'I ain't got enough to buy you a new one, Ma and barely enough for me keep, but it's all I've got.'

With downhearted efficiency, Maisie counted what was left in her purse; shillings, sixpenny bits, and copper, including a few farthings; barely enough to last her the week.

She rubbed at her bruised cheek and swore under her breath, words she wouldn't dare call him out loud. Her father had grabbed hold of her the minute she'd got back from the outing, swung her against the wall in the hallway and grabbed her handbag. Once he'd taken the silver and the ten-bob note, he'd flung the purse back at her.

Strangely enough, Sunday was one of the better days of the week, thanks to her father spending most of Saturday in the pub. His usual habit was to roll home after midnight. A few pubs hereabouts were known to serve after-hours and Frank Miles made a point of only frequenting those that did. The night before, he'd come out early because he'd run out of money, which is when he had taken most of what she had, then went back out again.

Maisie scowled as a resonant snore came from overhead, so powerful it seemed to shake the ceiling. She wished he wasn't here, wished he wouldn't come home, wished him dead.

The money he'd splashed around at the Duke of York represented most of her wages. It was only by hanging onto her purse that she had anything left at all, hence the blow she'd caught across her cheek.

The smell of burnt porridge came from the kitchen and her face dropped. Cooking was one of the things her mother couldn't get right and many a meal had been flung by her father across the length of the scullery, once hitting the glass window at the end. It had never been replaced, a piece of wood hammered into place over the gap.

'I've made porridge.'

'I'll have toast.'

Her mother, who had consigned what remained of the wireless to the bin, looked affronted. 'Suit yerself. It'll have to be marge though. There's only a bit of butter left and yer dad or Alf might want that.'

The fact that she was the one who had to go without made Maisie fume and raise her voice. 'Me dad don't go to work and I need to keep up me strength.'

'You're a girl,' her mother responded, as though in some way that negated the fact that she was the one who went to work.

Maisie couldn't believe what she was hearing. 'What's that got to do with it? I work. I bring in a wage!'

Her mother rushed towards her, hand raised.

Maisie, fuelled by the confidence she'd gained since starting work, caught her mother's wrist. 'Stick yer bloody butter and stick yer burnt porridge.' Her tone was venomous and had the desired effect.

'My porridge ain't burnt.' Her mother looked quite frightened to see her wrist grasped so tightly.

Maisie apologised and let go.

'I didn't mean to,' she cried after her as her mother rushed back into the scullery, a decrepit lean-to that almost always smelt of stale food and pungent drains.

Barely audible, the faint sound of crying took Maisie by surprise. She'd never known her mother to cry before. Even after a beating from her father, she tended to brush at her eyes and state that it was all her fault anyway.

'He could 'ave done better than me. I don't do things right.' That's what she used to say. Maisie had heard it time and time again.

It had to be said that her mother didn't have much going for her. At one time, she might have been good-looking, but not now. She looked shabby and battered.

'What's all the noise about?' Alf came in scratching his head and carrying his trousers over his arm having just got out of bed.

Maisie checked her reflection in the jagged piece of mirror perched precariously on the mantelpiece. Thanks to a dab of Woolworths' face powder, the bruise wasn't too noticeable. 'I refused to eat the porridge.'

He chuckled. 'I don't blame you.'

'I asked for toast.' Her stomach made a rumbling noise.

He glanced at the yellow dress she was wearing. 'You going out?'

'Yeah. Any objections?'

'Course not. Just interested. Where're you going?'

'Castle Street, window shopping. It's Sunday.'

Crowds descended on the city's favourite shopping street

every weekend. Not many had the money to spend in its upmarket shops, but window shopping was next best.

'Only window shopping?'

She threw him a sideways glance. 'Just as well it's Sunday and the shops are closed. The old man nicked me money last night. Left me with bugger all.'

Alf shook his head in disbelief, then delved into his trouser pocket and brought out what looked like pound notes and even a fiver. He pulled out a pink one. 'Ten bob for when you next go shopping proper. That all right?'

She took it gladly and thanked him.

He lit up a cigarette. Maisie winced, wishing he'd done that once she was gone.

He shouted for his mother to bring him a couple of slices of toast and a cup of tea then added, 'Our Maisie wants a cup too.'

The tea arrived and so did the toast. Alf took one piece and offered her the other. On seeing it was spread with butter and not margarine, she took it.

He looked her up and down. 'You're looking quite special. Have you got a fellah?'

Maisie swallowed the last bite of toast before she answered, wiped her lips and prepared to apply more lipstick. 'What if I 'ave?'

'It wouldn't surprise me. You're becoming a real looker.'

'You got a girlfriend?' Her sudden question was her way of coping with flattery which made her feel uncomfortable. She hadn't expected Alf to blush like a girl.

He turned his head to one side. His face was in profile. Sometimes she thought his looks were better than hers – as enigmatic as a stone angel above a churchyard tomb stone. He didn't answer but occupied himself with blowing smoke rings.

'Come on,' she said, suddenly tickling him in the ribs. 'Tell me what her name is. Come on. Tell me!'

He wriggled and squirmed, his soft hair falling like the fringe of a mop cap onto his forehead. 'Never you mind.' Suddenly he grabbed her wrists and held her away from him. His expression turned serious. 'Now you listen 'ere, Maisie. Let me give you a piece of advice. The sooner you're out of York Street, the better. I won't always be 'ere to protect you from the old man or Eddie Bridgeman.'

Maisie frowned. 'You've already warned me about 'im. I'll watch out. I can 'andle 'im.' She went on to tell him about kneeing him in the crotch and expected him to be amused. It surprised her when he wasn't.

Alf let go her wrists, a clouded look in his eyes.

'I've already told you 'e's got a reputation with young girls. Sweeps them off their feet, and then...'

'I won't be swept off my feet and don't care about his reputation. All I did was to get him access to the despatch sheets in the loading bay. I ain't done nothin' else.'

She had not needed to. The news had swept through the factory that a consignment of tobacco products had been hijacked. That was over a week ago. She knew it was the first and guessed there'd be more. Everything was based on those delivery schedules. If you knew where the lorries were going, the rest was apple pie.

'Anyway, what can I do,' she added. No other jobs had come through from any nice houses in the country, a job she wasn't sure she still wanted.

There was a new darkness in Alf's eyes and his face looked sad and drawn. He reached for a cigarette and a flash lighter, no doubt nicked from somebody with a few bob. 'Get married, run away or move in with a mate – and the sooner, the better. Move in with a boyfriend if you must – if you got one that is.'

'What about you? You going to move away from York Street?' she asked, filled with panic at the possibility that he was off to pastures new himself.

For a moment, there was a glassy look in his eyes and a tightening around his lips. She had the distinct impression he didn't want to answer the question.

'I'll go when the time is right.'

'You'll join up?'

He cupped her face with his hand. 'Not until they call me. But it's likely.'

His statement filled her with fear.

With a twist of his wrist that was both elegant and casual, he flicked the last of his cigarette into the stone-cold fire grate.

She left the room before he could say anything else. The prospect of Alf going scared her. Once he was big enough, Alf had done his best to protect her from their father, but he was right. He wouldn't always be here.

*   *   *

She was still thinking about what Alf had said on her way to meet Sid at the bus stop but it was all very well telling her to get out, to marry, to do anything rather than stay, but it wasn't so easy if you didn't have anywhere to go.

Halfway along Midland Road, she passed a car. It was black and shiny and a man she vaguely recognised was leaning against it. On seeing her, he straightened and banged on the roof of the car. She couldn't hear what he said but instinctively she broke into a run.

The car started up and she knew it was following her.

Her legs pumped the pavement as hard as her heart pumped against her ribs.

Ahead of her was the bus stop where Sid was waiting.

'Maisie!' he shouted and came towards her.

Out of the corner of her eye, she spotted another figure walking steadily and firmly along the front of the shops. In time he became a figure in uniform, a blank blur of navy serge and silver buttons.

The car passed in a blur of black and chrome and shot ahead of her in the direction of Old Market.

Her footsteps slowed. Her chest hurt and she was still panting heavily from running.

'Are you all right?' Sid was a picture of concern.

Hand held against her racing heart, she nodded.

Sid glanced in the direction of the car. 'What were they up to?'

'Are you all right, miss?'

Again a series of nods. 'I think so,' she managed to say at last. 'They saw you,' she said to the policeman. 'That's why they drove away.'

'Thank goodness they did,' he said, poking a finger beneath the peak of his helmet so it sat a bit further back on his head, the strap tight against his chin. 'I couldn't have done much by myself.'

Sid said that he could have given him a hand. 'Landing punches on two blokes is a bit more difficult than punching one,' he pointed out, though, quite frankly, Maisie couldn't see him being in the least bit aggressive.

The policeman seemed to see the same in Sid and grinned. 'Us or them?'

There was something sombre about their shared laughter, almost as though the occasion should be regarded with more respect.

'Off somewhere nice?' asked the constable.

'A bus ride to the country,' said Sid. 'Might be the last chance we get now war's been declared.'

The policeman adjusted his chinstrap. 'True. Have a good time.'

Maisie didn't admit that she'd not heard that morning's declaration. To do so would have meant explaining about her father smashing the wireless and she felt ashamed about it – almost as though it was her fault.

Instead she listened to Sid talking about the fact that he would soon be off to fight.

'I'd like you to write to me while I'm away,' he said to her. 'If you don't mind that is.'

She looked up at him and smiled. 'I don't mind. Unless I join up as well. I'd certainly like to.'

Joining up would solve all her problems, get her away from York Street, from Eddie Bridgeman and any likelihood of falling into a life of crime just like them – or even worse. Alf had given her wise counsel and she'd taken it on board. It was now a case of what to do about it.

'Not likely, Maisie. You're too young. Might have to wait a few years yet.'

'But then the war might be over!'

'Just as well,' returned Sid, his face full of sadness. 'The sooner it's over, the better.'

It was as if a whirlwind had hit the tobacco factory. Everything people did or said was influenced by the news that for the second time in the twentieth century, England – Britain and all its empire – were at war with Germany.

People were running, news flashing from one part of the production line to another and the subject of conversation was war, war, war. Rumours spread and gas masks were distributed to everyone in the factory.

'In case the Germans use mustard gas like they did in the Great War,' explained Aggie Hill, who seemed to be the font of wisdom on what had happened back then.

Volunteers were called to man the company's fire engines. Maisie and Bridget put their hands up.

Phyllis chortled as she retouched her lipstick. 'Only men drive big things like that.'

'Times are changing,' said Bridget.

'I got to drive a bus in the last war,' said Aggie. 'Managed it easy. Gave it up when the old man came back and said 'e wanted a pub. Wouldn't have done by choice, but some drivers were hauled off by mobs 'cause they thought the jobs should be done by men. Not that anybody dragged me off mine. They wouldn't dare.'

Nobody doubted it. It would take a brave man indeed to face the likes of Aggie.

'My mum used to make mustard gas when she lived down at Avonmouth,' said Sally Grey, one of the other girls. She eyed the mask she'd been given as though it were something that might bite her if she held it too close.

Maisie was taking in all the hustle and bustle with a faraway look in her eyes.

'Penny for them, Maisie,' said Bridget.

'I'd like to join up.'

'You're too young. I think the youngest you can be is sixteen, but even then only with your parents' permission.'

Bridget noticed her miserable expression.

'Would you really join up?'

She'd never pried into Maisie's home life but hadn't failed to notice bruised shadows beneath heavily applied face powder.

Maisie shot her a fierce look. 'If you lived where I do, you wouldn't ask that.'

Phyllis, who had only heard part of the conversation, chipped in, 'Get married. You can leave home then. If you want to that is. After all, that's what we girls are supposed to do, ain't we.'

'Don't mean we've got to.'

'Course not, unless there's a bun in the oven,' said Sally Grey, who giggled and rubbed her rounded stomach. 'Most parents insist on you getting married then – no matter what yer age. Mine did. Me dad went 'round Cyril's 'ouse and 'ad it out with 'is dad. Cyril's dad threatened to cut off 'is dangly bits if 'e didn't marry me. So that was that. Then they went down the pub.'

There was laughter until the factory loud speaker system

crackled into life. It was normal for everyone to fall silent when an announcement from management came over the loudspeaker. But now a silence such as never had been known descended on the stripping room; even the throb of the machines in the production and packing rooms seemed more subdued, almost as though they too were listening.

More crackling was followed by a clear voice. 'Attention, attention. On the orders of the War Office, all those men in the reserves, please get home, retrieve your kit and make your way to the train station. You'll be allocated a train once you get there. Your department managers will arrange temporary cover for your jobs. God bless you all and God save the King.'

Everyone stood up as the National Anthem was played.

There followed again the most complete silence, broken only by the sound of gasps and sobs. Bridget, Maisie and Phyllis put their arms round each other. Women discarded their work, some heading for the cloakroom, grabbing their things before rushing off home to say goodbye to their sons.

It was the sons who were going, those called up as reserves back in April and all between the ages of twenty to twenty-two.

Sid came barrelling through the double doors, heading straight for Maisie. 'Looks like I'm off, Maisie,' he said, his hands palm down on the table, his soft brown eyes looking into hers.

She was surprised how she felt; looking at his face, remembering their bus ride, feeling suddenly closer to him now he was going off to war than she'd ever done before. Poor chap, she thought. Ain't had much of a life yet. The urge to throw her arms round him was strong, but she held back, afraid of rejection. Her childhood had been bereft of affection, so much so that not showing it had become a habit.

She clenched her hands beneath the table. 'When's yer train?'

'When we get there. First come, first served I suppose. They're giving us time to collect our kit, then it's down to Temple Meads.'

She reaffirmed her promise to write to him.

'I'll get the BFPO address to you as soon as I can. I don't 'ave yours, but tell you what, I'll send my first letter to Bert with all the details. Would that be all right?'

She said that it would be. At the same time, she sensed the interested looks of her workmates. The younger girls were sighing and the older ones had sad eyes, as though recalling similar scenes in the past.

She knew he wanted to kiss her, but the saucy chap she'd met outside the Town Hall picture house was more subdued than he'd been then. He looked like a worried little boy, very aware, just as she was, that they were being watched and smiled on by the roomful of women.

'Go on. Kiss her!' somebody shouted.

Maisie rounded on the woman who had ordered them to kiss. 'We ain't 'ere to entertain you, Mrs Foster. Looking at us as though we're up on the screen at the pictures.'

Sensing he disliked being the centre of their attention, Maisie smiled.

'Sid Powell, I'm not providing entertainment for this lot. I'll meet you at Temple Meads and kiss you there.'

A hushed sigh travelled from one end of the stripping room to the other.

'I do love a good romance,' stated Aggie and brushed the tears from her eyes.

As for Sid, his whole body seemed to heave in a gigantic sigh of relief and his eyes danced with happiness. 'I'd like that.'

* * *

Factory management had given permission for the women to go home or to the station to say goodbye to their loved ones. The foremen and managers filled the gaps in the workforce, even though some of them had sons leaving on the train.

Maisie pushed her way through the crowds at Temple Meads Station, barely glancing at the gothic façade of one of the most handsome railway stations in the country, a long-time hub of the Great Western Railway, nicknamed God's Wonderful Railway by many.

Men in uniform with kitbags over their shoulders were being hugged by tearful relatives or girlfriends, so many of them that it was difficult to see the edge of the platform. Maisie clambered onto a seat so she could better see over the heads of the crowd.

Sid was in the midst of the throng and waved when he saw her, head and shoulders above the crowd.

She was back on the ground by the time he got to her.

'You came.' He sounded totally surprised but also apprehensive, as though suddenly understanding what exactly he had let himself in for.

'Said I would, didn't I?' said a cheery Maisie, her head held to one side like a cheeky sparrow.

The crush increased and she found herself pressed against Sid and fancied she could feel the beating of his heart.

His eyes were shining with excitement, like a young boy going away to scout camp for the very first time, but there was no doubting his nervousness.

It was odd the way she suddenly felt sorry for him and unwilling to let him go.

'You don't have to go. Do you?'

He laughed, a nervous hesitant sound as if he might be persuaded to stay – or to run away. 'I 'ave to go, Maisie.'

She smiled sadly. 'Silly bugger. Fancy being in the reserves and one of the first. What the 'ell were you thinkin' of?'

He suddenly looked quite relaxed. 'Doin' me duty. But I will be back, p'raps sooner than you fink.'

Maisie shook her head and tutted. 'I reckon there's only one way to win this war, and that's to send Aggie Hill. She could take on Hitler all by herself.' She tried her best to sound as though the bright side was the only side to look on and it did make him laugh.

His expression suddenly crumpled. 'You will reply to that letter I'm gonna send you?'

'Don't you worry about it. But you might get back before my letter arrives. Two shakes of a lamb's tail and you'll be 'ome.'

'Yeah.' He licked his lips thoughtfully and she could tell from his expression that there was something else he wanted to say. 'Maisie, I'm a bit older than you. I'm mindful of that. I'd appreciate you waitin' for me. Could be our ages might be evened up a bit by the time I get back.'

'It's only five years between us.' She tried to sound offhand about it but knew what he meant. If he stayed away long enough, she'd be at least sixteen by the time he got back, probably a lot older than that depending on how long the war went on.

She was feeling strange about being this close to him and for caring whatever might befall, not that she'd admit to that. These new, untested feelings frightened her. To ease her own discomfort, she became her old saucy self.

'You're gettin' all romantic with me, Sid Powell, and you know you shouldn't. I'm too young for that and will be for a time yet.

'I knows that, but you won't be forever. I can't stop thinking about you, Maisie. Wish you'd given me a photo to take with me.'

She couldn't tell him that she didn't own a single photo of herself so apologised.

'You'll have to depend on yer memory,' she said., twirling coquettishly on her heels.

'Right,' he said. 'Brown eyes, lovely dark hair, nice nose and pretty lips.' He smiled after mentioning her lips. 'I'll remember you, Maisie Miles.' He blinked as though he really was consigning her details to memory. 'There,' he said, 'Just like a camera.'

His gaze fixed on her lips. His head bent to hers and their lips came together. His kiss was gentle, a world away from the cocky chap who'd chanced his luck on their first meeting.

Suddenly she feared for him and didn't want him to go. He'd popped into her life and now he was popping out again. Her bottom lips quivered and tears threatened.

'I'll miss you, Sid.'

He nodded. 'Me, you.'

He kissed her again. It was then as if a gap had opened up between them, yet they hadn't moved. Their surroundings seemed no longer stable but a heaving sea of people, steam, screeching whistles, tears and cries of anguish.

The heaving throng began to move, circling and manoeuvring closer to the line of railway carriages lining the platform. The engine up front blew its whistle and a head of steam billowed upwards to hang like storm clouds in the rafters of the station roof.

The voice of a sergeant major boomed into the section they were standing in. 'Come on, lads. Let's be 'aving you!'

Kitbags bumped against each other and knocked mothers' hats from their heads.

'I 'ave to go,' Sid said, his hands still clung to hers.

This time, his kiss was quick and hard, the excitement of his adventure luring him away along with all the other young men who were going off to war.

'I'll write to you,' he shouted.

Then he was gone, just one man indistinguishable from all the others floundering in a sea of khaki.

Maisie stood on tiptoe and stretched her neck in an effort to get one last glance, but there were no longer individuals, just a mass of men. Sid was lost to view.

Weaving her way down the railway station concourse, she brushed at her eyes. Why should she be crying? It wasn't as though they were sweethearts, at least she didn't think they were.

'It's just not fair,' she muttered under her breath as she hurried along. Her friend Sid had shown her affection. The only other man who'd ever shown her that was her brother Alf. Like the girls in the factory, he had become a sweet and reliable friend, just twenty and off to fight a formidable enemy. He seemed too young to do that. Too young by half to get killed.

A light rain began to fall, dampening her hair and mixing with the tears that ran down her face. She had gone straight from the factory to the railway station so was still wearing her overall. Water trickled down her neck and plastered her hair to her head as the rain increased.

Turning up her collar and bending her head, she quickened her steps; water from the swiftly forming puddles splashed up her legs.

It was a long walk home from the station and was too late to go back to work. Production would be down, but the management had allowed for that. This was a sombre moment, one most of their workforce would remember for a very long time.

Maisie turned from Midland Road into York Street, keen to get indoors and out of her wet overall and glad she had a clean one for tomorrow.

As she passed the Duke of York, the pub doors banged open and a meaty hand grabbed her arm.

Her father's breath fell over her. 'You should 'ave bin 'ome by now.' His face was greasy and shiny with sweat. His eyes were bleary, mouth slack as though he had no control over its shape.

'I've bin to Temple Meads to see a friend off to fight the Germans. 'Ave you 'eard there's a war on, Dad, or are you too drunk or stupid to care?' There was no respect in her voice and sheer hatred in the look she gave him.

Certain that a blow was forthcoming, she raised arms in front of her face.

It came as something of a surprise that no blow came. Still keeping a firm grip on her arm, her father looked over his shoulder at the pub doors and dragged her towards them. 'Come on, girl. Somebody wants to buy you a drink.'

Her legs turned to jelly. Something bad awaited her within those doors. She could feel it in her muscles, in her legs, in her mind. 'I don't want one!'

She struggled but he held her too tightly.

'Well, you're bloody goin' to 'ave one. I'm yer father, and you, my girl, will bloody well do as I say!'

The pub was packed with working men having their customary pint or two – sometimes a lot more – before staggering home to a meal. They smelt dirty. Some of them stank of the rendering yards, rotting flesh and powdered bones. Some smelt oily and sooty, like the trucks that carried all manner of goods that they shunted round the marshalling yards.

Hard work resulted in hard drinking that would result in them spending the rest of their evening in a drunken stupor. Their bodies worn down with work and their brains addled with alcohol, their families were likely to suffer. There would be anger over the quality of their evening meal, wives beaten for the short-coming of having too little to spend on food, blamed for the hopelessness of their husbands' lives. Only as the evening wore on and their tiredness overwhelmed them would they finally pass out – much to their wives' – and children's relief. Other wives, other mothers, would be inconsolable, their older sons off to serve their country.

Years of cigarette smoke had stained the pub's walls and ceilings a waxy yellow. Thick as a winter fog, it fouled the air, adding an extra layer of sickly colour, sticking to glass, seeping into clothes. Men coughed and spluttered into handkerchiefs or onto the floor. Both the sound and the sight were sickening.

Her father dragged and pushed Maisie to the far end of the bar, where it was less crowded. Most of the men wearing caps, men who worked for a living, avoided that end. It was as though it was sacrosanct, not meant for the likes of them. Rough and tough as they were, there were those who were tougher, more ruthless and deeply involved in violent crime.

She knew it was not her imagination that the fug of cigarette smoke seemed bluer here. More expensive brands were being smoked. Passing Clouds, Gold Flake or cigar smoke; tobacco from Virginia went into the most expensive brands.

Three men were sitting down the far end of the bar. At the sight of them, divining what was being smoked went right out of her mind. She recognised one man as the driver of the car that had driven off in Old Market. Alf, her brother, sat next to him, his eyes cutting to her, holding her gaze as though trying to warn her, even to fear for her.

A cloud of cigar smoke rose in an upward spiral in front of Eddie Bridgeman's sallow complexion, the unblinking boot-button eyes.

'Here she is,' said her father in a sickeningly grovelling manner. 'Go on, Maisie. Sit down. Eddie wants to buy you a drink.' His fist thudded into her back and propelled her forward.

Eddie continued to stare at her. How black those eyes seemed, how totally lacking in warmth, like chips of coal left unburned in the fire grate.

Maisie stood defiantly, refusing to sit down. Her upper arms throbbed thanks to her father's overly tight grip. 'I don't want a drink. I need to go home and eat. I've been working all day.'

Actually, her mouth was dry, but she wasn't going to admit that. She'd prefer water or stewed tea rather than accept a drink from this man.

'And I won't do anything more for you at the factory. I wants to keep me job.'

She could hardly believe her own words. Working at a country house had always been her dream, but things had changed. Eddie's eyebrows lifted, then beetled, a single line of black hair across his brow. His eyes were like chips of glass, reflecting the outside world but giving nothing away of the inner one. 'A girl who don't want a nice port and lemon? Can't believe that. And there's me and your dad in business together. Could end up being a family business. Who knows? Now come on. Sit down. You're 'aving a port and lemon. I would order champagne for you, little darling, but I don't think the Duke of York runs to anything French. Asking a lot just to get a decent beer.'

Her father and the driver laughed at the joke. Alf merely looked at the ash from the end of his cigarette as he flicked it into the ashtray.

Eddie passed half a crown to his driver. 'Get the girl a port and lemon.'

The driver half rose from the table.

Maisie remained standing. 'I've already told you; I don't want one. My mum says it's not a good idea to drink on an empty stomach.'

Her mother never said any such thing. Working with a variety of women of all different ages had made her aware of what older women said. Most of them were mothers who gave their advice to anyone who would listen. She wished her mother was like them, but, unfortunately, she was not.

The driver looked uncertain. He knew his boss well and always carried out what he wanted, but this slip of a girl had attitude. The tilt of her chin, the way she held her head, the straight line of her lips. 'Boss... we do 'ave to go over to see—'

'Shaddup! That can wait.'

He stayed where he was, halfway between sitting and standing, waiting to see which way the dice would fall. Eddie usually got what Eddie wanted. The girl should wise up and get to know that.

Eddie's eyes never left her face. A thin smile spread across his lips. 'Don't bother with a port and lemon. Get the little lady a shandy.'

The driver moved more quickly than his big frame looked capable of before the boss could change his mind.

Her father's heavy hand landed on her shoulder. 'Sit down when I tell you, Maisie. There's a good girl.' The weight of his hand stayed resting on her shoulder, as though suspecting she would scarper if it didn't.

Her clothes felt heavy, her shoes and stockings were soaking wet, and she felt trapped, but despite that she stayed alert.

Eddie had only just stubbed out a cigarette but immediately lit up another with fingertips yellowed with nicotine. He offered her a cigarette. She declined.

'Your choice.'

Both her father and brother took up his offer.

Eric the driver came back with half a shandy and set it on the table in front of her.

She glared at the honey-coloured liquid as though it might kill her. 'I told you, I don't want a drink.'

Eddie flicked his hand casually. 'Your choice again, love.'

'I won't do anything else for you.'

Hearing about a whole lorry load of cigarettes being stolen had made her feel sick. She'd hidden it well from her workmates, had heard the outrage in their voices when the news broke, but had said little.

'No need for you to do anything, sweetheart,' said Eddie, his gold tooth flashing when he smiled. 'Not now we got the delivery notes and somebody to pass fresh ones to us.'

Inwardly, she breathed a sigh of relief. Outwardly, her face was frozen, eyes unblinking.

Eddie leaned forward, the cigar held between his face and hers, looked about to say something but was distracted when a crowd of noisy revellers burst into the bar. At the heart of the noisy group were three young men in merchant navy uniforms.

'Drinks all round!'

Eddie Bridgeman scowled at the interruption and turned to Eric. 'Go and tell them I can buy me own drinks and to piss off out of 'ere.'

Before Eric had chance, one of those wearing a uniform lurched over, glass in hand, face red and boozy breath falling over them like a damp blanket. 'We're off to war, chum. 'Ave a drink with us and wish us well.'

Eddie glowered. 'I'm not your chum.' His voice was menacingly churlish.

In a less than polite manner, Eric tried to persuade the man that his drinks weren't wanted.

During the sudden lull, Maisie looked over at her brother. Alf had not said a word since she'd arrived, and now he couldn't take his eyes off the three burly merchant seamen. He caught her looking, and although at first his face was implacable, she saw a glance pass between him and one man who didn't seem as drunk as the others.

The man who had offered to buy everyone a drink and was by far the most drunken, now turned surly. 'We're off on convoys,' he slurred in an aggressive tone. 'Don't you care that we're putting our lives in danger to bring over supplies from America?'

'I'd prefer you to shut your mouth,' growled Eddie. He gazed steadily through a pall of smoke.

Unsteady on his legs, the man's brawny hands tightened round an almost empty glass tankard. His eyes were red-rimmed, his lips were slack and his speech slurred. 'Shut my mouth, eh? Make me!'

Maisie jumped as he shattered the glass tankard on the edge of the table, leaving just the handle and a section of jagged glass in his hand.

An uproar ensued, Eric, her father and Alf getting to their feet, Eddie, calm as a cucumber, staying put yet seemingly in charge of whatever happened next.

The sailor's mates crowded round, faces grim with violence.

This was her chance! Maisie got to her feet and pushed her way through the crowd, away from her father and from Eddie Bridgeman.

She glanced back to where men were glowering at each other, the seamen and their supporters on one side holding back the man with the jagged glass in his hand. On the other side was Eddie, Eric and her father. She couldn't see Alf anywhere.

Eddie was on his feet now. She could see that much, but she didn't see what went on after that, so she pushed her way out of the double doors, leaving them swinging behind her.

* * *

Maisie fled the Duke of York and bumped into her mother half way down the street, a bundle beneath her arm which smelled of fish and chips.

'Look, I've got fish and chips. One fer yer dad, and one for us to share.'

Maisie blinked and looked tellingly at her mother. Stripes of grey and brown hair strained untidily back into a ragged bun. Her complexion was grey and a yellow-rimmed bruise had burst a blood vessel in her cheek.

'That greedy layabout gets one portion all to himself and we gets to share the other. Don't seem fair to me.'

For a moment, her mother looked visibly hurt, but the look passed. A more sour, defensive one returned. 'He's a bloke, ain't he? Men are supposed to get more. They need more.'

'I'm the one who's working, Ma,' Maisie pointed out to her.

A surprised look came to her mother's face as though only now had the truth sunk in.

'Why do you stay, Ma?'

Her mother's mouth dropped open. 'What?'

'Why do you stay with me dad?'

Her mother's eyes fluttered. 'He's me husband.'

Maisie looked bemused. To her mind, it seemed such a pathetic excuse. 'I know that. I didn't think 'e was Prince bloody Charming!'

Her mother's face clouded. 'Mind yer tongue, our Maisie. That's your father yer talking about.'

'Unfortunately.'

Once inside the house, a single portion of fish and chips was placed in the middle of the kitchen table. Together they ate straight from the newspaper, fish, chips and scrumps – the crispy bits of batter that you always asked for because you knew they were free.

When the paper was finally scraped clean, it was scrunched into a ball with an air both of finality and regret. Maisie definitely wished there'd been more.

'You goin' out with your mates tonight?' asked her mother as she washed her greasy fingers beneath the kitchen tap?

Maisie shook her head. 'Ain't got no money left.'

Her mother turned thoughtful. 'How about you go along to Hamblins and get a portion of chips and scrumps? I've got a few coppers for that.'

Maisie's stomach rumbled as though agreeing to this plan. She held out her hand.

'Seems like a good idea to me.'

* * *

Two figures stood outside the Duke of York smoking and laughing with one of the merchant seamen. She recognised him as the one with whom Alf had exchanged a familiar look.

On seeing her, another such look passed between them.

'My kid sister,' said Alf and smiled.

The man nodded at her. 'I'll be off then. See you in the usual place, Alf?'

Her brother nodded. 'You can count on it.'

There seemed to her to be genuine affection in the way they laid a hand on each other's shoulders, a farewell but also something of a promise.

Collar up against the rain, the man strode off. Alf watched him for a while before turning his attention back to his sister.

'Where you goin'?'

'Chip shop. Want anything?'

He shook his head. 'No. I ain't dressed for eatin' fish and chips in the street.'

Maisie smiled. 'Course not. Wouldn't want to mess up yer best suit would you.'

He laughed.

Maisie's thoughts turned back to earlier in the evening. 'What did Eddie Bridgeman want me for?' she asked him.

Alf stubbed his cigarette out under the toe of his shiny brown shoe.

'He wants you,' said Alf, his voice not much above a whisper.

'I won't betray my mates and Wills's. They're too good to me...'

'No, Maisie. You,' he said in a more stressed tone. 'He wants you.'

Maisie frowned. There was a dark worried look on her brother's face.

'I wish you'd go away from here, Maisie. I thought you wanted to work in a grand house out in the sticks. Don't you want to do that any more?'

Her mouth felt dry. She gulped. 'I don't want to leave my mates.' A nervous smile twitched at her lips. 'And you. I don't want to leave you.'

Alf stuffed his hands in his pockets and looked directly at her. 'Sis, you've got to know that when I get called up – and I'm sure to be, that's it, I won't be here to protect you. I'm thinking of joining the merchant navy before I get drafted into the army. Be one step ahead of it all. I ain't told the old man, yet, but the moment that call-up paper arrives, I'm off.'

She stared at him. 'I'll be all by myself.'

He nodded. 'That's what I'm afraid of. Get out, sis, before the old man does a deal with Eddie and you become a piece of his property.'

'I could join up.'

Alf shook his head and reminded her that she was only fifteen.

'I could lie.' She'd heard some of the old-timers in the pub say that they'd lied about their age back in the Great War.

Alf shook his head. 'And dad would tell them the truth and drag you back. Won't work, love.'

'What about the fight?'

He grinned, sucked on his cigarette, his lips pursed as he puffed the smoke up into the air.

'No fight. Not once I pointed out that these blokes would be better as friends than enemies. Them boats are going to be carrying stuff this country's going to need. Smuggling ain't dead you know. I think Eddie saw the light. Them blokes could be useful.'

'Alright for you going away to sea. And me stuck 'ere with 'im. What a bloody life!'

Alf gave her a brotherly hug. 'You're young but you've got a good brain in yer noggin. Use it. Don't just wait for something to turn up. Make it 'appen, and grab the chance when it does.'

18

PHYLLIS

Mrs Mason, Phyllis's mother, was all smiles. The best china was only laid out for Christmas and special occasions. Today was one of those special occasions.

It was Sunday and she'd seen Robert with his mother at the Methodist chapel that morning when she'd gone in early with fresh flowers cut from the garden. Gardening was her great pastime, and supplying blooms for the church a labour of love. Nobody would believe what wonderful flowers she had growing in her back garden. A council house it might be, but it was a large plot and she was a keen gardener.

The sermon had been especially depressing and she made a note to herself to mention her views to the minister. She'd closed her ears to listening to the news on the wireless or reading of it in the newspapers. She even rushed past newspaper sellers so she didn't have to hear them shouting about the war or read it on bill-boards. And here she was being bombarded with all this unpleasant news on a Sunday.

The one thing she was glad of was that she had a daughter

not a son, that's what she'd said to Mr and Mrs Harvey, Robert's parents.

'I couldn't bear it,' she'd said to Robert's mother.

On seeing the alarm on Mrs Harvey's face, she'd immediately regretted saying it.

Hilda Harvey had looked with undisputed motherly love at her son whilst dabbing at her nose with her handkerchief. 'I don't know what I'll do if they take him,' she'd replied. 'I'm not a well woman, you know. Perhaps that might keep him out on compassionate grounds.'

Phyllis's mother had sympathised and decided on the spot to be charitable and ask her, her husband and her son to tea.

Robert's father had looked to his wife before accepting her offer. 'Well, I'm not sure what we've got planned...'

It had long been obvious to Stella Mason that Hilda Harvey was the one who wore the trousers.

'Of course we can,' she'd responded with one last dab at her nose. 'It's not often I get to enjoy little treats like that. Come to think of it, I'm never indulged in anything particularly enjoyable.' She threw an accusing jibe at her long-suffering husband. 'I work my fingers to the bone...'

Robert's mother had gone on and on. Mr Harvey had tried to placate her but was told he didn't understand anything, had no sympathy and should shut up. It came as a great relief when Robert intervened, patting his mother's hand and telling her not to be such a silly girl.

'Right,' Mrs Mason had said, adopting what she hoped was a sincere smile. 'We'll see you at four.'

* * *

Phyllis came downstairs wearing a cotton dress scattered with yellow daisies and quite a low sweetheart neckline.

Her mother looked at her, then looked away. 'That's a very pretty dress, dear, but will you be warm enough?'

Phyllis knew that what her mother was really saying was that the neckline was too low. She hadn't been thinking of how Robert or his parents might view the dress. She'd found herself thinking of her typing teacher, imagining him saying how pretty it was, how pretty she was. Up in her bedroom, she'd picked up her lipstick. She was sure Alan Stalybridge, her typing teacher, would approve. But Alan wasn't Robert. He preferred the fresh-faced look, a prim hairstyle, a dress lacking in pattern, ribbons or bows. It was him she had to conform to, and now high tea with his parents. Unlike her mother, she was not looking forward to it.

'There's a seed cake in the kitchen. Could you bring it in, dear?'

Phyllis glanced at the pile of bread and butter, the jars of jam – one of strawberry and one blackcurrant. There was also an apple pie, a jug of cream and tinned salmon sandwiches.

'Did you use all the salmon?' her mother asked when she came back in with the cake.

'No. I left some in the tin like you usually do.'

Her mother's face creased. 'You shouldn't have. We don't want them to think we're paupers. We have to show some generosity.'

Phyllis had thought she'd done right, especially given the current circumstances. 'I thought that now we're at war, we have to get used to being a bit careful with food.'

Her mother threw up her hands in horror and closed her eyes. 'Don't mention war! Please! I'm sick of hearing about it.'

Phyllis wanted to say that closing one's eyes wouldn't make the war go away. It had to be faced. She stopped herself. Like a lot of other people, her mother had gone through one war and was finding it hard to face the fact that another had started.

The tablecloth was a sparkling white, and although they were now in September, the whole appearance was of a summer tea.

Stella Mason's hands flitted over the table cloth. 'Do you think they'll be impressed?'

'It's only Robert's parents coming to tea, not the King and Queen,' Phyllis replied.

'No need to be sarcastic,' her mother snapped.

A knock on the door heralded the arrival of their visitors. Robert shooed his mother in through the door first, her elbow resting in his hand. His father came in behind him, took his trilby from his head and everyone shook hands. Robert gave Phyllis a little peck on the cheek.

Mrs Harvey scrutinised the room, as though measuring its dimensions and assessing the quality of the drapes and furniture. 'Hmm,' she murmured a trifle sniffily. 'Is this your only parlour?'

Phyllis saw the slight pinkness on her mother's face.

'I was going to put in for a parlour type – you know – two reception rooms, but there's only Phyllis and me, so not much point.'

Mrs Harvey sniffed. 'Well, as long as you can manage. We own our house. It was the best thing Tom ever did. Course I had to persuade him. Make him see the sense in it.'

To Phyllis's ears, Mrs Harvey made it sound as though Mr Harvey was totally useless, yet to Phyllis he'd always seemed a kind, long-suffering man. Married to Mrs Harvey, long suffering must be a way of life.

Small talk accompanied the eating of sandwiches and cakes, the drinking of copious amounts of tea. It was very noticeable to Phyllis that they were purposely talking about the weather, the food and what the men were doing at work. It was noticeable too that they did not touch on Phyllis and her job in the tobacco factory. She felt as if she was being banded with her mother and Robert's mother, her employment not important. Her destiny was mapped out. She would become as they were – a stay-at-home housewife and mother.

Robert's mother picked up a sandwich, sniffed then frowned at it. 'Is this tinned salmon?'

'Yes,' said Phyllis. 'Freshly made.' She wanted to add that she'd taken ages cutting the bread into neat triangles but doubted Mrs Harvey would be interested. Her mother looked nervous.

'Is it red salmon or pink salmon? I know red is more expensive, but it has to be red salmon for me. Pink salmon unsettles my stomach.'

A warning note sounded in her head. If she married Robert, that difficult woman would become her mother-in-law and no doubt she'd see more of her. The trouble was, for all her natural effervescence with friends, Phyllis quailed in her shoes faced with this lot.

In an effort to cope with Mrs Harvey's constant whining, she escaped into her favourite daydream, walking out with Alan Stalybridge, laughing with him, hearing him saying how pretty she looked. He hadn't so far, but at least she could dream.

Robert's voice broke into her faraway thoughts. 'There's going to be a lot of uncertainty, Phyllis, and a chap going away to fight needs to feel that there's somebody waiting for him at home worth fighting for. I believe we've been engaged for long enough. I want us to get married before I get called up.' He wasn't looking at her as he said it, but at his parents. Her jaw dropped. Even her own mother looked taken by surprise.

'Robert, I thought we were going to save up first. I mean...' She searched around for excuses – any excuses. 'Where will we live?'

He shook his head and smiled at her as though she were only a child. 'Silly goose. That's hardly a problem. There's plenty of room for us at home with my parents. They'll need some company whilst I'm away.'

For a moment Phyllis was speechless.

Finally she found her voice. 'Robert, I don't know what to say.'

He lit up a cigarette. 'I've given it considerable thought. I'm going to get called up so might as well get married as soon as we can.'

Her eyes followed the smoke in its upward twisting and turning. It was very likely that she'd had a hand in making that cigarette. She wondered how many other young men would be smoking with shaking hands as Robert was presently doing. She'd never known his hands shake before but had heard that smoking helped calm the nerves of those about to go into battle.

His mother gave little muted sobs. 'My poor boy.'

'Now, now dear,' said his father. The hand that patted his wife's shoulder was shrugged abruptly off.

'When do you think...?' Even to Phyllis's ears, her voice seemed far away.

Robert was adamant. 'I think we should get married the moment I receive my call-up papers – whenever that's likely to be. By special licence if need be.'

Her acceptance taken for granted, Phyllis was speechless. She wasn't required to agree.

Later that evening after the Harveys had gone home, the dishes were done, light music was playing on the wireless and a magazine lay on her lap. All the things she wished she'd said were whirling round in her head. In her head she was brave. In actuality she found it difficult to stand up for herself as though what everyone else wanted was more important than what she wanted.

Her mother had no such misgivings. As far as she was concerned, Robert could do no wrong. However, his mother was a different prospect. 'I do like, Robert, I really do. His father seems a decent sort too. But his mother... a difficult woman. She can't be easy to live with,' she mused.

Phyllis turned a page of the magazine. The words were a blur. Even speaking of Mrs Harvey made her prickle all over. Finding the courage to call off the engagement seemed to her a mammoth task. They'd been together for some time and she hated the thought of hurting Robert.

She glanced up at her mother. Her eyes were closed and she was humming along with the music.

In a sudden moment of increased bravery, she decided to declare her reservations. However, she didn't get the chance.

Her mother got in first. 'Don't think I don't know what you're thinking, my girl. There's two sides to you, just as there was to your father. One side accepts routine, the other wants to fly to the stars. Well, life ain't like that.' Her eyes, darker than those of her daughter, held a warning look. 'You're too exuberant at times. Robert won't want that, so calm yerself down. No man wants a wife who draws attention to herself and 'e don't want no Dolly Daydream either.'

The moment of bravery vanished. 'He does have the odd pint, and 'im being a Methodist.'

An odd pint! It sounded so trivial but was all she could think of.

Her mother sprang to his defence. 'Not enough to worry about. That's what I like about that young man. Everything in moderation.'

Her mother reclosed her eyes and resumed humming along with the music coming from the wireless.

'Did my father like a drink?'

'In moderation.'

The subject was finished.

Behind her closed eyes, Stella Mason remembered how things had once been. George Mason had been dead some years now. She regretted his passing, regretted no longer hearing his voice and that accent he'd picked up during his years in Canada. Sometimes, when the mood took her, she'd retell the stories of his experiences to Phyllis, especially when her daughter had been younger. She hadn't done it for some time now. He'd gone over to Canada as a two-year-old child taking passage on the ship that had crossed immediately before the ill-fated Titanic. He'd been sent back as a grown man, unable to find work in his adopted country. The laws of Canada had turned cruel, sending back the unemployed to a country they had no memory of.

Stella had fallen head over hills for him, married in haste and although she hadn't exactly repented at leisure, over time his bubbly personality had become slightly tiring. She'd found herself wanting somebody of a steadier nature, who didn't get involved in moneymaking schemes that never quite came off. If he had, perhaps they could have bought their own house, not be living in one rented from the council. Thinking of her situation brought Hilda Harvey to mind.

'Mrs Harvey thought this house was small,' she said suddenly. 'You've got an aunt in Canada with her own house. Hamilton,' she exclaimed suddenly as if she'd only just remembered. 'Hamilton, Ontario.'

Phyllis stared at her mother, waiting for her to say more. 'Have you ever heard from her?'

Her mother didn't answer but went back to closing her eyes and humming along with the music. Phyllis recognised that the moment when the past had broken through into the present was over – until another time perhaps.

19

BRIDGET

Mary Milligan heard the front door shut, followed by her daughter calling out that she was home from work. She gave her a few minutes to take off her coat and overall, wash her hands and come in from the hallway, then stand in the kitchen doorway.

She saw Bridget's blue eyes, that so matched her own, glance at the mantelpiece and knew she was looking for a letter from the young American who'd picked her up in that posh motor car.

Her mother's heart bled on seeing the look of disappointment on her daughter's face. He hadn't written and neither did Mary Milligan expect him to. Her daughter and the young man lived in different worlds. It was her opinion that they were unlikely ever to see each other again.

'How was your day at work, darling?' she said and smiled as though all was well with the world, when in fact it most certainly was not.

Her daughter smiled in return; more smiles as she watched the younger siblings gobble down the last of their dinners and waited to see what sweets she'd brought home today. They were not disappointed.

'Two bars of Fry's Five Boys to be divided between each of you. Make the most of it. Sweets are going on ration and they're getting harder to come by.'

The cream-filled dark chocolate bars, manufactured in the Bristol-based chocolate factory at Keynsham, were greeted with wide-eyed pleasure.

'You've your tea in peace this evening without being surrounded by bits of clock,' said her mother.

'Just this lot.' Bridget laughed as she ruffled Katy's hair, then did the same with Michael. 'Where's dad?' she asked her mother.

'Gone to some meeting about air raid Wardens. Given half the chance and his leg back, I'd swear he'd be joining up.'

Mary went to finish drying the dishes whilst Bridget finished her meal, then offered her a cup of tea. Once there was a cup set in front of them, her mother sat down and took a sip. Bridget was her first daughter and she fancied she knew what she was feeling.

'You know,' she said, wrapping both hands round her tea cup, 'I worried the moment I saw that big shiny motorcar pull up that you might start wishing for the moon...'

Bridget sat silently, eyes downcast, tea untouched.

To her mother's mind, this was not normal behaviour for her girl who was rarely stuck for words.

Mary sighed. 'I know he promised to write to you. Sure, you get to the letter box before I do on a morning.'

Bridget too sighed, sucked in her lips and gingerly picked up her tea cup. 'I was so sure. He'd promised and I really believed him. 'Tis a bitter pill to swallow. I keep asking myself, where do I go from here?'

Her mother reached out and smoothed her daughter's hair back from her forehead and recalled the first time she'd stroked Bridget's head. She remembered her being born, that first cry, the slight disappointment that she hadn't presented her husband with a boy, the reassurance and the sudden rush of love she'd felt as she held that pink bundle for the first time. 'Him with all his money – he belongs to a different world. Like marries like. As will you, me darlin' girl. The right man is out there somewhere in the future just waiting for you to come along.'

Talk of the future made Bridget look up. 'Will you read the leaves, Ma?'

Mary hesitated, but the pleading in Bridget's eyes was too intense to ignore. 'Why not? Drink up and we'll see what the leaves foretell. Lucky I didn't use the tea strainer. There'll be more than enough leaves to read.'

Once Bridget's cup was empty of liquid, her mother placed a saucer on top of it before turning it upside down so that the leaves were left in the saucer.

'One, two, three,' she counted as she turned the cup round in the saucer before righting it. 'Now let's see what we have here,' she finally said, clasping the cup with both hands aware that Bridget was watching her avidly.

Mary had gained a reputation with the neighbours as being a very accurate reader of the tea leaves. A piece of silver – even if only a sixpence – had crossed her palm many a time. The one thing she rarely did was a reading for her family, preferring to keep the future a closed book rather than see things she did not wish to see.

She felt Bridget's eyes upon her, anxious to know if the young American was coming back. It seemed for a moment as though all Mary could see were leaves and not the pictures they seemed to coalesce into. Deep down, she knew it was her blocking the pictures, not wishing to disclose what her daughter wanted to know. Blocking out the pictures did not last. They were a natural phenomenon that could not be denied. Suddenly it all came into focus.

Bridget was getting anxious and impatient. 'What can you see? Mother? What do you see?'

Just as she opened her mouth to reply, the house shook to the sudden banging of the front door, followed by Patrick Milligan announcing that he was home.

He came into the room still wearing his hat and coat, looked from one to the other and said, 'What's the two most beautiful girls in the world up to, then?'

'Mother's reading my tea leaves.'

Her mother noted the hope shining in her daughter's eyes and her heart lurched.

'Your meal's out on the saucepan,' she said to her husband. 'I won't be a minute.'

Bridget sighed and looked up at her father. 'You've interrupted my future,' she said, her voice laced with more amusement than accusation.

'Sorry, me darling.'

He went back out in the hallway to hang up his coat and hat. 'I could eat a horse,' he said as Bridget's mother placed the steaming meal in front of him.

Mary flicked the tea towel at him, an amused look on her face. 'I couldn't get horse meat, but I did get pork cuttings, so think yourself lucky.'

'I'm a very lucky man.'

She blushed when he winked at her. 'Get on with you.'

Bridget looked from one to the other. She was used to seeing them laugh and joke together in an intimate manner that was theirs and theirs alone. This was the way it was now. 'Am I missing something here?' she asked.

There followed a bashful exchange of looks between her parents, the people she loved most in all the world, before they faced her and told her their secret.

'There's another Milligan on the way,' her father said proudly, his face wreathed in smiles. 'Isn't that marvellous, Bridie? Isn't it just?'

The news rang like a bell inside her head. Her mother was pregnant. Again?

Images of the last time came into her mind. The pain, the blood-soaked bundles burnt on a bonfire.

Her mother's face came into view, floating disembodied in front of her. 'Bridie? Are you alright?'

'Fine,' she said, but Bridget felt far from fine. 'I've just remembered I promised to go round to Phyllis's. I'll see you later.'

All thoughts of reading the tea leaves now forgotten, she ran all the way to where Phyllis lived and had already knocked on the door when she realised that her best friend wouldn't be there.

'I'm sorry,' she said, when Mrs Mason answered the door, a headful of curlers tucked beneath a plaid headscarf. 'I forgot that it's Phyllis's typing class tonight.'

The moment the words were out, she saw the colour drain from Mrs Mason's face.

'What typing class? What are you on about? She said she was going out with Robert tonight.'

Bridget was all of a dither. The news that her mother was having another baby had come as such a shock. Without meaning to, she'd dropped Phyllis in it.

She tried her best to make amends. 'I'm sorry. I didn't mean to come here. I was thinking of somebody else. Sorry to disturb you, Mrs Mason.'

She didn't ask for her to tell Phyllis that she'd called but hoped nothing would come of her unfortunate mistake. The one thing she did know was that Phyllis would be livid once she found out.

* * *

Mary Milligan looked at her daughter's teacup sitting on top a pile of dishes. From the living room came the sound of her husband's gentle snoring. Knowing he so hated war, she smiled at his willingness to get involved with the local ARP unit. It was his way of doing something constructive that didn't require him to kill somebody but might help save lives.

Before plunging the teacup into the hot sudsy water, she took one last look in case she'd missed something. Her eyes narrowed. The leaves were unchanged and so were their message, one that would upset her husband no end if she chose to tell him. She could see explosions, tumbled masonry and many frightened people. Worst of all, Bridget was in the thick of it. There was little sign of the American her daughter so hoped would come back, though that didn't mean he never would. The tea leaves were like a diary and only pronounced so far ahead. She resolved that at some time in the future she would have another go, but for now she would say nothing of what might happen.

Having made her mind up, she plunged the teacup into the water, the tea leaves dispersing and floating on the surface, along with a future she wished would not come.

20

PHYLLIS

Phyllis swelled with pride when Alan Stalybridge told her that she'd taken to typing like a duck to water. He also said that it wasn't just her determination to succeed that had a hand in it, but she really did have a natural skill to feel her way over the keyboard.

'As long as you pass your exam you'll get your certificate round about March,' he said to her. 'I've no doubt you'll pass and then you will be the proud recipient of a certificate for RSA Stage I in Typing.'

'I can't wait,' she said, thinking how she would brim with pride when he handed it to her. 'I'd like to leave the factory floor and go to work in the office.'

She felt she was walking on air when he said to her, 'I wish you all the luck in the world.'

With a sudden pang of regret that she realised that after March she would never see him again, she admitted, 'I'll miss coming here.' She bit back the other things she wanted to say, such as how much she admired him, how relaxed she felt in his class. He was in her dreams every night and she regularly woke to find herself tangled in the bedclothes. She'd convinced herself that he also dreamed of her, both of them in a fairy-tale castle. March would come around too quickly to her mind. On top of that, she felt that she hadn't lived enough yet to settle for marrying Robert. Necessity led to uncommon courage. 'Do you drink?'

At first, her question seemed to take him by surprise and then he looked pleased. Creases appeared at the sides of his eyes and his mouth. She didn't think they were age-related, in fact she thought they suited him. For a start, they matched his shirt, which never looked as if it was ironed. His hair remained overlong and his corduroy trousers seemed to hang too low on his hips, perhaps because his hands always seemed to be stuffed in his pockets as he gave the class the benefit of his knowledge.

'Is that an invitation?' A tic of amusement lifted one side of his mouth.

'Oh! Well... um...'

He drew in his chin and raised his eyebrows. 'I'll be disappointed if you say no.'

Phyllis was sure that her cheeks were turning the same colour as her lipstick. She made a point of always wearing lipstick to class. It made up for the nights out with Robert when she couldn't wear any make-up.

In that moment, it seemed as though Alan's eyes were the only thing in the world that existed, the world around him appearing fuzzy and unfocused.

* * *

The Bunch of Grapes was an interloper in a street of terraced houses that she'd spotted on her way to class. Women who looked older than their years stood with crossed arms at their respective front doors, all of them wearing crossover aprons.

A cold wind blew. The nights were getting darker and the public bar in the Bunch of Grapes did not give much extra light. Blackout curtains had been fitted at every window. Only the flickering of gas wall lights lifted the leaden gloom, their smell mixing with that of sawdust and strong yeast.

Old men in cloth caps and baggy trousers leaned on the bar. Nobody wished them good evening or eyed them too intently. Much to Phyllis's relief, nobody seemed to care who they were or where they were from.

Her heart thudding, she sat on a bench seat under the window whilst Alan ordered two drinks. He came back and placed them on the three-legged circular table.

'I forgot to ask you what you wanted to drink. I've bought us two whiskies. Are you all right with that?'

'That's lovely.' The truth was, she was so beside herself, she hadn't noticed that he hadn't asked her what she wanted. She didn't like whisky but refrained from telling him.

Having brushed against the blackout curtains, he rearranged them so no light could escape. It made her feel cocooned, safe.

A barrel of a man behind the bar nodded approvingly at his action.

'Never upset a pub landlord,' Alan murmured softly as they clinked glasses.

Phyllis raised her glass. 'Cheers.'

'Cheers.'

She gulped too appreciatively, coughed and patted her chest. 'My word.'

Alan smiled, sipped and spoke. 'I won't ask you if you're enjoying the course, because I know you are.'

'Are you enjoying teaching it?'

'Yes.'

'You're not from Bristol.'

He smiled and set his glass down on the table. 'You noticed. I'm originally from London and came here to teach English at Clifton College, but I got fed up with it. Public-school boys are irritating. They feel they have a divine right to lord it over other people – including their masters. I stuck it for so long and then left. Worked at the tobacco bonds for a while, weighing the casks to evaluate customs duty – hard work, but I enjoyed it. Then I got the yearning to teach again. I'd always fancied going into journalism, hence my proficiency with a typewriter. It's a competitive occupation and I wasn't as good at it as I thought I was. So here I am teaching instead – which suits me very well. So that's me. Now tell me about you.'

Feeling a little light-headed from the moment, Phyllis looked down into her glass, which was now empty, and blamed her nerves for knocking it back so swiftly. 'There's not much to tell really.' She fingered her empty glass, turning it round and round on the tabletop.

'I don't believe that. For a start, I know you live in Bedminster and that you work at the tobacco factory. Is that making cigarettes?'

He seemed genuinely interested and she found herself opening up. 'Yes. It can be quite fun at times. I have two friends, Bridget and Maisie. We go out together.'

'No boyfriend?'

She tried not to look guilty and was glad she'd left her engagement ring back on the dressing table in her bedroom. The lie rolled off her tongue. 'No. I did, but we finished. What with the war happening, we didn't think it a very good time to get married.'

'Gather ye rosebuds...' he said in a lazy drifting voice.

'Rosebuds?'

'It's about time flying. Seize the day. Live for today in case tomorrow never comes. Get married if you like or stay single and indulge in the day-to-day pleasures of life.' He sighed and there was sadness in his eyes. 'I wonder how many young men are going to regret not living enough by the time this war is over.'

Most young men she knew were keen to fight, full of bravado without being fully aware of what they were letting themselves in for.

'Are you not going to fight?' Phyllis asked him. He carefully avoided mentioning that he was older than the present upper limit for the draft. That was another thing she liked about him. He was more mature than the young men she was used to.

His response was crisply delivered. 'Not if I can help it. I don't agree with war. I firmly believe in life. Whether I die on the battlefield or as an old man in my bed, I want to look back on moments when I felt incredibly alive. Do you understand what I'm saying?'

Her eyes shone. The face that filled her dreams held her attention now and his words made her feel as though she were flying; never before had anyone spoken to her so poetically. With words, he'd taken her to another place.

'Yes. I know what you mean.'

For this frozen moment in time, the details of the dingy back-street pub were no more than blurred outlines, as though seen through water.

To her great surprise, he leaned forward and the sudden touch of his lips on her forehead seemed to burn into her brain, its heat remaining even after the kiss was over. The first thought that came to her was that Robert's closed-lip kiss left no such lingering warmth and did not seem to melt into her skin as Alan's lips did or make her wonder what they would feel like on her lips, on her neck, her throat, her shoulders... She shivered at the prospect.

Alan checked his wristwatch. 'Good lord. I'm afraid I have to go.'

Phyllis gathered her things together. 'Yes. So do I or I'll miss the last tram.'

She didn't really know whether she would or she wouldn't miss the last tram or bus, it just seemed she had to counter his words, make herself believe that they were both just flirting. The truth was, she didn't want it to be just flirting. His words about living for today had awoken something deep inside. The logic was like a door in her mind that she'd never noticed before, a locked door that had never been opened.

She sighed as he helped her to her feet, cupping her elbow, winding his arm round her back as he escorted her to the door.

The doors closed behind them. The night was pitch black, yet she felt him there, saw the faint silhouette of something not quite so dark against a night that was very dark.

She hoped he wouldn't think her a fool when she said, 'You're right. Who knows where we'll be this time next year or the year after?'

He took a deep breath of the chill night air. 'Or the years beyond that. I want to make memories, to be able to view my life as a book of many chapters, and a lot of them before I reach the end.'

She was genuinely impressed. 'That's lovely. I've never thought of it like that.'

He cupped her elbow again. 'I'll give you a lift home.'

'That would be nice.'

She felt like a queen sitting beside him in the front seat of the car and she couldn't help thinking of that day Bridget had been picked up in a car. Of course, this one was much smaller than the Rolls-Royce Bridget had ridden in, the top of her head hitting the roof each time they went over a bump in the road or brushed the curb.

At her request, they turned into Littleton Road.

Alan peered over the wheel at the houses. Some of them were semi-detached and built of brick and others were terraced and/or covered in painted pebbledash. 'Is this your house?'

'No. It's a little further along.'

She purposely didn't want him to know her exact address and not only because she felt embarrassed that she came from a lesser background than him. Her mother would ask questions about the man who had brought her home, most of which she was disinclined to answer. After all, she had told him she was meeting Robert in town.

'I'll see you next week then.'

She half expected him to kiss her and was disappointed when he didn't.

'Yes. I'll see you then.'

When she was halfway out of the passenger seat, he offered to give her extra tuition. 'I can see you want to get on. How about we fix up an extra night?'

'At Redcross Street?'

She suspected it wouldn't be there but wanted him to say what he meant – what he really meant.

'I have a rather sumptuous flat in Redland, the whole of the ground floor in fact. It includes my private office. Hang on.' He extracted a notebook from his pocket and began writing on it. 'I've included the tram and bus details,' he said as he handed it to her.

Though her mother's voice inside her head warned that one thing could lead to another, she blanked it out, thanked him and was walking on air until she was inside the front door and faced with her mother.

Arms folded across her chest, hair curlers quivering with fury, she ordered Phyllis to sit down and listen to what she had to say.

'You lied to me. You told me you were going out with Robert tonight. Well, I know better. Your friend Bridget's been round and spilled the beans.'

'What?' Phyllis's jaw dropped. She couldn't believe Bridget would do such a thing, but she could see the truth in her mother's face. 'I want to better myself,' she said as bravely as she knew how. 'I want to work in an office.'

Her mother's metal curlers rattled with the ferocity of her shaking head. 'You don't need to better yourself! Robert wants to marry you. Isn't that enough that you've bagged a bloke who can look after you, who don't expect you to ever work again?'

I'll look like you in time, thought Phyllis as she stared at her mother's lined face and blurted, 'I'll never be as young as I am now and never come this way again and have a choice of which path to take.'

A look of sheer incomprehension came to her mother's face. 'What are you on about?'

Phyllis realised that her words reflected a lot of what Alan had said to her.

She leaned forward, hands clasped, her expression shining with the expectation of something grand happening in her future. 'I'm having second thoughts about marrying Robert.'

Her mother flopped herself into the other armchair, looking totally puzzled. 'I can't believe I'm hearing this.'

'Don't tell 'im,' Phyllis entreated. 'Let me be. If I don't pass the exam, I won't get an office job anyway and I don't want to work in the factory forever, so marriage it will have to be.'

Her mother had the stunned expression of somebody who had unexpectedly been hit over the head.

Phyllis took the opportunity to get up and go to bed. In the semi-darkness of her room, she examined the diamonds on the engagement ring Robert had bought her. They seemed lost, a bit like she was in a way. She could still feel Alan's kiss on her forehead. How would it feel, she wondered, on her lips. She blushed as she thought of how it might feel on more intimate areas of her body. There was shame in those feelings but also excitement.

The saying the other man's grass is always greener sprang into her mind. That was exactly what she wanted, to sample not just the grass but the man himself.

21
———

It was the end of September and sandbags were springing up outside every building of importance. Most of them in Bedminster were stacked round the police station in case the Germans decided it was a prime target. Other important buildings, such as the General Hospital, were also having sandbags piled round the entrances. Every window in every building, every house and also shop windows were criss-crossed with strong masking tape. If windows should be damaged in a bomb blast, the tape would stop the glass shattering and flying off in all directions.

Bridget, Phyllis and Maisie peered down into the prepared bomb shelter beneath the factory. What they saw impressed them very much.

'I hear it will take a thousand people,' Bridget informed her.

'Will that be for men and women?' asked an intrigued Maisie.

'I'm afraid so,' said Bridget. 'Just think of it; trapped in there all night with all that snoring going on round us. Worse than the bombs!'

They peered into the gloom a bit longer, each imagining how

it might be. Benches had been placed between and beneath the steam mains and in the alcoves between the boilers.

'It's gonna be nice and cosy down by them boilers,' proclaimed Maisie.

Bridget frowned at the thought of it. 'Let's hope we never have to find out.'

'We're gonna be 'avin' drills,' said Maisie. 'Did you 'ear that air-raid siren? Loud enough to wake the dead.' She rubbed at her ears at the memory of it. 'Louder than Aggie,' she added with a giggle.

The siren that would warn of a coming raid had been fitted onto the roof. Its wail had already sent people scurrying to reach shelters before being told it wasn't for real.

Bridget sighed at Maisie's comment. 'A drill I can cope with. It's the real thing that frightens me.'

They made their way to the canteen, where Maisie bought herself a plate of chips and a cup of tea. The other two had pies with theirs.

Bridget had recovered somewhat from the shock announcement that her mother was expecting again, news she would keep to herself. But it had become common knowledge about her acting as guide to the young American who had visited the factory with his father, and Bridget was coping with the aftermath of questions.

'Will you see 'im again?'

'Did 'e try and take advantage of your good nature?'

'What was it like riding in that big car?'

She fielded the questions well enough whilst enduring her disappointment that he never wrote to her. She needed something to divert her and thought about going to the pictures. Phyllis was staring into space when Bridget suggested going.

Phyllis jerked herself out of her reverie. 'Can't. I'm going somewhere.'

'How's the typing going? I mean, is your mother alright about it now?' Bridget bit her bottom lip. 'Sorry I let the cat out of the bag.'

'At least she's keeping it to herself.'

The fact was her mother wanted at all costs to preserve the engagement to Robert so was keeping it a secret.

Phyllis looked very proud of herself. 'My teacher says I'm a natural. I'm doin' extra classes to make sure I pass.'

'Does that mean you'll be leaving us and going to work in the office?'

'I will, but not yet... I mean I've still got a lot of learning to do.' Her faraway look was replaced by one of pride. 'I've been told I'm making excellent progress, best in the class in fact.'

Maisie smirked. 'So you're teacher's pet?'

Phyllis was adamant. 'Of course not. Alan really rates me...'

Bridget's eyebrows arched. 'Alan?' There was a cheeky smile on her face.

'Aye, aye,' said Maisie, a judgemental look aging her young face.

Phyllis pushed her plate of half-finished food across the table. 'I'm off to the toilets. Don't get me any pudding.' She pushed her chair back and tottered off on three-inch heels.

Bridget frowned as she watched her go. 'Is it my imagination, or has she been acting a bit vague of late?'

Maisie opened her mouth to answer until she became aware that Bert had arrived, a flushed, excited look on his face.

'I got something for you,' he said to Maisie and handed her a letter. It was of the official kind, written by a member of the forces on flimsy paper. He winked. 'It's addressed to me, but there's a bit for you. He couldn't send it to you direct 'cos 'e didn't know yer address.'

'Because I chose not to give him my address,' said Maisie blushing as the bitter sweet memory of saying goodbye flooded over her. 'I'm too young to be anyone's sweetheart.' The fact was she was secretly pleased that he'd written. She hadn't been sure that he would.

As she unfolded the crisp paper, Bert rubbed his hands together with feverish excitement. Bridget sensed Maisie wanted to read it for herself and not with Bert or anyone else hanging over her shoulder.

'Thanks for bringing it, Bert,' she said. 'You'd better be getting back to work.'

Instead of taking the hint, Bert sat himself between them. He leaned slightly towards Maisie and peered over her shoulder.

Maisie folded the paper and glared at him. 'Do you mind?'

He looked hurt. 'I already know what it says.'

'That's not the point. It's rude to read over somebody's shoulder. Either knock it off or I'm off to the lavatory to read it.'

Recognising he'd been put in his place; Bert turned his attention to Bridget. 'Fancy going to the Saturday matinee. I'm on fire duty that night so can only go in the afternoon.' He beamed proudly. 'I'm still in training, but we'll be up on the roof, ready to deal with incendiaries, gas or anyfink that falls on us.'

'I thought you were joining the RAF?'

He looked crushed. 'Me dad won't let me. Told me to wait until I'm twenty and they call me up anyway.'

'I thought you were twenty. That's what you told me.'

He looked embarrassed. 'I get fed up of everybody thinking I'm a boy, so I lies about me age.'

'Lying about your age won't make any difference to how you

look. Anyway,' she said, patting his hand amiably, 'I like your boyish looks.'

'Do you mean that?' His smooth cheeks turned pink with pleasure as he eyed the hand she'd patted.

'Yes.' *It will do me good*, she told herself. *Better than staying at home mooning about somebody who I'm never likely to see again.*

Maisie chewed her lower lip before saying, 'Sid wants me to write to him.'

'That's nice,' Bridget replied.

'But I need an address. You know how it is with me; not sure where I'm likely to be.'

Their eyes met in mutual understanding. Even if Maisie had not confided in her about her home life, she would have guessed it. Bridget only wished there was room in the Milligan household to have her there. There'd be even less with another baby on the way. She hoped this baby would go full term, but whether it did or not, she didn't want to be there.

Her concerns were pushed from her mind when Bridget told her that Sid could send his letters to her house. 'And I promise not to read over your shoulder!'

Even Bert laughed.

22

MAISIE

Reaching home was like walking out of sunshine into shadow. The smell and look of York Street never failed to depress Maisie. The windowpanes looked greasier than usual, which led her to wondering when her mother had last cleaned them. On reflection, it seemed that everything that had looked half tidy about the house now looked dirty and tired. It had also become noticeable that her mother was now often in bed when she got home from work, which meant she had to find her own meal. Not that it worried her. She was no great cook but certainly better than her mother.

The sense of menace and hopelessness had increased since Alf had voluntarily joined the merchant navy.

'I'm going with me mate,' he'd said to her. 'You know; the one I was talking to outside the Duke of York.'

Maisie had been devastated. Life at York Street without her brother would be unbearable. The idea to leave popped yet again into her mind. She'd miss her mates at work, but her only protector had left. Young as she was, she understood what he'd told her about Eddie Bridgeman. He bought young girls like her and her father would gladly take the money.

She'd hardly got through the door when she heard her father shouting.

'About time you got 'ere. Where's me bloody dinner?'

'Where's Mum?' Obviously she wasn't upstairs in bed or he would have dragged her out by now.

'How should I bloody know?'

The way he was eyeing her over the top of a glass of beer unnerved her.

'What you looking at me like that for?' she said as she took off her coat. Feeling the clammy coldness of an unheated house she shrugged herself back into it and went through to the kitchen. Dishes were piled in the sink and the blackout curtains hadn't been drawn. 'We're gonna get a fine if you forget to draw the blackout curtains.'

'Stuff 'em.'

The only sound in the kitchen was the dripping of the tap. The most dominant smell was from the pig bin, where leftover food was scraped, including the dried peas burnt to the bottom of a saucepan.

Dingy before she pulled the curtains, the room was plunged into impenetrable darkness. Maisie felt her way across to the light switch at the side of the door dividing kitchen from living room. When it came on, there was her father.

'Are you gettin' on with it then? I ain't 'ad a thing to eat all bloody day!'

'You could 'ave bought something down at the caff.'

'I ain't got money to throw away like that,' he shouted.

The fact was that he did have money. He spent it on himself, allotting only the most minimal amount to housekeeping. He couldn't seem to get it through his head that he was responsible for feeding and providing a roof over the head of his family, and keeping it in good repair would give them comfort. He didn't care about their comfort and didn't see the cracked plaster or smell the pungent drains.

Maisie turned her back on him, took off her coat and flung it onto a chair.

'You couldn't be bothered to wash the pots then,' she growled as she rolled up her sleeves.

'That's woman's work!'

Ignoring him she began to pile the dishes into the sink, filled the kettle from the tap and put it on the gas, her movements quick and angry. 'Yeah, and that's all women are fit for, ain't it. Work. I work all day and am working still.' Some of her anger was scrubbed out with the pans, but not all of it. She knew he'd retaliate.

'Don't you talk to me like that! I'm yer father.'

She turned round glaring at him, and saw him wince, almost as though he expected her to land a blow on his greasy face rather than wash the dishes.

Once he realised this wasn't going to happen, a darker look came to his fleshy features, a look that made her shiver and back onto the hard ridge of the sink. It wasn't the first time he'd looked at her like that, an odd mixture of hate and lust. His eyes were narrowed and there was a bulge in his flies.

Maisie gripped the rim of the sink, her body tense and her heart drumming against her ribs as he stared at her, drinking her in from head to toe. She knew him well, how he thought, how self-centred he was, having things his way no matter what. That was what she was seeing now.

She was still in her overall. It felt confining, tight round her ribs or perhaps it was that her ribs were expanding with fear. The overall had fitted her well when she'd first started work, hanging on her thin carcass. Thanks to the canteen food, her body had filled out. She no longer had the figure of a scrawny adolescent girl but the burgeoning form of a young woman and this was what her father was seeing.

It scared her to see the hunger in his eyes and the way he ran his tongue along his bottom lip, as though he relished the prospect of tasting her.

Maisie understood what was going on. It sickened her, frightened her, but she still owned that same defiance that had brought her through.

'Don't,' she said, shaking her head as his wet lips came closer.

Stinking of stale tobacco and booze, his breath fell on her face. The hardness in his loins was pressing against her. She tried to slide sideways out from beneath him, but although she'd filled out, he was heavier and older than her. As the gap between them narrowed, she quickly assessed her chances, backed up as she was against the sink and draining board. He'd called it women's work, yet there, amongst the pots and pans, the plates and cups, were weapons. She reached back into the sink, her fingers closing around the handle of a carving knife.

His flaccid lips snarled into her face. 'You little tart. You're no better than yer mother. Open yer legs fer anyone, well, I'm gonna 'ave my share. Now! Right now!' His hand groped for the hem of her overall and his slobbering breath was damp against her ear.

She pummelled his chest with her empty fist, the other behind her back pulling the knife from the water. 'Do it to yer own daughter? You sick sod...'

'You ain't no daughter of mine,' he growled, his lips wet on her ear.

Fired with lust, he slammed against her, pinning her against the draining board, his fleshy lips seeking hers, his hands mauling at her hips and her breasts, grappling to raise her skirt.

The steel knife flashed as she brought it round. He froze as its tip nicked the flabby, fat flesh of his throat.

'Let me go or I swear I'll slit your fat throat!' she hissed and was amazed that she believed she really would do it.

A globule of blood ran from the tip of the knife and began to trickle down his neck. For a moment, she was fascinated by it, wanting the flow to quicken, to see the life diminish in a man she hated. It would be so easy to plunge the knife into his neck. Just a little bit more force...

The sudden awareness that they were not alone stopped her. It was hard to read the look on her mother's face; the kind of look when somebody is awakened too quickly from deep slumber.

Frank Miles's reaction was swift and sudden. First he grabbed the sopping-wet tea towel and applied it to his wounded neck. Eyes glassy and his slack mouth spitting anger, he turned away and pushed past her mother. 'I just wanted me dinner,' he grumbled and went crashing out into the hallway, his footsteps beating time all the way up the stairs.

Maisie took in the look on her mother's face. She had to have heard what was said yet showed no reaction.

The words her father had spoken were seared in Maisie's mind. *You're not my daughter.*

Her mother withdrew a packet of cigarettes from her pocket, sank onto a kitchen chair and lit one up. Her hands were trembling, her fingers fidgeting with the packet of cigarettes and box of matches. It was difficult to see where she was looking or what she was thinking, but not once did she lift her eyes and dare to meet her daughter's questioning gaze. Even Maisie placing a cup of tea in front of her didn't encourage her to look up.

There was silence between them, and although Maisie had

planned to go out, she felt it her duty to stay, though goodness knows why. After all, they'd never been close. She'd been brought up – fed and clothed after a fashion. But never in all her life had she received the motherly love she'd seen others receive. As for her father... he seemed intent on showing her a different kind of love, which made her believe he'd spoken the truth. It begged the question that if he was not her father, who was?

Reeling from the revelation, she busied herself as she waited for her mother to make comment. She washed the dishes, lifted the lid on the pot of stew already set on the unlit gas. She could see from the fatty skim on its surface that it only needed reheating and hadn't – as yet – been burnt.

The dingy kitchen smelt of stew and cigarette smoke. The windows were tightly shut so neither aroma had anywhere to go but gathered like smog in the cramped room.

Her mother coughed and smoked, coughed and smoked. No matter how hard she tried to clear her throat, to control the coughing, the harrowing, gargling sound continued.

'I'll get you a handkerchief,' offered Maisie.

She looked through the heap of laundry piled on the kitchen table but couldn't find one – not a clean one anyway, so she handed her mother a tea towel, clean but ragged and fit only for the bin.

Her mother coughed into it, her shoulders, bonier than Maisie could ever remember them, hunching forwards and seemingly likely to meet at the front of her chest.

Once she'd finished, she handed the cloth to Maisie. Weaker stomachs might have retched at the sight of the dark red stain and mucus. Her mother looked diminished in size, though she'd always seemed quite tall, taller than her that's for sure. Her dark hair, greying now, looked dry and lifeless. Her face was gaunt, cheeks sunken and dark circles hung in the puffiness beneath her eyes.

For one brief moment, Maisie raised her hand, meaning to pat her mother's shoulder and say all would be well and not to worry, but the unloving past was still there, a barrier to whatever might have been.

The door suddenly burst open and shattered the moment. The man who had dominated her mother and reduced her to this sad caricature of the woman she might have been was standing in the doorway. He was wearing his khaki gabardine trench coat and brown trilby.

'I ain't 'anging round 'ere. I'm off down the pub.'

Maisie could hardly believe her ears. 'Going out? I thought you wanted yer dinner!'

He totally ignored her and spoke directly to her mother. 'I need some money.'

Her mother looked dazed and didn't answer.

'You've got money from stealing the fags,' said Maisie. 'Where's that gone?'

His eyes blazed with anger and for one moment she thought he was going to hit her. 'That ain't spending money. That's money to be kept quiet for a rainy day.'

She wanted to say that if this wasn't a rainy day, she didn't know what was, but to do so would be a waste of breath.

His attention was centred on her mother anyway.

Lowering his head, he trumpeted straight into her mother's ear. 'Don't pretend to be deaf, you stupid cow! I need some money. I know you got some.'

She shook her head and in a small voice said, 'I ain't got it no more.'

'I know you had some in the tea caddy. Where is it?'

Her mother winced as Frank Miles, the man Maisie was glad to know was not her father, gripped her mother's thin shoulder.

Maisie stepped as close as she dared, wishing she still had the knife in her hand. 'She's just told you. She ain't got none, cloth ears.'

He began pulling out the dresser drawers, sending things crashing from the shelves with one sweep of his arm. When he came up empty-handed, he caught hold of his wife and shook her.

Quick on her feet, Maisie got to the sink and picked up the knife, sliding against his shirt collar. 'Leave 'er alone!'

Her mother broke down, her head hanging forward, face hidden in both hands. Between great, hollow sounding sobs, she confessed where she'd been. 'I paid the doctor. I ain't been well.'

'What d'ya mean, you ain't been well.' Frank Miles looked angry rather than concerned.

'This cough...'

'Oh, for Chrissakes, we all got coughs, ain't we? A good puff on a Woodbine is all it needs.'

'No,' she said, shaking her head, face still hidden and tears beginning to stream down her face.

'I don't care about yer bleedin' cough. I want some money.'

'Here. Take what I've got.' Maisie reached for her purse, dived in determinedly and flung her father half a crown and a two-bob piece followed by a shilling, the sole piece of remaining silver shining amongst the pennies. 'Bugger off down the pub.'

He snatched it up. 'Ten bob would be better, you tight cow.'

She stood her ground, still gripping the knife. 'I just told you, that's yer lot. Take it or leave it.'

Almost as an act of defiance against her and the knife, he slapped the side of her mother's head before leaving.

After the front door banged behind him, her mother subsided into a new bout of coughing, the sobs turning to hiccups.

Maisie gave her a cup of water. 'Drink it slowly.'

Not all the water went down. Some trickled out from the corners of her mouth.

When her eyes closed, Maisie thought how tired she looked, yet at the same time her face seemed less lined, perhaps more like the young woman she'd once been. Something was very wrong. They were not close, but she was a constant in her life and seeing her mother like this scared her.

Maisie took the bloodied rag and it over the gas ring until it was burned through. Once blackened, she took it outside to the ashbin.

The night air proclaimed that colder weather was on its way. Summer was gone and autumn dying. Surrounding houses where windows had burned with light were now only unrelieved blocks of blackness. Overhead, a thousand stars twinkled in defiance of the blackout.

Maisie stood there for a moment to catch her breath, to think of what she'd done. The feel of the knife handle had felt good. She'd felt powerful, in charge of her life. One thing above all was that she'd been glad to hear Frank Miles declare he was not her father. In time she might find out who was, but for now she was satisfied that she was not his.

She went back into the house, heated up the stew and, after ladling a portion into a bowl, put it in front of her mother along with a mug of cold water. She ladled some into a dish for herself, took a seat and urged her mother to tell her what the doctor had said.

'The doctor said I ain't got long,' she said at last after a bout of coughing. 'My chest is bad.'

How long was long, Maisie wondered. Despite everything she

needed her mother still to be here at least as a buffer between her and her father. She reached and began to spoon food into her mother's mouth and was disappointed when it ran from the corners and down her chin.

'You need to rest. Go to bed and stay there. Never mind what the old man wants, let 'im get it 'imself.' Her voice trembled, yet she felt suddenly strong, suddenly in control of one of the people who had controlled her for most of her life.

The shocking comment Frank Miles had made was still with her. She sorely wanted to know if what he'd said was true. If it was, she wanted to know the identity of her father, but her mother was having trouble breathing let alone speaking. Everything about her was breaking down. Eyes that had once been as dark as her own had faded, as though all the life and all the energy had been washed out.

Suddenly she placed her hand over that of her daughter and eyed her intently. 'When I'm gone, get yer 'ands on that caddy on top of the dresser. Not the 'ousekeepin' one, the other one on the top shelf. Don't do it before then and don't do it whilst that old sod's around. It's for you. All that I've got to leave you.'

Maisie swallowed. She couldn't remember ever having a close conversation with her mother and despite everything she couldn't help the lump that came to her throat.

'How long have you got?' she asked.

Her mother shook her head sadly. 'I won't be yer for Christmas.'

Maisie was shaken. The house in York Street was like a ball and chain. She'd sought to escape, but now her mother was dying. Arguably she owed her nothing but an obligation she never thought she would feel anchored her to this place. No matter how she'd been treated, she knew very well that if she left, her mother would receive no help from her father. She'd get no meals and the fire grate would remain unlit. It wasn't just that her mother would die more quickly, it was the fact that there would be nobody to take care of her. No matter her shortcomings as a mother, Maisie couldn't bear to let that happen. Simply put, she would blame herself for her mother's early demise. She had to stay. She had to see this through.

23

PHYLLIS

A wave of panic gave wings to Phyllis's feet as she rushed to change buses from the one that went up Park Street to Redland. The bus had been slow thanks to diminished headlights – another precaution to deter enemy bombers. Thanks to the blackout, there were no street lights, no warm glow falling out from shop windows. It was a case of finding your way home by instinct. 'Reckon I could 'ave walked faster,' Phyllis muttered to herself.

Not that she was going home any time soon. She half entertained the idea that Alan really intended giving her extra typing tuition. The other half of her bristled with expectation. She really wanted more than that.

Her heart had pounded in her chest when he'd invited her to visit him at home for extra lessons. She took the tram to the city centre and a bus to Whiteladies Road. On alighting from the bus she checked the address he'd given her. Large Victorian houses loomed behind tight front gardens. The avenue was lined with trees their bare branches starkly naked against a twilight sky.

Her shoes clattered quickly as her eyes searched for the

number of the house. Eventually, she found a number seven painted in white on one of the pillars standing to either side of the garden gate. The imposing house with its vast bay windows had long been turned into two separate flats.

Taking a deep breath, Phyllis caught hold of the cast-iron knocker sending its sound echoing in the hallway on the other side of the door.

Alan was some time coming and for a moment she questioned whether she was at the right place. Damn the blackout.

But then he answered and stood there in the doorway, his figure a feeling rather than a visual presence. She sensed rather than saw his smile and his pleasure that she was here.

'I wasn't entirely sure you'd come, but did prepare accordingly,' he said as he closed the door behind her and turned on the light. 'Welcome.' His voice was soft and sensual.

Phyllis's heart was hammering and her mouth turned dry at the sight of him before he took her arm and guided her through the door to his flat.

She saw a room with high elegant ceilings and shelves piled with books on either side of the fireplace. Music was playing from a wind-up gramophone – the same one he used at class? She couldn't be sure. The smell of something cooking came from the kitchen. Light sparkled and danced from a crystal chandelier. A table lamp cast a low orange glow from a side table on which sat a glass of dark red wine.

'Let me take your coat,' he offered.

Phyllis eased off her coat to reveal the pale blue woollen dress she was wearing. It was a great favourite and one she'd never worn to the evening class.

'Do take a seat.'

The sofa was covered in dark green velvet. The cushions were plump and their covers seemed to be made of silk.

He offered her a glass of wine. 'It's French. Likely it could be in short supply before very long.'

'Because of the war,' she said with a sigh. 'I still hope it doesn't happen.'

'Let's drink to that, shall we?'

They both raised their glasses in that hope.

The wine slid easily down her throat.

She admitted to him that she'd never tasted wine before.

'Have some more,' he said on seeing her glass was empty.

She looked round for the typewriter. Choosing to believe that he really was going to give her extra tuition, she'd brought some paper with her, plus a rubber.

'It's broken,' he said. 'I had to leave it back in Redcross Street. I've cooked us dinner instead. Would you like to come through?'

Her legs feeling like melted butter, Phyllis followed him into a rather splendid dining room of wood-panelled walls. Candles burned from a five-armed candelabra in the centre of the table. The plates were already in situ. He'd admitted to being unsure that she'd come, yet here was a romantic table setting for two.

'I've taken the liberty of plating up. Chicken supreme, green vegetables and small potatoes.'

The food melted in her mouth. More wine was consumed. They laughed and they talked until he suggested they take their wine back into the living room.

Halfway there, they bumped thighs and suddenly she found herself pressed against the wall.

'I've been waiting for this all day,' he said, then kissed her.

His lips tasted of wine, such a pleasant taste. It felt as though she was drowning but was disinclined to come up for air. The whole length of his body was hard and pressed against her.

'I have wanted to take you to bed, ever since we met.'

Her breath caught in her throat before his tongue probed between her open lips.

The dreams she'd dreamed had become reality. Helped by the wine, she gladly walked into the scenario she had so often fantasised about. 'My prince,' she said in a laughingly foolish voice.

He laughed too. He led her into the bedroom. Phyllis was only vaguely aware that it smelt of him, a masculine, almost salty smell, coupled with that of shaving soap and strong tobacco. He didn't turn the light on, but left the door slightly ajar so the glow from the living room lit the bedroom. The light was muted, just enough to see by and not enough to embarrass her. She'd never let a man strip off her clothes before. Alan did it slowly, his lips sliding over each area as it became exposed.

If he noticed she was a virgin, he made no comment. The girls she worked with had said that the first time was the worst, that it was painful and there was blood. But for Phyllis, there was no pain, only intense pleasure.

Smoking afterwards, she looked up at the ceiling and at the way the triangle of light from the hallway fell all the way across to the top of the window.

She watched the smoke rings from her mouth rising up to the ceiling.

'Anyway,' he said, swiftly stubbing his cigarette in the bedside ashtray as he leapt out of bed, 'You're getting a new teacher. I've jumped the job. No more typing lessons from me – certainly not in Bristol. I'm off to London in a week or so for a job interview. If all goes well, I'll be moving sometime in November. Possibly no more than two weeks' time.'

'London?' She watched as he began to dress, following each movement, the way he pulled on each item in the same sensual way he'd taken them off.

A moment ago she'd soared like an eagle. Now she felt as

though she'd plunged down a deep, dark well. She'd expected to see him regularly. It now looked as though this would be a one off. She felt shame, but more than this disappointment.

He ran his hands through his hair. 'I have a possible job offer closer to home. My home is in London. Bristol is not my home. And neither is this place.' When he waved his hands to indicate his flat, his hair flopped over his forehead.

'This flat isn't your home?' Phyllis swung her legs out of bed and reached for her clothes. Her gaze kept returning to him, his hair, his eyes and the cat like way he moved across the bedroom.

'No. It is not.'

When he kissed her on the forehead, she felt like a child who needed to understand what was going on. Judging by the sudden creases in his face and the depth of his frown, he was making up his mind to tell her something. 'My family are in London.'

Phyllis felt her expression stiffen as she digested this, which in itself aroused questions, one question above all others. Did he have a wife? The truth was she couldn't bear to ask. A sense of panic took hold of her. 'Can I see you before then?'

'There won't be enough time before I go for the interview.'

'How about November? Please. Just one more time before you go away for good?' She could hear the pleading in her voice, but the wine had blurred her vision, she wasn't sure of the response in his face.

'I still won't be able to pick you up.'

'I'll come on the bus like I did tonight.'

His smile was a little sad. 'Yes. I suppose you will.'

'You're not leading me up the garden path, are you?' she asked.

He laughed as though it was the most ridiculous thing she could have said. 'As if I would do something like that to someone like you.'

She thrilled at the touch of his fingers beneath her chin and felt she could drown in his eyes. No matter what he said at this moment in time, she would accept it. Whatever he wanted to do, whatever he told her was right, because she simply didn't want it to be any other way.

Later, as he escorted her to the front door, she asked him whether she could visit him in London and whether he would come back to Bristol to see her.

His answer could be taken in a number of ways. 'We have many options, all of them feasible.'

Feasible. What would Bridget say to that? Bridget who knew lots of words she'd never heard of.

'Does that mean you'll come or doesn't it?'

'As long as the trains are still running. Now come on, you'd better get going or you'll miss your bus.' He did his best to sound reassuring, then added, 'I have so many things to organise if I'm to get to London and make arrangements to come back and see you.'

'I'll see you before you go?' she pressed.

'Of course you will.'

On the journey home, all Phyllis could think of was being in bed with Alan. She could still see him, feel him and smell him. Her eyes closed in an effort to hold that moment and relive the thrill all over again.

By the time the bus reached Wedmore Vale from where she could walk home, she had made her mind up to visit him before he left. It would be a surprise and an opportunity to tell him exactly how she felt. He was the man she wanted to go to bed with for the rest of her life. Not Robert. Now she'd met Alan, she knew it could never be Robert.

24

BRIDGET, PHYLLIS AND MAISIE

Phyllis made no comment when Bridget came back into the stripping room following her training, up on the roof, learning how to deal with incendiary bombs. Her thoughts were still with Alan Stalybridge.

'You can see everything from up on that roof,' Bridget declared as she sat down, her face flushed with enthusiasm. 'I saw the wages trolley being rolled across from the bank by two women from the wages department. Right down there in the street in front of me. Pushing all that money across the road.'

'Two women pushing the wages trolley,' said one of the older women, a shocked expression on her face. 'That's a man's job. He'll want it when he gets back from the war. It's not a woman's job doing that.'

Bridget looked deflated for a fleeting second before she bounced back with a sharp observation. 'If a woman can push a baby in a pram, I'm sure she can push a trolley across from the bank.'

She immediately found herself basking in murmurs of approval.

Maisie winced, hoping against hope that her father didn't find out that it was two girls who pushed the wages from the bank to the factory.

Bridget was chatting amiably enough with the rest of the girls, when she became aware of a sudden silence from her immediate neighbours. She looked up to see Bert standing at the end of the table. His hands were clasped in front of him and his expression was a mixture of pride and nervousness.

'I came to tell you I'm off, I got called up. Nothing me dad could do to stop it, so I've joined the RAF.'

A great cheer went up, followed by a clapping of hands.

Bridget got to her feet and threw her arms round him. 'Good for you, Bert. You did it.'

Thrilled to finally have Bridget's arms round him, Bert's face turned bright pink.

'I'm going to train as an aircraft mechanic,' he stated and looked proud – it was almost as though he'd grown another three inches.

'I thought you wanted to be a pilot?'

'They said I lacked experience, but never mind,' he said brightly. 'Who knows where it might lead. I could get a job anywhere as a mechanic – even on aircraft.'

Bridget smiled at him. She didn't like to say that if he was always working on aircraft then he might be in the RAF forever. She found herself wondering what that life might be like, living on an RAF base anywhere in the world. She then reminded herself that one of the biggest aircraft factories in the country lay to the north of Bristol. There were always bound to be jobs there.

'Are you off now?' she asked.

'Yes. I've got me orders.'

Bert had always looked young for his age, today even more so. She found it hard to imagine him wearing the smart blue RAF uniform and blinked the tears from her eyes. 'You be careful, Bert. Do you hear?'

His hands looked to be strangling his cap and his cheeks remained flushed. She sensed there was something else he wanted to say.

'Do you mind if I...'

Before he could go any further, she kissed him on both cheeks, then on the lips.

Phyllis did the same and was closely followed by Maisie and a number of other girls. If Bert had been pink before, he was puce now, more so when Aggie wrapped him in a bear hug, almost squeezing the breath out of him!

Their goodbyes and applause followed him the length of the stripping room.

'Poor lad,' said Bridget, blinking the tears from her eyes. 'He just doesn't seem old enough.'

Once he was gone, the three friends settled back behind the piles of pungent tobacco leaves. Their conversation was less virulent than usual, restrained by their thoughts. Every day somebody from the factory bid farewell and swapped their overall for a uniform.

'It's all 'appening so fast,' said Maisie. 'My brother's gone. Wish they'd take me dad too. Shame the old sod's too old!'

In a low voice, Bridget asked how her mother was doing. Maisie had told her how terribly ill she was.

'She's coughing 'er lungs up, and me dad ain't no 'elp. If I weren't there, they'd both starve to death and drown in filth. He moaned like mad about 'er paying the doctor to take a look at 'er chest – as though it weren't so important as 'im going down the pub.'

Bridget winced. She didn't want to ask what Maisie intended doing once her mother was gone but knew her plan had been to leave home. Her mother's illness had stopped her doing that. Somebody had to look after the poor woman. 'How about your brother, does he know his mother is ill?'

Maisie nodded. 'I've got a telephone number. Quicker than writing, ain't it.'

Bridget agreed. 'We live in a time of wonder.'

Everything was changing. The comfortable old life was being severely disrupted.

'I wonder how long it will be,' she mused, 'before people stop writing letters?'

'People will always write letters. Won't they?' asked Phyllis.

Her comment made Bridget wince. 'I suppose so.' It still hurt that Lyndon had not written to her as promised. She'd only half expected him to visit, seeing as many people from neutral countries had fled Britain the moment war was declared. All the same, he could have made the effort to write. He'd sounded so sincere about it.

Her thoughts turned to Phyllis who had also changed, though it was hard to put her finger on exactly how and what might have caused it.

'So how about Robert, Phyllis? Has he got his call-up papers?'

'Probably.'

'Will you get married before he goes?'

Phyllis shrugged. 'We'll have to see, won't we?' She sounded totally dismissive.

Bridget was alarmed. Phyllis had been exceptionally secretive of late and she had the impression something was going on, but no matter how hard she pressed, Phyllis brushed her questions aside.

Later, in the white-tiled ladies' toilets that smelled of carbolic and disinfectant, Bridget confided her concerns to Maisie.

'She's changed, don't you think? I wonder what's going on?'

'Another man. That's what's going on.'

Bridget flicked the water from her hands and looked in the mirror. 'What makes you think that?'

Maisie leaned her backside against one of the sinks and crossed her arms. She was one of the youngest girls in the factory, yet came across as wise beyond her years thanks to a hard home life. 'The way she speaks for a start. Ain't you noticed? She's going all posh.'

'Ah yes, but it's because she wants to get a job in the office. You've got to speak a bit proper for that.'

'Proper is as proper does!'

Bridget looked puzzled. 'I don't know what you mean.'

'She didn't start forcing 'erself to speak proper until after she'd started the typing course. Don't you remember what she said? About her teacher?'

'Ah,' said Bridget as the truth hit her. 'A male teacher, a Mr...'

'Alan. Alan Stalybridge.'

Bridget blinked. 'Maisie Miles, you have an incredible memory. I never would have remembered it.'

Maisie shrugged. 'She'll come out with it when she's ready. Mind you, I wouldn't blame her about Robert. I only met 'im the once, but to my mind it wouldn't be a marriage wed to him, it would be a bloody life sentence!'

Bridget could tell by Maisie's expression that she was preparing to pursue the truth. Maisie resembled a bulldog, willing to fight and bite if she had to.

* * *

Even when Phyllis and Bridget were finding their way home by torchlight across the waste ground and past the gasometer, Phyllis didn't say very much.

'How's the typing courses going?' Bridget asked in an effort to get some conversation out of her.

'Very well,' returned Phyllis trying to sound as upbeat as possible. 'Alan Stalybridge, my former teacher has given in his notice. He's got a lot to do: give up where he lives now and find a new place in London.'

Mrs Porter, her new typewriting teacher was very good, but Phyllis's thoughts were in London. Alan had not been in touch. By her reckoning he should be back from the job interview and preparing to move sometime in November. There was plenty of time to see him before then, and at the first opportunity, she would take the bus and visit him.

'Sounds as though you thought a lot of the teacher who's just left,' said Bridget. 'Were you sweet on him?'

Even by torchlight Bridget detected Phyllis's pale complexion, a vivid contrast with her reddish blonde hair, turn paler. 'He was just my typing teacher.'

'Is he joining up?'

'No. He's going for a new job in London.'

'You look as though you're gonna miss him. Was it just typing or were you going out with him as well?'

Phyllis's pallor increased.

'I never went out on a date with him!'

On noting Phyllis's panicky expression, Bridget decided to change the subject.

'I know it's a bit early, but do you have any thoughts about the Christmas dance. We're all going, I take it.'

A look of relief swept over Phyllis's face. 'Yes. That would be nice.'

She still sounded distracted.

Her thoughts are in London, thought Bridget and wondered what Phyllis wasn't telling her.

25

PHYLLIS

It was over two weeks since Alan had gone to London and some time before he was due to leave for good when Phyllis had made up her mind to surprise him. She caught a tram to the Tramway Centre and a bus up the steep hill that was Park Street, past the Wills Memorial Tower and the City Museum and Art Gallery. She got off close to his address in Redland.

With one hand over her racing heart, the other holding the torch, she picked her way over the damp pavements.

A chill wind blew and the hand that had been covering her heart moved to the brim of her hat. It was new and the loveliest shade of lilac, bought specifically to match the black swagger coat she was wearing over a lilac dress. She'd taken a lot of time getting ready for this event, determined to look her very best, so Alan would carry the vision of her loveliness with him to London. Her reasoning was that the lovelier she looked, the quicker he would return to Bristol.

The torch flashed over the pavement and onto the walls enclosing the front gardens of the stone-built houses. The beam of light picked up the number seven etched into the gatepost.

The gate opened silently, and she made her way to the front door.

Although she couldn't see the names on the three doorbells, she knew his was the bottom one because he lived in the ground-floor flat. She pressed it firmly and heard it echo in the long hallway of black and dark red tiles.

Nobody came.

She pressed again.

There was no sign of movement inside.

Phyllis tried peering into the ground-floor window, an impossible task. The blackout curtains were impenetrable.

She was just about to press the next bell up when she heard footsteps pattering over the solid tiles on the other side of the door.

Licking the dryness from her lips, she fingered her collar, lips slightly parted as her excitement grew.

Suddenly the door opened onto the unlit hallway.

'Yes? Can I help you?'

The voice was that of a woman and although all was darkness, Phyllis could just about make out her outline.

At first she felt furious, assuming that her place had been usurped by somebody else. It then occurred to her that this was an older woman and quite small.

'I've come to see Alan. Alan Stalybridge. He's not expecting me, but...'

'I'm sorry, my dear. Mr Stalybridge has left for London and I've moved back in just for tonight whilst I tidy things up. Do you want to rent this place by any chance? The rent's quite cheap for a flat of this quality in this area.'

Phyllis imagined the elderly eyes peering through the gloom in an effort to ascertain whether she was likely to be a respectable tenant. Obviously she'd decided she was.

'When did he leave?' Her voice trembled and her knees were shaking.

'Now let me see... two weeks, I think. A Saturday, I think it was.'

Saturday! Her hopes plummeted. The day after the Friday two weeks ago when she'd visited, drank wine and he'd cooked her dinner. That precious moment when her body had soared to heights she'd never known existed.

'Was he expecting you, dear?'

At first, Phyllis couldn't answer. It felt as though her tongue had stuck to the roof of her mouth. When she eventually spoke her voice was hoarse, her throat suddenly painful. 'No. No, he wasn't.' *I was going to surprise him before he left, but he's surprised me.* The words stuck in her throat.

'I'm sorry I can't help you.'

'Did he leave a forwarding address?'

She was vaguely aware of the blacked-out diminutive figure shaking her head. 'No. I'm afraid he didn't. If he does get in contact, shall I tell him you called?'

'Yes. Tell him Phyllis called. He knows my address.'

It was as though her whole body had gone rigid. She'd anticipated his joy at seeing her again. Instead he'd already flown the nest. The love nest, she told herself, though going to bed with him just one time hardly qualified.

She brushed at the tears streaming from her eyes and staggered into the darkness, not bothering to switch on the torch, not caring whether she tripped over a paving slab and fell flat on her face. She'd already fallen flat on her face, emotionally if not physically.

It was on the way to work on a Monday morning that a flushed Phyllis gave Bridget the big news. 'Robert's got his call-up papers. We're getting married on Saturday. Just a small affair. You and Maisie are my attendants – not bridesmaids exactly, but there should I faint or something.'

Or run away, thought Bridget, but held her tongue.

Phyllis repeated the big news to Maisie before announcing it to the rest of the girls. She also confirmed that she would be leaving. Unlike some other factories, W. D. & H. O. Wills's female employees were not sacked on their marrying, but Robert had been adamant.

'As my wife you'll get a portion of my army pay. You don't need to work and I don't want you to work.'

To Phyllis, it felt as though her life – certainly her freedoms – were coming to an end. She had agreed to everything he wanted because she had no choice. Her life would be ruined if she didn't become the respectable woman, he wanted her to be. It had been just over a month since her night in the splendid flat in Redland, such a small amount of time in the greater scheme of things, but long enough to suspect that something drastic was happening inside her body. Alan had disappeared from her life, but Robert was still here. She was two weeks overdue and just knew that she was expecting Alan's child. It was early enough, though, to pass it off as her would-be husband's.

Congratulations kept coming, along with a chorus of 'Here Comes the Bride.'

Blushing and smiling, Phyllis accepted them all and also tried to pretend that she didn't notice Aggie traipsing round the room with a collection tin. It was the habit for a collection to be made amongst the workforce when one of their own was getting married. There would also be a bonus in her wage packet when she left at the end of the week.

The congratulations and ad-lib singsong would have gone on indefinitely, but the air-raid siren on the factory roof intervened, gradually working its way up to a full-throated wail.

Heads jerked up at the sound of the very first note and all conversation came to an abrupt halt.

An ARP warden, who also worked unloading trucks in the area where the tobacco casks arrived, shouted out that everybody should only take essential valuables.

Chair legs scraped over the floor and some fell over in the women's haste to get down to the factory's cavernous cellars and boiler room.

Bridget interlinked her arms with those of Maisie and Phyllis and, loudly humming the wedding march, they made their way to the cellars beneath the factory.

Hugging Phyllis's arm tightly to her side, Bridget had an urge to ask Phyllis if she was sure she was doing the right thing. She decided it wasn't her business. Phyllis had made her decision and that was it.

Aggie shouted, 'Let's stick together, girls. It's dark down there and I don't like spiders.'

Actually, it wasn't that dark and it was too clean for spiders.

The three friends tucked themselves into a warm little corner close to the boiler house door.

'I could murder a cup of tea,' said Maisie.

Bridget rummaged in her overall pocket. 'Can't oblige, I'm afraid, but I do have these.' She pulled out an opened packet of strong mints.

Maisie took one gladly. Phyllis declined and said she'd prefer a smoke.

Bridget thrust the open end of the packet at her. 'It's no good fancying a smoke. Not down here. You'll have to make do with a mint.'

Phyllis took one. 'I will, especially seeing as I've had no breakfast.'

'You trying to lose weight so you can look your best in your wedding dress?'

Her friend's cheeks turned pink. 'I want to look my best, though it won't be a white dress. No time to buy or make one. You two can wear what you like too.'

'Will there be a party?' Maisie asked brightly.

'Robert's parents don't drink. My mother does, even though she attends a Methodist chapel. Still, that doesn't mean to say we can't have a drink and we most certainly will.'

She tried to sound excited about getting married. The truth was, she was scared but didn't feel she had any choice. A baby, and she was sure one was on the way, needed two parents. She had to get married, to do otherwise would mean her life was in ruins. There would be no working in an office, no bettering herself and going to work in smart clothes. Everything she had to do now was centred on this baby.

Bridget patted her hand. 'Best of luck to you both. When does he leave?'

'Four days after the wedding. We're having a couple of days' honeymoon in Clevedon.'

It was Robert who had insisted on Clevedon, a quiet little resort overlooking a pebble beach and the grey waters of the Bristol Channel. She'd accepted his choice. All she wanted was a big bed and the marriage consummated – then all would be well. A short time after that she would break the news that she was in the family way.

Bridget sighed. 'Seems funny to think you'll be Mrs Harvey.'

'You definitely going to live with your in-laws then?' Maisie's question burst the happy little bubble that was Phyllis playing the would-be blushing bride.

Phyllis looked down at her hands, which were tightly inter-locked, as though she was trying to hold onto something that was gradually slipping through her fingers. 'It's the most sensible thing. Robert thought it would be for the best.'

Bridget and Maisie exchanged a swift glance. From what Phyllis had told them, Robert's mother was far from a bundle of laughs.

After they had been counted, a whistle was blown and they all trooped back upstairs again. Thankfully there had been no air raid for real; it was only an exercise.

'The real thing will come soon enough,' mumbled one of the older women.

'Must remember to bring me knitting,' said another.

Aggie declared that she was going to ask management for a wireless.

'We're gonna run out of things to say if we're stuck down there for any length of time. Listening to the wireless will pass the time.'

Everyone agreed that what Aggie asked for she always got. Either she asked in the right way or management couldn't stand her loud-mouthed demands and gave in just to get rid of her.

On their way back upstairs, Phyllis excused herself and dashed into the toilets.

'We'll wait for you,' Bridget called after her.

They leaned against the wall outside the door, arms crossed as though defying anyone to tell them to get on back to work.

Bridget lit up. Her thumb stroked her lower lip as she frowned through the smoke.

'Well, I'm glad I'm not her, going to live with Hilda Harvey. A right snapdragon from what I hear.'

Maisie jerked her head towards the toilet door through which Phyllis had disappeared. 'That's the third time she's thrown up this morning.'

Bridget looked astounded. 'Thrown up. How do you know that?'

'I was in there earlier when she was on the other side of the cubicle to me. She didn't know I was there. Don't tell 'er that I was.'

Bridget met Maisie's open expression. 'What are you thinking?'

Maisie shrugged. 'It's not for me to think. Mr Gorman the foreman said that to me the other day, that I weren't employed to think.'

'He's related to the Wills family.'

'Says who?'

'It's well known that they like the family to learn from the bottom up.'

Maisie banged on the door. 'Come on, Phyllis. What the bloody 'ell are you doin' in there?'

Phyllis came out, looking flushed.

'You all right, Phyl?' asked Bridget.

'I'm all right. Just a bit of a tummy bug.'

'Could be worse,' said Maisie. 'You could be in the family way.'

* * *

'That's it! Off 'ome the lot of you.'

As usual, Aggie Hill's foghorn voice stirred more bottoms from chairs than the factory hooter.

'How about putting Aggie up on the roof to replace the air-raid siren? She might frighten the Germans off as well – if they ever come!' suggested Bridget.

There was laughter and excited chatter as they collected their hats, coats, mufflers and gloves. The days were turning colder, the nights even more so.

A whole gaggle of women workers spilled out onto the pavement, all talking nineteen to the dozen and heading to catch a tram or a bus to wherever home happened to be. Some of them were clutching carrier bags containing a bit of shopping.

Maisie was one of those who hadn't done any shopping, though she did have to think about a wedding present for Phyllis. It had come as something of a surprise that they really had been invited to the wedding.

Bridget had mentioned getting a practical present like towels or bed linen. Maisie fancied buying something totally unexpected, though wasn't quite sure what that might be.

Pulling on her gloves as she hurried along, her wage packet tucked inside her handbag, she was happy that the end of the week had come round again.

Suddenly she was pulled from behind. A beefy hand caught

her shoulder in a cruel grasp, her hat fell off and it felt as though her hair was being wrenched from her head.

Her attacker shook her as though she was nothing but a bag of rags. 'Come on! Hand over yer wages!'

There was a great intake of breath. The torches everyone carried to see them through the blackout focused on what was going on. The women that had been crowded together now formed a circle.

One voice boomed over all the others. 'Well we ain't 'aving that is we, girls!'

Suddenly, the rough hands that had been holding Maisie tight were gone. By torchlight, she spotted her work colleagues hammering her father to the ground. When he tried to rise and throw them off, he was met with the full force of Aggie Hill's right hand. His head jerked backwards, and although he tried to get up, more blows landed and the rounded toes of sensible shoes thudded into his guts.

'Give 'im what for, girls. We ain't 'avin' none of that thievin' round 'ere.'

At first, Maisie could hardly believe what she was seeing. Once she could make it out, a smile of satisfaction crept across her face. This was the moment she'd been waiting for. The tough man she feared was pulled to his feet by the very workers who made the cigarettes he'd stolen. It was a kind of revenge, payback for what he'd done to their beloved factory.

She could see that his head was bare, his hat flown off to goodness knows where. A large pair of fists hoisted him upright until his face was level with that of Aggie, the beam of her torch picking out his bloodied nostrils, cut lip and half-closed eye.

'Now just you get it through your 'ead, mister. Maisie worked for that money. If you want money, then get off yer arse and earn it yerself.' Fists twice the size of his gave him a good shake and glared along the line of the torch beam into his battered face. 'You ever touch 'er again, you'll 'ave me to deal with. And them,' she added, jerking her head at all the other women. 'Ain't that right, girls?'

There was a resounding shout of affirmation. Somebody found his hat and slammed it on his head. Aggie turned him roundabout, kicked him up the rear and sent him staggering on his way.

'Right,' she said, slapping her hands together as anyone would after a job well done. 'Cross the tobacco girls at your peril. And anyone who fancies their chances will 'ave me to deal with!'

'One for all and all for one,' shouted Bridget, quite carried away with excitement, though she was one to shun violence if at all possible. It surprised her that a load of women sorting out a single violent man was amazingly uplifting. There was only one thing that worried Bridget.

'Will you be all right going home, Maisie? Will he take it out on you when you get there?'

'Bridget, would you dare defy Aggie Hills?' There was defiance and joy in Maisie's tone of voice.

Bridget laughed. 'Not on your nelly!'

27

THE WEDDING

The registry office was in a place called Quakers Friars in the centre of Bristol, the building all that remained of a fourteenth-century priory. Its windows were Gothic and the worn faces of gargoyles looked unseeing on a city that had changed irrevocably since it was built.

The gathering for the ceremony was small: Phyllis's mother, Robert's parents, plus a clutch of cousins and uncles and aunts from both sides. Robert had asked a friend from work to be best man, whilst Maisie and Bridget were Phyllis's attendants. They wore their own dresses, each with blue hats, and carried small sprays of blue silk flowers.

Phyllis's wedding outfit was a speckled blue and gold suit with a cinched-in waist. Her hat was golden mustard with a fake blue rose at one side. The last of the blooms were picked from her mother's garden to make the bouquet, gathered round in a series of lace doilies and tied with blue ribbon.

To Phyllis, the whole ceremony went by in a blur. Her mother being a widow, there was no father of the bride to give her away or give a speech. Her uncle, a man she hardly knew, who owned a butchers' shop in Bath, agreed to stand in.

The best man said something about Robert being a real steady Eddie, so good husband material, though he wasn't sure how come such a beautiful girl as Phyllis would agree to marry him.

The wedding reception was held in a room above the Engineer's Arms, both bride and bridegroom's family contributing to the spread. An aunt had baked the cake, a single-tier fruit cake covered in white icing and decorated with blue sugared roses.

Mrs Harvey, Robert's mother, told everyone that they owned their own house.

Maisie whispered to Bridget that she should declare it in the newspaper so everyone would know.

Robert's mother eyed the cake with shrew-like eyes and a pinched mouth. 'I still think it would have looked better with the bridal couple we used on our wedding cake. It did for us.'

'But it was yours, and anyway, iced blue roses match my outfit,' Phyllis countered.

The moment the words were out, she knew she'd spoken out of turn.

Mrs Harvey's expression turned even more disapproving. 'Well, if ours wasn't good enough, sorry, I'm sure.'

'I didn't mean to—'

Another sniff up her haughty nose, and Mrs Harvey turned her back on her son's new wife but found her way blocked by Bridget. 'Hello, Mrs Harvey. I'm Phyllis's friend, Bridget Milligan.'

All she got for her trouble was a cold blank look. 'Milligan? That's an Irish name, isn't it?'

'My parents came from there originally.'

'And now you're here.' Mrs Harvey made it sound as though she'd committed a crime.

Bridget found herself staring at Mrs Harvey's back and quite lost for words.

Maisie raised her eyebrows at Bridget. 'Glad it's not me that's got to live with her,' she whispered.

Bridget shuddered. 'You're right there.'

* * *

Phyllis leaned on the basin in the ladies' toilet and looked at herself in the mirror. The blushing bride staring back at her looked vulnerable and drained of energy. A little make-up would have given her some colour, but Robert wouldn't approve.

She'd come out here not to renew make-up but to escape her mother-in-law's all pervasive criticisms and continual bragging about having her own house in Bedminster Road. Following their return from honeymoon, that's where the newlyweds would be living – or at least she would be. Robert would be away serving in the army and had made his mind up that he wouldn't remain a private.

'I'll make my mark, Phyllis, just you wait and see.'

He'd been happy at the prospect of bettering himself and although she'd shown happiness for him, inside she was considering her own prospects. Her waiting and seeing would take place in Bedminster Road alongside Robert's parents. The prospect of living there was getting grimmer.

There'd been no word from Alan. For days after his leaving, she'd checked the post each morning, an action that had aroused her mother's suspicion.

'Who are you expecting a letter from?'

Phyllis had voiced the excuse that she might get called up before she had chance to get married. It was the only acceptable excuse she could think of.

The door to the ladies' toilet swung open and there were Maisie and Bridget.

'We came to see if you were all right.'

Phyllis looked from one to the other, then burst into tears.

'There, there. No need to take on like that.' Bridget patted her arm, then put it round her. 'Now pull yourself together. This is supposed to be the happiest day of your life.'

Maisie, a few inches shorter than Phyllis, looked up into her face. She'd already noted the lack of lipstick. 'Borrow my lipstick. Put a bit of colour on your face.'

Phyllis brushed the tears from her eyes and shrugged. 'It doesn't matter.'

Maisie drew her chin back into her face, a look of disbelief. She tutted like somebody older might do. 'You without yer lipstick?'

Phyllis shook her head, and got rid of the residual wetness that stained her cheeks on the back of her hand. 'I'm just a bit overcome. It's been such a busy day...'

'Are you up the spout?'

Bridget gasped. As usual, Maisie hadn't held back.

'Ah,' said Maisie when Phyllis didn't answer, her face frozen with shock. 'Who's the father?'

'Maisie!'

Phyllis turned her back on the pair of them, snapped open the clasp of her handbag, got out powder and puff, mascara and lipstick. Although Robert had forbade her to wear it, she'd brought it with her anyway.

Bridget was apologetic. 'She didn't mean it, did you, Maisie?'

Maisie said nothing but wondered at the swiftness of how quickly the make-up was applied.

Phyllis's eyes were ablaze with indignation. 'How could you say such a thing, Maisie Miles! How could you!'

The door to the ladies' toilets slammed behind her and the two girls found themselves staring at the closed door.

Bridget shook her head. 'You shouldn't have said that.'

Maisie was unmoved. 'Did you see the look on her face? Did you? You saw how she behaved. I'm right, Phyllis. You know I am.'

Bridget sighed. 'Let's get back in there and try to make amends.'

* * *

Clevedon was cold. The tide was out, but what little could be seen was grey, as was the mud further into the rocky shore. The brightest glow had been from the candles and shiny ornaments decorating the Christmas tree in the reception area.

Their room at the Salt House, a large hostelry situated on the promontory at one end of the bay was buffeted by the winds of the Bristol Channel. The sash windows were ill fitting and rattled with each gust.

Robert's mother had provided them with sandwiches and cake to take with them. 'So you won't need to eat any of the foreign muck they might provide. You might have enough left over for breakfast. Good job you're only staying for one night.'

Why Hilda Harvey thought they'd be served anything but English food was beyond comprehension; Clevedon was in Somerset, not Italy or France.

Once the sun had set, Robert drew the curtains and by the muted glow of the bedside lights he portioned out the sandwiches and cake.

Phyllis declined, stating that she was not hungry. She'd ate little at the reception, both her taste buds and her sense of smell reacting to whatever she tried.

Her stomach heaved with emptiness and the smell of the Brylcreem on Robert's hair made her feel sick.

She made obvious her aversion to look at the double bed in which tonight she would pretend to be the virgin bride. The eiderdown was green with a dark red trim, two contrasting colours that didn't really match – a bit like her and Robert really.

The wind rattled the glass in the windows and startled her.

Robert took it as a ripe opportunity to take her into his arms. He made soothing sounds as she trembled. 'Sweetheart,' he said, his lips brushing her hair. 'It's time to put on our nightclothes.'

Nightclothes? Her first inclination was to laugh out loud and exclaim that it was quite ridiculous to undress, then put on clothes to wear in bed, especially on their honeymoon.

The comparison sprang swiftly to mind. With slow, languid attention, Alan had stripped off her clothes one item at a time. Between each item of her clothing, he'd taken off one of his own until, finally, both of them were completely naked. She recalled the silky cool of the sheets, the warmth of his body against hers.

Robert retrieved a pair of green striped pyjamas from his suit-case. 'I'll leave you to get undressed in here. I'll go along to the bathroom at the end of the landing.'

She wanted to laugh out loud but merely nodded.

He smiled before going out of the door.

Phyllis was alone. For one frantic moment she wanted to draw back the curtains, open the window and jump out. Would she land on the rocks or in the water to be swept out to sea?

Slipping from between a layer of tissue paper, her nightdress fell out of her hands and onto the bed. It was a pale shade of pink trimmed at the neck and hem with a band of matching lace. How would it be, she wondered, going to bed with Robert, her husband? Despite not being ignorant of the act about to happen, she shivered.

Robert came back, his pyjamas beneath a dark red dressing gown.

'You match the eiderdown,' she said to him in an effort to inject some humour into the situation.

He frowned. 'What are you talking about?'

Her smile was hesitant as she pointed at the bed. 'It's the same colour as your nightclothes.'

He didn't laugh. He didn't even smile but looked at her indulgently, as though she really couldn't help saying and thinking silly things.

With great deliberation, he stretched, yawned, took off his dressing gown to reveal the striped pyjamas he was wearing. The dressing gown was folded neatly before he set it down on a chair.

'Let's get to bed, shall we? It's been a long day.'

There was only a slight catch in his throat – not excitement, more as though there was something here that needed to be accomplished in a certain way – his way.

They each climbed into their designated sides of the bed. The sheets were just as cool as the ones on the bed she'd shared with Alan. The warmth of Robert's body was the same too. Closing her eyes, Phyllis pretended it was Alan and, to her great surprise, she found herself responding, moving her body against his and opening her legs to his probing hand and then his ultimate intrusion.

When small exclamations accompanied her movements and the movements intensified, Robert stopped what he was doing.

'Quietly, Phyllis,' he said a trifle gruffly. 'We don't want the whole hotel to hear us. A woman is supposed to stay quiet and still.'

Up until that moment, she'd very successfully forgotten who he was, that it wasn't Alan whose body had moved in time with hers, his exclamations of ecstasy matching her own. Her fantasy punctured, she stopped moving, stopped uttering her pleasure, and instead remained silent and completely still as Robert had instructed until he had finished and rolled away from her.

It was the longest night she'd ever encountered. Whilst he slept and snored, she lay there until the early hours staring at the ceiling but seeing time like an ever-rolling stream, winding its way through the years in a life chosen by circumstance and the dictates of society.

28

MAISIE'S MUM

It was the first day back at work without Phyllis's bright face at the same table and Maisie had found that she missed her.

Neither she nor Bridget felt like going out anywhere after work. Besides, she had her mother to consider. She had to go home to York Street whether she liked it or not.

A gloomy sky hung over York Street as Maisie carefully pushed open the door. Before closing it behind her, she looked and listened for any sign of her father, but there was none. It had been that way ever since her mother was taken ill. He couldn't bear to be there and not once had he gone in to see her.

Once the door was closed behind her, she drew the blackout curtain before turning on the light. The single bulb hanging from the ceiling did little to brighten the dark green walls and brown floor.

Maisie turned her nose up at the smell of mould that no amount of scrubbing could ever get rid of. Before leaving school, she'd only done what housework she was forced to do, aided by the threat of a good hiding if she didn't do as she was told. As a child, she'd avoided being home, running wild and not getting

back until her stomach was growling with hunger. When she'd
been a child, her mother's cooking had been eaten with gusto
though only because she knew she'd get nothing else. The need
to leave had increased and perhaps she would have gone by now.
Her mother falling sick had intervened with her plans.

Maisie poked her head round the living room door to where
her mother lay on the sofa, no more than a bundle of bones
enveloped in a blanket.

'Maisie... is... that... you?' Her mother spoke between inter-
mittent gasps. As her illness had taken hold, she was no longer
able to get up the stairs, so Maisie had made her a bed on the
sofa. Whether her father noticed that he slept alone was debate-
able. He made no remark on the subject, simply avoiding the
living room and only going into the kitchen or upstairs to bed. He
just moaned about his food not being on the table and when was
he going to get another cup of tea.

Maisie checked the curtains were closed before switching on
the light. She listened to her mother's breathing before her
shadow fell like a black veil over her mother's face. Was she imagining it, or did her mother's eyes look more sunken, the hollows
beneath her cheekbones more pronounced? A brown sticky
liquid trickled from the side of her mouth and even from a few
steps away her breath smelt foul.

'Get... me... a... fag, will... you?' Her voice was strangulated
and rasping, as though a pair of unseen hands were crushing her
windpipe.

Maisie's response was abrupt. 'No.'

'Get me... a fag!'

'They're killing you.'

Her mother raised her head from the pillow and tried to voice
her anger. There were no words just a vile spitting and gasping

before her head fell back on the pillow. Eventually, she managed to gasp out that Maisie was a cruel little bitch.

'Well that's the pot calling the kettle black,' she said under her breath.

Maisie tugged at the blanket that covered the thin frame, tucking the cold spidery hands inside in an effort to make them warm. As she did so, her hands brushed against the swift though weak rise and fall of her mother's ribcage. Like a pair of broken bellows, she thought.

Eyes that had never looked on her with love closed, as though they were too heavy to keep open. The breathing was still erratic, the ribcage still pumping up and down in a futile attempt to take in air.

Maisie's eyes strayed to the packet of Woodbines sitting on the arm of a ragged armchair. She picked up the packet and took one out. At first, she rolled it between her finger and thumb, eyeing it with curiosity, wanting to understand why people had to smoke.

It wasn't just about curiosity when she slipped the end of the cigarette between her lips. She wanted to know if this small stick of white paper and tobacco could suddenly grab her allegiance and rule her life just as it had her mother – her father too.

She struck a match. The flame flared before the lit tobacco reduced to a red glow. She took a deep breath and sucked it in. Before she had chance to blow it out, she was coughing against her closed hand, her eyes watering and her throat feeling as though somebody had rubbed it down with sandpaper. She disliked both the taste and the habit, but not smoking was the exception rather than the rule.

After she'd finished coughing, she looked over her closed fist at her mother and noticed that her eyes were open, staring up at the ceiling. They were brown like her own, though faded. When was the last time she'd looked into them? Why hadn't she ever noticed their colour before?

Without being asked, she passed the lighted cigarette into her mother's nicotine-stained fingers. They were like those of an old woman or the tendrils of dead ivy strangling its host.

Her mother drew deeply, which resulted in a frantic coughing fit. Her eyes bulged and a pink round spot erupted on each cheek. It was the first colour she'd had in a long while.

Gradually, the coughing subsided.

Maisie watched dispassionately. Her mother had never loved her and the feeling was mutual. She questioned whether it was her fault. Had she tried hard enough to love her mother?

Certainly not her father. All the trying in the world wouldn't make him loveable. So why had her mother married him? Had it been love like she'd seen at the pictures, a charmed romance played out in black and white on the silver screen? Had she always been cowed by him, always trying to get on his good side? Or had they had something special when they were young?

She didn't know. She couldn't know.

Another bout of coughing ensued.

Maisie balanced an ashtray on her mother's chest and watched as it rose up and down like a boat on the sea. Some of the ash landed in it, some scattered like very fine grey snowflakes over the blanket.

The moment the coughing subsided, her mother went back to drawing in the smoke.

Maisie checked her eyes again as they swept back to her; dark brown and almost youthful. 'Have you had anything to eat?'

'I don't want nothin'. Stomach's upset. Tha's all it is.'

A low-seated gargling came from her throat.

Maisie grabbed a piece of folded newspaper and held it up with one hand for her mother to spit in, her other hand on the nape of her neck raising her from the pillow. The phlegm was copious and a nasty colour. Turning her head away, Maisie threw the crumpled-up newspaper into the fire, added a few more nubs of coke and stabbed at it with the poker. She watched the paper burn and, glancing momentarily at her mother, saw the reflection of the flames in the new brownness.

The cigarette was halfway gone now.

The brown eyes slid sidelong to meet those of her daughter.

'You need to get out of 'ere.' She said it in one spurt without a single gasp, though her voice was rough and hushed, like grit being ground beneath the sole of a boot.

It surprised her that her mother's speech had not faltered uttering those words.

Despite the smell of decay and death, Maisie knelt beside the bed, her small brow frowning. 'I need to get out of here, do I? And where do you suggest I go? And when should I go?'

'When I'm dead.' She took a series of gasping breaths before continuing. 'Your grandmother.' Another deep breath before continuing. 'Go to Granny Wells. She lives in Totterdown. Tell 'er...' Another bout of coughing ensued before she caught her breath and attempted to speak. 'Tell Granny Wells that I'm sorry. Can you do that?'

Maisie heard that throaty guttural sound again and replied that she would.

Her mother reached out a hand and the finished cigarette dropped from her fingers.

Taken by surprise, Maisie's mind raced. No relatives had ever been mentioned, and certainly no grandmother.

In a sadly feeble fashion, her mother reached for her and rubbed her poor, thin fingers down Maisie's face. They felt icy cold, like spines of frost running down the windowpane. The sleeves of her nightdress fell back from her arms. What little flesh

there hung from her bones – no more than wrinkled skin. 'Get...
away... Promise.'

Maisie nodded. 'I promise, but, Mum...'

Her mother looked desperate to hear whatever it was she was
about to say.

'What about dad saying 'e weren't me dad?'

Her mother looked at her, glassy-eyed, and pointed at the tea
caddy sitting high on the top shelf of the dresser. There were no
more words, just a struggle for breath.

Maisie held her mother's hand, willing her to say more,
anything that might make some sense of all that had happened of
late.

Once again, she pointed one spindly index finger at the
dresser. Then her arm fell back and she was gone, eyes closed
forever.

* * *

The factory allowed Maisie a day off to attend the funeral. Luckily
her mother had been paying a penny policy for years to the Liver-
pool Victoria, so there was just about enough money to bury her.

The day dawned as miserable as the occasion. The rain was
coming down like stair rods and the sky was thick with marbled
clouds, so many different shades of grey that they resembled a
mausoleum.

Alf's ship had docked in the Port of London and he'd been
granted leave. He came to the funeral in his uniform, his head
bowed, hair trickling with water. He asked her how she was.
Maisie told him she was fine. He looked fine. He looked happy.

'I love my life,' he said to her. 'I'll be sailing the world even
when this war is over.'

'Are you still with your friend?'

A bashful look came to his face as though she was referring to some girl he'd met.

'We're close as that,' he said with his fingers crossed.

Few people were gathered round the graveside, a sad reflection, thought Maisie on the loneliness of her mother's life.

She almost exploded with anger on seeing that her father was in the company of Eddie Bridgeman.

'What's 'e doing yer?' she hissed.

'I asked the same question,' said Alf. 'Here in 'is capacity of the old man's business partner.'

Maisie choked back her anger, to which was added the discomfort of feeling Eddie Bridgeman's eyes on her, his attempt to elicit some response to his smile which seemed for her and her alone.

The rain continued. Maisie eyed the muddy grave, the co n perched on the side ready to be lowered into the hole.

Her father was impatient to get it over with and addressed the vicar to that end. ''Ere mate. Get a bloody move on will you. It's raining cats and dogs and I'm working up a thirst. Pubs soon be open.'

Her father dared to laugh.

Everyone else looked embarrassed.

Maisie had purposely not arranged a wake which would have been paid for by her. Her father was furious.

'It ain't respectful. That's yer mother being buried.'

Maisie's voice was laced with sarcasm. 'Is that right, Frank Miles! Shame you didn't show 'er some respect while she was alive!'

He'd taken a step towards her, but Eddie Bridgeman's restraining hand held him back.

Bristling with indignation, Maisie turned away. Raindrops glistened on her eyelashes, mixed with a salty splash of tears.

Later, after the first clods of earth had landed on the co n and after she'd declined a lift from Eddie, Alf put his arm round her shoulder and led her away. Their father went with Eddie.

'We're off for a drink,' he shouted.

Maisie and Alf ignored him.

* * *

Back at York Street, Maisie chewed her bottom lip as she looked into the last embers of the dying fire, its warmth only going some way to easing the chill of the graveyard.

'I wish you could stay longer,' she said to Alf, who was sitting beside her, toasting a piece of bread speared onto the end of a toasting fork. The butter dish sat between his feet.

He passed her the slice of toast. 'You have this piece; I'll have the next.'

Her stomach growled. The toast smelt delicious and the bright yellow butter melted into its warmth.

She was thoughtful as she ate.

Her brother buttered his own toast. It was cosy to be together and they both enjoyed the silence that came along with the toast.

For Alf, it was a time of reflection, memories of where he'd spent his childhood and where he expected to spend his future.

For Maisie, too, it was a time of reflection, but also of decisions. Before she made those decisions regarding her future, she had questions to ask. Alf was the one person who might be able to answer them.

As she swallowed the last piece of toast, she felt his eyes on her.

'A penny for 'em.'

Maisie smiled sadly. 'Bridget's always saying that. I know I get thoughtful a lot, but then there's a lot for me to think about now ar mum's gone. It's funny, we were never that close, but I do miss 'er.'

She shivered at the thought of just her and her father in the house. Thanks to her exploit with the knife, he'd so far eyed her with uneasy respect. At night she jammed a chair against her bedroom door. Sometimes she heard the door knob rattle, a slight push and when it didn't give, the sound of her father's footsteps trudging off along the landing, occasionally followed by a rumbling as he fell down the stairs.

'You got a chap?' asked Alf.

She thought about Sid and the letter he'd first sent via Bert. She'd had a few after that, though not of late. 'I'm too young.'

Alf nodded. 'You're right. There's plenty of time for all that. Live a bit first. Decide what you want.' He stood up and stretched. 'I'm whacked. That train took four times as long as normal gettin' 'ere in the dark. You gonna wait up for the old man?'

Maisie sprang so swiftly to her feet; Alf was forced to take a step back.

'Down here all by meself? No. I'm bloody well not!'

'Then I'll stay down 'ere with you. I'll sleep on the chair; you take the sofa. Fancy another cup of tea?' A slow smile crossed his face. 'With another tot of whisky?'

They drank a few more of what was to her mind a good cup of tea, a real pick-me-up after standing at her mother's graveside. The whisky also gave her courage to ask one question in particular, the one that had kept her awake at night.

'The old man said that 'e weren't my dad. Did you know that?'

Alf's dark blonde hair flopped over eyes the colour of summer skies and he hesitated before answering. 'I don't know what to say.' He looked uncomfortable. He could remember something. She could tell.

Maisie studied the handsome profile, the high brow, the thick hair tumbling like waves over it and at the nape of his neck. Almost girlish, she thought, and nothing like her own mass of dark, tangled locks.

It irked her that he was taking his time replying. She was impatient to know. The truth was important to her. Soon, Alf would travel back to his ship. If he knew anything at all, it had to be now. To that end, she told him about the day Frank Miles had attempted to rape her, the day when he'd stated that he was not her father.

Alf was dumbstruck and suddenly a great change came over him. He stared into the fire as though somehow the answer lay amidst the flickering flames and glowing coals.

'Can you remember anything around the time I was born?'

Alf frowned as he fought to break through the fog of half-forgotten memories. 'I think there was a time when Ma wasn't around. A few months, I think. I was just a kid. Dad left me to get on with it though 'e did 'ave some woman in for a time to look after me and 'im.'

'A woman? Was she a relative?'

He shrugged his shoulders. 'I don't remember. I was just a kid. Shortly after that, there was me mum again and you in 'er arms.' He shook his head. 'Sorry, sis. That's about all I remember.'

'What about Granny Wells?'

He looked blank. 'Never 'eard of 'er.'

'Can you get me that caddy down?' She jerked her chin in the direction of the top shelf of the dresser.

'Sure.'

Alf obliged, standing on a wooden chair to reach it. He placed it on the table in front of her and blew the dust from the top. 'It's a bit dusty.'

'And a bit rusty,' Maisie added as she tried to prise off the lid. A kitchen knife finally did for it.

Inside was a faded sepia photograph of a young woman – no doubt her mother – in a formal poise and wearing a dress with leg-of-mutton sleeves. Her hair was swept up into a cottage-loaf style. Her eyes were dark and looked full of hope and excitement, a young girl on the threshold of her life.

Alf looked over Maisie's shoulder at the torn half of a bigger photo, a baby nestled in her mother's arms. She wondered who had been on that other half.

'This must be me.'

Alf agreed.

Maisie poked around in the tin for the other half. There were no other photographs, just birth certificates and her mother's marriage certificate. Alf's birth certificate was there. His date and place of birth were given. Her own birth certificate was dated sometime after her birth and she wondered at the reason why.

There was also an address scrawled on a piece of paper. She recognised the name her mother had uttered on her deathbed, Mrs G Wells. She vaguely recalled the G stood for Grace. Mrs Grace Wells. The address was in Totterdown where flat-faced terraces clung to hilly streets above the city. The houses were a bit better than York Street, but it was still just a working-class area.

Her heart beat faster at the prospect of getting to know this old woman. Perhaps she could shed some light of who had been in the other half of the photo.

Alf agreed that she should do as her mother had said and visit her grandmother. 'Wish I could go with you,' he added. 'Don't forget to tell her that she's got a real 'andsome grandson.'

Maisie gave him a playful slap, then pushed herself into his arms and burst into tears against his chest. 'I wish you weren't goin' Alf. I can't stand being 'ere all on me own with 'im in the 'ouse.'

Alf held her away from him and wiped the tears from her eyes with a sparkling white handkerchief. 'Don't you worry 'bout that. I'll fit a bolt on your bedroom door before I go. That should 'old until you sort yerself out. Now promise me you'll go and visit this grandmother we didn't know we had.'

'I will.'

She had every intention of doing so in the hope that she might be taken in, that she might at last live somewhere safer than the place she was currently in.

29

GRANNY WELLS

The houses in Totterdown did exactly that, their foundations clinging to a steep hillside between the upper road to Wells and the lower road to Bath so they really did appear to be tottering and in grave danger of sliding down onto the road and into the river. Precariously positioned, they were of similar age as those in St Phillips, but the air up here was pleasanter, unsullied by bone-yards and soap factories.

Metal bollards set deep into pavements of crumpled slabs, most dating from the middle of the last century, were there to help pedestrians climb up the hill.

A milkman's cart was parked halfway up, a heavy metal weight wedged against its back wheel to aid the brakes and stop it running downhill.

The little Maisie had gleaned about her grandmother had been imparted during her mother's illness. 'Just tell 'er I'm sorry.' She'd kept repeating that. Maisie wondered what she'd been sorry for.

Number twenty-seven was a flat-fronted house with a brown door that opened directly onto the street. The windows were clean, the net curtain thick and white, impossible to look through. Overall it looked far more appealing than anything York Street had to offer.

Other people knew their grandmothers, but she'd never known hers so was unsure what to expect. Some were tough old boots like Aggie Hill. Others, like the kind in story books, sat in a rocking chair and knitted things.

Taking a good grip of the knocker, Maisie rammed it three times against the door. Three was always the logical number to choose: if the first knock wasn't heard, the second had a better chance, the third better again.

Maisie heard no sign of movement from behind the brown door but out of the corner of her eye got the impression that someone had peered out from behind the net curtain.

Just as she was about to knock one last time, the door was tugged open a little way. Another tug and it was open halfway and a face appeared.

She had dark crinkly hair, dark eyes and her skin was pale brown in colour. Her figure was stout and her dark grey dress shimmered as though it was made of some kind of silk.

Her face beamed and her eyes shone with delight as she looked on Maisie. 'Ah! My long-lost granddaughter. You'd better come in. Managed to find me all right then?'

Astounded that her grandmother appeared to be expecting her, Maisie followed.

Granny Wells indicated the passage running alongside the staircase, the top of which seemed to disappear into a dense gloom on the upper landing. 'Go on through to the back. I keep everything we need in the scullery,' she said in a more business-like voice.

Puzzled, Maisie said nothing but did as she was told.

The room at the back was shabby but scrupulously clean,

fresh curtains at the single window that looked out onto the back garden. The smell of a newly baked fruit cake came in from the scullery.

A cat lounged in an armchair. Her grandmother shooed it away.

'Well, don't stick there gawping, girl. We've got work to do. Off with your coat – unless you've changed your mind.'

Maisie obeyed. It seemed her grandmother was expecting her, but how could she know she was coming? She'd told nobody.

'How did...'

She was going to ask how she knew, but Granny Wells didn't give her chance.

'Right,' she said after Maisie's coat was hung up. 'Shall we get the business side out of the way first? That'll be ten pounds.'

Maisie looked down into the wrinkled palm and frowned. This wasn't at all what she'd expected. Why did she want money? What was it for? She found her voice. 'Ten pounds for what?'

The amiable expression vanished. The hand was withdrawn.

'My time costs money. I don't do it fer nothing!' Before Maisie could speak, Grace Wells grabbed an enamel bowl. Maisie glimpsed a rust-coloured rubber hose along with something metallic. Grace Wells shoved it in front of her face. 'This is what you've come for, ain't it? You got yourself in the family way and the bloke don't want to marry you. 'Appens all the time. You ain't the first. Far from it.'

Maisie's jaw dropped. 'You get rid of babies?'

On realising they were talking at cross purposes her own surprised expression was mirrored in that of the woman she understood to be her grandmother.

'Who the bloody 'ell are you? What are you doin' 'ere? Get out of my 'ouse. Go on. Get out!' Grace Wells barked.

Maisie shook her head in disbelief. This was not the kind of person she'd expected; this was not the kind of grandmother she wanted. She took a deep breath. 'My name's Maisie Miles. My mother was Gwen Miles. She told me to come here and tell you that she was sorry. Now I've said it, I might as well go,' she mumbled, turning on her heel

'Gwen sent you? Why didn't she come 'erself?'

'She's dead.'

'Well, I'll be...'

'I didn't know where you lived till after she was gone. She kept your address in the tea caddy. She didn't want it opened until she was dead.'

It was suddenly as though she was hit by pain and sadness. Tears stung at her eyes and all she wanted to do was get away from here.

When a timid knock sounded at the front door, she grabbed her coat fled down the passageway and tugged it open.

There, right in front of her, was the girl she must have been mistaken for. She had huge eyes, and hunched shoulders. An older, worried-looking woman was with her, perhaps her mother if the similar eyes were anything to go by.

Feeling both shocked and disappointed, Maisie stiffened. 'Down there,' she said, jerking her chin towards her shoulder to indicate they should proceed along the passageway.

She knew now the reason her grandmother had welcomed her as her granddaughter was for the benefit of the neighbours. She'd said it loud enough to be overheard.

A quick glance over her shoulder and she saw Grace Wells staring after her, the girl who had come for her help standing there looking totally confused.

She ran on, heard the slam of the front door and knew for sure that Grace Wells was not coming after her.

Earlier that morning, she'd had such high hopes; she'd truly imagined she'd be welcomed with open arms. The ending – or new beginning to her life's story – had seemed like a fairy tale. And that, it seemed, was all it was.

She'd really hoped to be taken in so she could leave York Street and her life there behind. It seemed now that the only option left for her was the almoner at the factory whose job it was to help the girls out with personal problems. In a way, she should be feeling grateful that the company went out of their way to have a happy workforce, but one room in a shared house wasn't really what she wanted. She craved a home. She craved a family.

As Maisie made her way back to York Street, she attempted to blank her grandmother from her mind, but there was just one little thing that kept coming back. What was the history behind her mother's message that she was sorry? What was she sorry for? She wished she'd asked. And what about Frank Miles? Did Grace Wells know who her real father was? She hadn't got chance to find out.

Twilight bathed York Street in that strange half-light that made the houses seem as though they were fading into slate grey before full darkness descended. Doors were being shut for the night. Curtains were being drawn. A lone rat crossed her path, a cat in hot pursuit. The sound of rattling metal bins was joined by the rattling of goods trains from the marshalling yards.

For a moment, Maisie thought she heard something else, the low burring of a car engine. Few cars ever entered York Street. Baker, fishmonger, milkman and greengrocer all used a horse and cart. There was only one car she knew of that would have any business here at this time of night. Only one car and one owner sprang to mind.

Her footsteps quickened, but the car was quicker. It slid to a stop beside her and Eddie Bridgeman jumped out.

'Maisie.'

He stopped in front of her, the width of his body as wide as the pavement.

He tilted two fingers beneath the brim of his hat and smiled like a cat might before pouncing on a mouse. 'Good evening, Maisie. I see you're as lovely as ever.'

'Get out of my way, Mr Bridgeman.'

'No need for such an unfriendly tone. Call me Eddie.'

'Get out of my way, Eddie.'

His gold tooth flashed when he smiled. 'Now, now. No need to be disagreeable.'

'What do you want?'

'I wanted to make you an offer you'd be daft to refuse. A job in my club, and get this, princess, I can offer you a nice little flat in St Pauls. All mod cons. Furnished and with a nice view over City Road. Out from under yer old man's feet.'

The prospect might have appealed to her if it hadn't been coming from Eddie Bridgeman. The thought of having her own flat was appealing, but she knew it would come at a price, one she was not prepared to pay. 'I've got a job and I've got somewhere to live.'

'Yeah. But come on… St Phillips? Let's face it, it's a right dump and I know what yer dad's like. You'd be no better than a skivvy, at 'is beck and call. Tell you what, if you don't like the flat in City Road, how about one somewhere else of your choosing. How would that be?'

'You're too late. I've got somewhere lined up,' she responded defiantly, though the truth was she didn't have anything just yet. It all depended on the almoner at the factory.

She brushed roughly past him, her footsteps clattering along the uneven pavement to number five.

'I could pay you a good wage. And you could have the flat for nothing. My treat. We'd work out later how you could pay me back.'

Overwhelmed with fear and anger, Maisie slammed the door. Everyone in the street would have heard his offer and made assumptions. The neighbours couldn't be seen, but she knew they were there, peering out through narrow gaps in the blackout curtains.

Eddie Bridgeman was giving her a choice. He could ruin her reputation by rumour if she turned him down, or she could accept his offer and become one of his 'girls', as much of a commodity as the booze and fags for sale in his nightclub.

Maisie leaned against the door and closed her eyes and resolved that he wouldn't get her. No matter where she had to live, she would assert her own will, her own dreams.

30

THE CANADIANS

Mrs Harvey was peering over her spectacles at her knitting needles and then glaring at the pattern as though it was somehow responsible for the stitches she'd dropped.

'Well, this isn't right,' she said, her lips pursed and her brow furrowed. 'And why do they make the print on these patterns so small? Well, I'll tell you why. It's to make you think they're cleverer than anyone not able to afford a proper shop-bought cardigan. That's why they do it. Of course I can afford one, but I won't be wasteful.'

In the short time Phyllis had lived with her in-laws, she'd heard Mrs Harvey's view that everyone was out to put her down as somebody who couldn't afford the better things of life. Whether it was the window cleaner, the butcher, the baker or the man who came round on his bicycle to sharpen knives and pairs of scissors; she treated them all with suspicion and cynicism.

Although Robert had only been gone for just over a week, his mother missed him and said so in both words and actions. For a start, she refused to let anyone sit in his favourite chair or use his own special mug that commemorated the coronation of King George the Fifth and Queen Mary. She'd bought it for him, of course, and in order that nobody – especially Phyllis – used it, kept it in a glass-fronted display cabinet in the front room. Above the cabinet were pictures of the current royal family: The King, George VI, his Queen, Elizabeth and the two princesses, Elizabeth and Margaret. Along-side was Edward the Eighth, the former Prince of Wales she'd retained a soft spot for even though he had chosen to abdicate and marry the American divorcee, Wallis Simpson. 'Once a royal, always a royal,' she frequently said as she dusted down each picture.

'I'm not sure about using the front room this Christmas,' she said to Robert's father. 'Did you hear what I said? About the front room?'

Robert's long-suffering father came out from behind his paper. 'It's four weeks until Christmas. You don't have to make up your mind right now. Anyway, we always use the front room at Christmas. It's nice to see it so cosy.'

He's right about that, thought Phyllis. The front room was usually the iciest in the house. It would be interesting, if nothing else, to see it decorated for Christmas.

The knitting needles resumed their clicking, each stitch stabbed into existence.

'Robert isn't here, it won't be the same. And not only that, I don't really want to invite relatives round. They ate and drank enough at the wedding. Do they think we're made of money?'

'Phyllis's mother did pay for most of it,' Mr Harvey offered.

'Not all of it. I'm not criticising your mother, Phyllis or objecting to doing our bit. I know she's a widow so has to be care-ful, but it's usually the bride's father who stumps up.'

'My father's dead.'

Mrs Harvey's pale, watery eyes flashed at her before falling back to the knitting. 'Unfortunate,' she said as the needles resumed their relentless rhythm.

'I was grateful for all of it,' said Phyllis, feeling a need to defend her mother and also to try and get on with her mother-in-law. 'I've still got some wedding presents to pick up – some sheets from Baker Baker in Castle Street. I think I might do that now – if you don't mind that is...'

'Why should I mind? Huh. Though it seems lazy to me, not wrapping a present up to give on the actual day. Not good manners in my estimation.'

'Perhaps you'd like to come with me?'

She awaited the answer with her heart in her mouth hoping she would not.

'I've got things to do. I don't expect any help doing them, which is just as well, because I doubt I'm likely to get any.'

Phyllis breathed a sigh of relief and ignored the insinuation that her mother-in-law did everything round the house. It was best to pretend she was right rather than have her fall into a bad mood.

'I'll get ready then,' said Phyllis, laying down the *Good Housekeeping* magazine she'd been pretending to read.

Hilda Harvey's attention was already elsewhere. 'Cyril! Never mind reading that paper. Help me with this. I need another skein.'

Sighing as he set down his paper, Robert's father held up his hands.

'For heaven's sake, keep still,' his wife admonished as she stretched a skein of wool between his hands and commenced winding it into a ball.

'I'll be off then,' said Phyllis, 'Whilst it's still light.'

* * *

A Salvation Army brass band was playing on the corner by a very ancient timbered building called The Dutch House. Each of its floors jutted out over the one beneath and in broad daylight Bridget likened it to a house made of playing cards, the upper layers likely to implode one on top of the other. Bridget and Maisie sang along with the band, each slipping a farthing into the collecting can that was rattled in front of their faces.

A number of shops were still open and as it was Saturday, the food shops would be open until nearly ten o'clock. There were queues outside some of them and the shop doors were only gingerly opened, the light kept from spilling out by a double door or blackout curtain, one on the inside and one out. The war, thought Bridget, is changing everything. Lights would normally be twinkling from shop windows, but war meant that the only light was from the moon and stars and those lucky enough to have a torch.

Leaving the band and the shops behind them, they headed for one of their favourite pubs, a very ancient hostelry that, despite its frowning overhang and low ceilings, would be well lit and cheerful inside.

'Take a look at my dress,' said Bridget. 'My Ma made it.'

Maisie shone her torch at Bridget and picked out the dark green wool dress beneath a swagger coat of wide check with big pockets.

'You're lucky,' said Maisie, and felt a pang of envy. If only she'd had a mother like that, but what was the point of wishing? And what good now that her mother was dead.

'Now you,' Bridget said laughingly. The narrow beam of her torch picked out a blue dress peeking out from beneath a black coat. Maisie was also wearing a blue and white muffler round her neck. 'You expecting snow?'

'No. Frost.'

They turned the upward glow of their torches onto their faces.

'I don't think we're supposed to shine our torches upwards,' said Bridget, 'in case enemy bombers see them.'

Maisie looked up at the sky and laughed defiantly, the torch beam picking out her rosy features. 'I don't see any enemy bombers.'

Their features stood out in the crowd of dark faces, so much so that Phyllis, wandering by just then spotted them.

Her voice rang out. 'Maisie? It's me. Phyllis.'

The beams of a trio of torches shone upwards as they fell into each other's arms.

'The three Ms are together again,' cried Bridget. 'One for all and all for one.'

This was the first time they'd seen each other since the wedding, which had seemed strange. Just because she was married didn't mean to say she shouldn't keep in touch.

Maisie had suggested to Bridget that Phyllis was being held prisoner. 'And fed only bread and water,' she'd added.

They'd laughed about it, but deep down were both worried. How was Phyllis coping? Phyllis's mother had refused to answer the door when Bridget had called round. 'Yet I know she was in there,' Bridget had told Maisie.

The first question Bridget asked now was about the honeymoon. 'How did it go?'

'Fine.'

'Is he gone now?' asked Maisie.

'Yes.' Phyllis had no intention of going into detail about her life with the Harveys. Even thinking about it was too depressing for words.

Bridget asked her what she was doing in town.

'I've been shopping for some extra bedding,' she replied. 'I'm on my way... back.' Maisie noticed the hesitation and couldn't resist making comment.

'Not happily by the sound of it.'

'Whatever makes you say that, Maisie Miles?' Phyllis responded. She sounded defensive and also hurt.

Maisie was unperturbed. 'Home, you should have said home, Phyllis. That's where you live with your husband, isn't it? Or his family.'

In the depth of the blackout, nobody could see Bridget rolling her eyes. Yet again, Maisie had made and voiced an accurate observation, though she could have been more tactful about it, but then, that was Maisie.

'How's Robert? Have you heard from him?' asked Bridget, doing her best to smooth over the situation.

'He's fine. He's been writing.'

Phyllis attempted to sound upbeat and not betray that she was missing her friends and even stripping tobacco leaves. She spent her days trying to keep busy helping to run the house, though strictly in line with Mrs Harvey's guidelines.

'There's only one way to do the housework in this house, young lady, and that's my way.'

Phyllis couldn't bring herself to tell her friends that she cried herself to sleep at night, one minute wishing Robert was there, and then equally wishing he never came back. It was a wicked thought, but as far as she could see, the only way out of her predicament, but she had the baby to think of, the child of another man. All the same, it was a lonely life. Working at the factory had provided more than just employment; that's where her friends were. She had thought about visiting Bridget, but a sense of pride, plus the temptation to unload all the reasons why she'd married, why she'd had to get married, had stopped her.

'We're going to the pub,' said Maisie. 'You're welcome to tag along. She'd be welcome, wouldn't she, Bridget?'

Bridget said that she would be, though didn't expect her to accept. She was a married woman now and it wasn't done for wives to frequent pubs when their husband was away fighting.

Phyllis hesitated. 'Well, I shouldn't really...' Thinking of what awaited her at home, his mother criticising everything she did, insisting that Robert wouldn't like her gadding about without reason – she'd just about got away with the excuse that her aunt had ordered new sheets as a wedding present from Baker Bakers and she was going to collect them. 'I lied,' she whispered. 'I don't have an aunt who ordered sheets. I made it up. Any excuse to get out,' she finally shouted, threw back her head and laughed fit to burst.'

Her friends saw the joke and laughed along with her.

'That's it, then,' said Maisie. 'You can tell the old bat they ain't arrived yet.'

Bridget remarked that Phyllis's mother-in-law might not be an old bat at all.

Phyllis put her right. 'She's all of that and then some! Don't I wish I had me own place, but there, I made me bed and got to lie on it.'

Maisie's arm slid through hers. 'How about we have a pre-Christmas drink?'

'I will,' said Phyllis feeling better than she had for weeks.

'Right,' said Bridget as she slid her arm through on Phyllis's other side. 'That's decided. Cat and Wheel or Bear and Rugged Staff?'

Through the thick darkness of a blacked-out night, they trudged along a cobble stoned street through jolly crowds to the ancient pubs, their torches flashing over the ground ahead of them. Someone had told Bridget that they dated back to the fourteenth century and Bridget being Bridget, she couldn't resist passing on the information.

'The Bear and Rugged Staff is the oldest known pub name and refers to baiting bears – a form of sport back in the Middle Ages; too gruesome for modern tastes. The origin of the Cat and Wheel is pretty gruesome too. It means Catherine wheel and refers to the martyrdom of St Catherine. She was fastened to a wheel and rolled along the street then burnt...'

Phyllis burst out laughing. 'Bridget, you don't change a bit. You still sound as though you've swallowed a whole library.'

One after the other, they pushed through the door of the Cat and Wheel and found themselves faced with a solid crowd between them and the bar.

'Blimey! Looks like there's a party going on!'

The air was thick with smoke which over the centuries had turned the walls and low ceiling a dirty shade of mustard.

Getting to the bar was difficult. Uniforms dominated, men making the most of their freedom before heading off to fight, young women hanging onto their every word.

'We're never going to get a drink in here,' cried a disconsolate Bridget.

Her words were lost in the noise. If she'd been in the least bit claustrophobic, she would have rushed out by now. Made of sterner stuff, Maisie pushed her way through, clearing a path so Bridget and Phyllis could follow.

Broad-shouldered men surrounded them, a whole orchestra of male voices in various accents all seeming to want to outdo each other, to have their last shouting match, their last song, their last drink before going off to war.

A particularly broad-backed man turned suddenly, almost knocking Bridget backwards and separating her from her friends.

'Oops, sorry, lady... Hey,' he said. 'Haven't we met before?'

It was on her tongue to say that she didn't think so, but having noted his uniform, she reminded herself that he was a long way from home and here to help win this war. There was also the matter of his accent. It wasn't quite the same as Lyndon's had been, but it was similar.

Her smile was warm. 'I don't think so.'

'That's a shame. How about I buy you a drink to make up for it?'

'I'm with friends,' she said, raising her voice and pointing to where Maisie and Phyllis had ducked their heads beneath the low-hanging beam that ran the length of the bar. Other heads were homing in on them, also ducking to avoid the many pint mugs hanging from the beam.

'Come on. I'll get you through to your friends.'

He was as good as his word, one arm wrapped protectively round her shoulders as he propelled her through a whole sea of uniforms that looked much the same as his. His pushing was matched with loud commands. 'Come on, you guys. I'm the sergeant here. Get out of the way, will ya?'

Phyllis and Maisie giggled in unison and exchanged wry looks with a very flushed Bridget when she reached them. Before any of them could counteract, their new Canadian friend had ordered and paid for the drinks. The girls thanked him, though Maisie apologised for not raising their glasses. 'Not in this crowd. One awkward elbow and I'd end up wearing it – or you might.'

He laughed with them, but his eyes were for Bridget.

'I forgot to ask your name.' He shouted above the din almost as loudly as he'd shouted at his colleagues.

'My name's Bridget Milligan,' she shouted back. 'And these are my friends, Maisie and Phyllis.'

Dancing eyes and a pleasant face smiled at each of them in

turn. 'Pleased to meet you all. My name's Stef O'Toole. I'm from Canada.'

Bridget remarked that it was an Irish surname, just as hers was. 'Though I don't recognise the name Stef as being Irish.'

'It's Swedish. My mother's father was a lumberjack.'

'Hence the broad shoulders,' shouted an amused Maisie. 'Unless your father was also a lumberjack.'

He laughed and shouted back that his father was an accountant. 'But still a big guy. And what about your pa? What does he do?' His question was aimed at Bridget.

'Mends clocks,' she shouted back.

They hardly knew each other and were shouting in order to be heard, yet their interchange was oddly intimate, as though the noisy crowd of men – plus a sprinkling of women – were only stage scenery.

The crush grew so intense that she found herself pressed up against him. The feel of his body reminded her of Lyndon, though they'd hardly had time to get this intimate.

She accepted Stef's offer of another drink at the same time telling herself that he was just a ship in the night. They were passing strangers and there was no need to get het up about a relationship developing. The future she feared, becoming a married woman and a mother, would not happen yet and anyway nobody could move her the way Lyndon O'Neill had moved her. She wondered how he would be spending his Christmas and tried to imagine what it was like in Virginia, whether it would be snowing and how big was the family that gathered round a tree she was sure would be quite enormous.

Maisie too had another drink bought for her by some good-looking young man with a shiny face and very short hair. She didn't bother to tell him that she was underage and the barman was too busy to notice.

Phyllis was offered drinks, but was pushing herself away from the bar. She wore an anxious look and something else besides. Bridget interpreted it as regret; regret she had to go, regret she was married and, more especially, that she was expected to keep 'respectable' hours. 'I have to go.'

'I understand,' said Bridget and offered to walk with her as far as the bus stop. In the old days when Phyllis was single, they'd walked together all the way home. Bridget perceived that a gap had opened up between them; it was as though they were on separate sides of a bridge that had been thrown up by a power determined to keep them apart.

Phyllis shook her head. 'No. You stay here.' Her glance at Stef was accompanied with a short-lived smile. 'Enjoy yourself – while you still can.'

Once she was gone, Bridget felt a sense of guilt. Phyllis had always been a happy-go-lucky soul before she'd married Robert and the change saddened her.

'What time does this pub close?' asked her Canadian companion.

'Ten thirty,' replied Bridget.

She felt his chest heave against her when he sighed.

'Then we have to compile a schedule. I have to get back to base, but have to walk you home first.'

'But I'm with my friend....' She indicated Maisie, who was listening to the young man with the shiny face, nodding between sips of whatever it was she was drinking.

'I dare say my good friend, Greg, will make sure she gets home safely. Does she live near you?'

She shook her head. 'No. In the other direction in fact.'

'Then let me make arrangements.'

Half an hour later and they were standing outside on the pavement. Both men got out their torches.

'Army issue,' said Stef and gave it a good thump when it didn't turn on at the first attempt.

Goodbyes were said, Stef and Bridget heading for the city centre where they could get on a tram to Bedminster Bridge.

'Where we going, honey?' Maisie sidestepped the arm Greg wound round her waist. She'd kept Sid at bay and had every intention of keeping him at bay too.

'I have to tell you, I'm only fifteen.'

'So what? You still need to get home safely. I'll even pay your bus fare.'

'I'm walking home.'

'Is it far?'

She marched quickly so even a man used to marching had to quickstep to keep up with her.

'A bit of a way,' she declared over her shoulder. 'I can get there by myself.'

He was striding after her. 'I won't let you.'

Cold air pinched at her cheeks, but Greg made her feel quite warm. A big smile came to her lips. 'Don't you have to get back to barracks?'

'I'm pretty sure we're going in the same direction. It's at a place called Old Market? It's just up a bit from a pub called The Stag and Hounds. Do you know it?'

Of course she knew it, and he was right. They were both heading in the same direction.

'Yes. I know it. Locals call it the Pied Powder.'

'Really? Why is that?'

She tried to remember everything that Bridget had told her. 'It's the English form of the French name for dusty feet. Hundreds of years ago, a market was held here and people arrived with dusty feet. I'll walk with you as far as that. I can find my own way home after that.'

'Hey, sister. I like to think of myself as a gentleman, and a gentleman always sees a lady to her front door. I insist.'

She gritted her teeth. Greg was a nice guy, but she wasn't ready to have a boyfriend. And she didn't want him to see where she lived or deal with the embarrassment of bumping into her father and his thieving friends.

Still, she had to admit it was a very kind gesture.

The darkness of night plus the blackout was all consuming. At times, the only way she knew for sure that he was still with her was the sound of his footsteps.

Thankfully, she could find her way home with her eyes shut, which was probably why, to some extent, she was leaving him behind.

'Cut me some slack, sister,' he said as he wound his arm round her for a second time. 'A stranger could easily get lost in this black pond.'

'We're nearly there,' she said as her hand brushed against one of the pillars supporting the gabled first floor of the Stag and Hounds.

'You sure?'

'Can't you smell it?'

'Smell what?'

'The faggot and pea shop. It's just up here on the right. The air round here always smells of faggots and peas. That's my secret. If you can't see where yer going, follow yer nose.'

'Clever girl.'

Maisie began to get nervous. He'd walked her all this way and if she didn't get rid of him shortly, he'd still be with her when she reached York Street. The blackout would hide most of the details of the shabby street, but she had other reasons. Frank Miles was one of them.

She disliked getting home this late in case her father was

there. If he was, she'd have to make a dash for her room. Unless he was out cold in a drunken stupor. She hoped he was.

Maisie stopped abruptly. 'I'm fine from here.'

'I said I'd walk you all the way, honey.'

'No need. I can take care of myself. Bye, Greg.'

She spun away from him and broke into a run, determined to put distance between them. The blackout worked in her favour. She knew her way home without street lights. She'd lived here all her life.

Once she was sure he wasn't following, she stopped to catch her breath. She listened for the sound of footsteps following behind but heard nothing. She smiled to herself. All in all, it had been fun meeting up with Greg and Stef. The foreign troops oozed a glamour the English lads just couldn't compete with.

As the smell of the bone yard chimney and the clanging of the marshalling yards assaulted her senses, Maisie's high spirits plummeted. Boys and young men were all very well, but she had some serious issues to address for one so young. For a start, she had to take her mother's advice and move out. She didn't need a picture drawn of the possible consequences if she didn't. She also had a yearning to find out the identity of her real father. The only person who knew that had to be Grace Wells – the granny she never knew she had and wasn't exactly what she'd expected.

As she turned into York Street, she heard measured, heavy footsteps echoing between the rows of miserable houses. Her steps slowed as her heartbeat quickened and she tried to guess who it might be.

The footsteps stopped suddenly and her racing heart slowed to a more temperate pace. Perhaps she'd been imagining things, or otherwise whoever it was – a man, judging by the sound of his footsteps – had gone into his own front door; perhaps a neighbour home early from the pub.

Fearing to linger in case she was wrong, Maisie hurried on, desperate to push open the front door. The house held unfortunate memories but was all she had for now. The door would not be locked; nobody in the street locked their doors. Nobody would dare trespass in Frank Miles's house, besides which he'd busted the lock ages ago after returning drunk from the pub.

Tension fell from her shoulders and her breathing was calm and collected as she reached home. She was just about to push the door open, when a big, black form loomed over her, features indistinguishable in the all-prevailing darkness.

'Miss Miles?'

The voice startled her. It was difficult to see who it was, but she smelt damp serge and quality tobacco.

Her heart began racing again.

'What do you want?'

'I'm Sergeant Evans. I patrol round here.'

She put two and two together. 'What's happened? Is he dead?'

Her hopes were dashed when the sergeant told her that if she meant her father, he was not. 'Can we go inside?'

She sensed him taking off his helmet before she opened the door. The air in the narrow passageway that led to the back of the house smelt damp, though not as filthy as it sometimes did.

Once inside, she drew the blackout curtains, turned on the light and took the policeman through to the kitchen.

Everything was in disarray.

'What's happened?'

The policeman cleared his throat as she straightened the kitchen rug and picked up the kettle from the floor, the upturned chair and the fragments of china scattered everywhere.

Her stance turned angry. 'Well, this is a right mess. Perhaps we'd best go through to the living room. Would you like a cup of tea?'

'That might be for the best.'

This had something to do with her father. She tried to guess what it might be as she put the kettle on and went into the living room with him.

Like the kitchen, the floor in this room was also covered in debris. A statue of a woman with two huge dogs lay smashed into chalky pieces over the floor. The fireguard was turned onto its side. Maisie picked them up dispassionately and without suspicion; when drunk, her father tended to throw things around. She took off her coat and hat, set it to one side. Her heart was racing yet some deep-seated instinct told her not to worry, that whatever it was would be for the best.

'So why are you here? Is it my dad?'

The policeman's fingers circled the inside of his helmet, his eyes following their progress. 'I'm afraid so. We've arrested him for his involvement in stealing a lorryload of cigarettes. Another bloke involved was caught for some minor crime and in order to get off fingered your father. We caught your old man red-handed about to steal another load. He'd have made a fortune selling them around Christmas.

'Robbery?' She sounded as though it had come as a complete surprise. In her heart of hearts, she still felt guilty about putting her father in touch with the man responsible for the delivery schedules. 'Was his name Red, this bloke who fingered my father?'

The police sergeant confirmed that it was. 'We got his fingerprints on more than one job and we've got some of the stuff back, though not all of it. You wouldn't know where he might have stashed it, would you?'

A puzzled frown creased her brows as she shook her head. 'No.'

The police sergeant ran his fingers through his hair, elbow resting on his knee.

Maisie made tea for both of them and brought it through. The sergeant sipped lustily. 'Well, that's warmed my cockles,' he said appreciatively.

'Will he go to prison?' she asked. It wouldn't be the first time. She vaguely remembered her mother mentioning something about him going to prison in the past.

'Very likely. It's a minimum of two though we're hoping he'll get six years, but you can never tell in these uncertain times. Deals are done. Every hand to the pump in a war situation.'

She wanted to say, please keep him as long as possible and throw away the key.

'There's a rumour he was in league with Eddie Bridgeman. Have you heard of him, young lady?' the sergeant asked.

She nodded.

He downed the last of his tea and looked at her. 'You don't seem that worried.'

'Every cloud has a silver lining. It's his cloud and my silver lining. I hope he stays in prison for years.'

The policeman got to his feet. 'Not the best dad in the world, eh?'

'Possibly the worst.'

He smiled and she thought how friendly he looked and how kind he'd been.

'Better be going. Thanks for the tea.' He picked up his helmet which he'd placed on the table when he'd been drinking his tea.

'I'll see you out.'

Half a foot before the front door, the sergeant stopped and turned to face her. 'Look, love. If there's ever anything you want to tell me, or if you're afraid or anything, you let me know. Will you do that?'

'I'll do that all right.'

Maisie danced round the room after the sergeant had gone. Her father was going to prison. She'd have the house to herself. It was the happiest she'd felt for ages. Something else hit her that made her feel even happier. She did not need the help of the factory almoner – at least not in the short term, and who knows where she'd be when her father was finally released from prison. Two years at least. That's what the policeman had said.

Her attention was drawn to her smiling reflection in the cracked mirror hanging above the fireplace. Defiance shone in her eyes and a smile played around her mouth, which became a chuckle and then laughter. *This*, she decided, *is the best day of my life*.

31

THE HARVEYS

Phyllis opened the front door of the house in Bedminster Road as quietly as she could as she returned from seeing Bridget and Maisie. The hall was in darkness but a sliver of light showed from beneath the living room door. Her heart sank. Somebody had waited up for her.

Her first inclination was to creep up the stairs to her bedroom. She thought of the freezing room with its solid and highly polished furniture, the ugly lino and the pink and green rug that made her feel sick just looking at it.

Before she had a chance to move one single step, the living-room door swung open and she cried out. A figure stood there, dark and almost featureless against the muted glow from within the room.

'Phyllis. Where the bloody 'ell do you think you've been?' Robert was home.

'Robert!' She was stunned. 'I didn't know – we didn't know...' The words shuddered into existence, startled hesitation preventing her from speaking coherently.

He opened the door wider. 'Get in here. Quickly.'

His anger was controlled, his voice kept purposely low.

As she entered the room, the mantel clock was showing nine o'clock so she guessed his parents had already gone to bed. She was late back and knew he wouldn't like that. She cloaked her nervousness with a wobbly smile.

Feeling apprehensive, she fiddled with her gloves, pulling off one, then the other in a rather haphazard fashion and became aware of the door closing softly behind her.

'Well this is a surprise. Darling, I wasn't expecting you. How nice...'

He didn't give her chance to continue. His face was unsmiling. 'Obviously. Where've you been?'

Under his watchful eyes, Phyllis put down her bag and took off her coat and hat, fumbling with each item in turn to prolong the procedure so she had time to think of what to say. 'I went into town shopping. I needed to collect my Aunt Maude's wedding present – those sheets – remember?'

He folded his arms. They seemed bigger than she remembered, his biceps better filling his sleeves. His brow was beetled. 'Can't say I do. Anyway, seems to me we've got plenty of sheets.'

Another excuse occurred to her. 'We'll be needing more soon, what with the war and... You look very well, Robert.'

It was true. As with his biceps, his facial features seemed far more prominent, as though army training had taken all the fat off him.

'I've been training. We need it if we're to defend this country.'

'Do your mum and dad know you're home?' she asked brightly.

'Of course they do!' He sounded as though she was stupid to think otherwise. 'Mum was a bit worried as to where you'd got to. Tired herself out thinking about it, so I said I'd wait up.'

She noticed that he hadn't mentioned his father. It was taken for granted that where his mother went, his father went too.

'It's not so late. The shops are still open until ten – and it's nowhere near that yet. Anyway, I had to go to the centre to get a tram back. The buses were crowded. So was Skivvies' Island come to that, but I managed to get on a tram back to Bedminster.'

His bottom lip curled with contempt. 'Skivvies Island? You got no business going there. All them little tramps waiting for a soldier to come along and pick them up. And you a married woman!'

The tra c island was in the middle of the Centre where all the trams pulled in. Years ago, domestic servants working in big houses arranged to meet their sweethearts there. Phyllis thought its reputation romantic. Obviously Robert did not. His comment and dark scowl were enough to emphasise the insinuation he was making.

He came close and looked directly into her eyes. She gasped when his hand gripped her shoulder.

'The tramway centre is where loose girls meet their soldiers. Are you mucking about with some other bloke when I'm not around?'

'No!' She shook her head, eyes wide with surprise. She'd never seen him like this and wondered where he'd got the idea. Then it came to her. She received one letter a week. So did his mother and the moment she had it, immediately wrote back scribbling away at the writing bureau over in the corner by the window, determined to write back to her son before Phyllis did and tell him...What did she tell him? That his wife would be out gallivanting if she didn't keep her under control, that she pined to be with her friends, that she couldn't even polish the sideboard without leaving smears and dust untouched. 'I've told you I was down there to collect the sheets. I had to wait around, and then they told me they hadn't come in so I'd have to call in again.'

He stood over her, nostrils flaring, eyes dark with something she'd never seen there before. 'Before she went to bed, Mum said there are plenty of sheets and she don't know why you had to go down and collect some more.'

She swayed back from him as he leaned into her and turned her head, hoping the cigarette she'd consumed on the tram was enough to veil the smell of port and lemon. 'We do have enough for our bed, but I wanted to alter the order. I wanted smaller ones for...'

His eyes were blazing. 'For what?'

She sighed and reached out for the chair arm. 'I need to sit down. There was such a queue – everyone buying things that are likely to become scarce soon. I've never seen Baker Bakers so busy.' Her knees began to buckle and she sank into a chair. 'I'm so tired,' she said, letting her head drop onto one hand.

Robert made no effort to help her sit down, but neither did he heed her. She could tell he was rolling all this over in his mind; what he knew, what she said and what his mother had said. There was only one thing likely to placate him, one thing that she hadn't been going to voice just yet. But there it was, the time for telling him she was pregnant had arrived more quickly than expected.

'I need to buy sheets now for a cot... for when the baby is born.'

There was a sudden moment of stillness, when it seemed as though the pair of them were as heavy and fixed as the furniture. She heard his sharp intake of breath before he spoke. She prayed he was savouring what she'd just told him, that he didn't suspect anything.

'A baby?' He looked astounded.

She nodded. 'Yes. Early days, but I'm quite sure.'

She did the figures in her head. A month since they'd been married. Enough time for it to be his. When it was born, she'd just say it was premature. She'd heard the women in work discuss premature babies born before full term.

His expression altered in one blinding moment. It was as though the clouds that had been there were suddenly blown away and the sun had come out. 'A baby! I'm going to be a father?' He sounded totally astounded that it was happening to him.

She nodded. 'That's what it means.'

He paused as a thought hit him. 'Mum didn't mention it.'

Confident that what she'd said had hit the right chord and sure of what she had to say next, she looked up at him in the way she had once looked up at Alan Stalybridge. 'I thought it only right that you should be the first to know. I didn't want to put it in a letter unless I had to. I wanted to share the moment with you, face to face. It's our baby after all. Nobody else's.'

She held his gaze and, as she did so, noted his flushed his face.

He fell on his knees, clasped her hands within his and regarded her with awestruck wonder. 'That's good. That's good,' he said thoughtfully. 'It's only right that I should know first. Have you told your mother?'

She shook her head. 'Of course not. It had to be you. I didn't think it right to tell anyone until I'd told you.'

Suddenly he jerked her to her feet, put his arms round her and began to dance and sing, 'It had to be you, wonderful you...'

Phyllis found herself laughing tears of joy as he hugged her closer. This was the most wonderful, most intimate moment they'd had in the course of their relationship. On top of that she found herself feeling pleased because he was pleased and actually looking forward to the birth when perhaps they would become a proper little family – even though it wasn't his child. But he didn't know that. He would never know that.

To her great relief Robert interpreted her tears as joy that they were going to have a child and she was grateful that she'd got away with it. He believed her and was happy to accept that the child did indeed belong to him. He'd never guess the truth and hopefully nobody would ever tell him that it wasn't so. She had indeed made her bed by saving her reputation and guaranteeing her unborn child a stable home life. It was hardly a soft feather mattress but as good a foundation as she could make it.

32

CHRISTMAS

Maisie had festooned the house in York Street with paper chains and picked some ivy from the stone walls of the railway bridge, which she ran along the mantelpiece.

She was all alone yet the house felt so much better than it used to feel. It even felt warmer for she made sure there was a big fire in the grate, not something niggardly that barely raised a flicker.

Knowing that she'd be all alone at Christmas, Bridget had invited her for Christmas dinner with her family. Maisie had been reluctant at first, but Bridget had insisted.

'I'm not letting you stay by yourself with just a sandwich or a fry-up. You're coming with us. No argument. I will warn you that you'll be expected to wear a paper hat, pull a cracker and stand for the National Anthem. And listen to the King's Christmas speech of course.'

Christmas was over and the New Year had almost arrived when Maisie got the worst kind of news she could possibly get.

The sergeant who had called on her to say that her father had been put in prison came by to tell her that he'd given evidence against Eddie Bridgeman and would most likely receive a suspended sentence.

'He might even be home with you before the New Year.'

The bad news weighed heavy and Maisie couldn't help taking it into work. Her expression downcast and she was certainly not concentrating, she cut her fingers and looked surprised to see she wasn't wearing any plasters.

Bridget saw her expression and asked what was wrong.

Maisie gulped and looked at her without really seeing her. Then suddenly she was up from the table and running out of the door.

Bridget went after her and found her staring out through one of the diamond-shaped spaces made by the strips of protective masking tape on the window. 'What's the matter?'

Aggie joined them, her strong face frowning and full of concern. 'Come on girl. Not like our Maisie to look as though she'd found a shilling and lost a ten-bob note.'

'I don't want them in there to know,' said Maisie, her chin almost touching her chest. 'My dad's in prison.'

Aggie exchanged a glance with Bridget. They could understand her not wanting everyone to know that.

'Nobody will hear it from us,' said Bridget and Aggie agreed with her.

'Let's go into the lavs where we can talk in private,' Aggie suggested.

They found themselves alone. Aggie rested her wide backside against the door so that nobody could come in. The two of them stood there, patiently waiting for Maisie to speak.

She heaved a sigh, resigned to let it all come out.

Bridget and Aggie listened.

'They're lettin' 'im out. I thought I was goin' to 'ave the 'ouse to meself, but they're lettin' 'im out. He grassed on a bloke. It's gonna be dangerous livin' there. I can't do it,' she said, shaking her head forlornly. 'I just can't do it.'

With Bridget's arm round her shoulder, Maisie gulped.

'Tell us everything,' Bridget said softly

'Eddie got arrested. Me dad shopped 'im in return for a shorter sentence. He'll be out by the end of next week.' Another bout of helplessness threatened. 'What am I gonna do? Where am I gonna go? The almoner says she can't get me anything for another month, what with the war and time of year. I can't stay in York Street. If 'e don't kill me, Eddie Bridgeman might.'

Aggie expressed great surprise. 'Well, why didn't you say so before? I got more rooms than I know what to do with above the Llandoger. You can 'ave one of them, two if you like. I don't let out to anybody. I'm a bit choosy like that. Oh we do 'ave a few ghosts. One's got a wooden leg and there's a woman who smells of jasmine, but they're no real trouble.'

Both Maisie and Bridget looked at her in outright amazement. They had heard that Aggie let rooms out but thought it was only to passing trade, like commercial travellers. Her offer of accommodation was an answer to Maisie's prayers.

'I can't pay too much rent,' Maisie exclaimed.

Aggie laughed and crossed her big arms; they were as big as a bloke's, with fists to match. 'Do a stint in the bar a few nights a week if you like. That would do it for me, though I warn you, it can be 'ard work, fun as well. What do you say, girl? Come on. Speak up.'

It was a more ebullient Maisie who accompanied them back to the stripping room.

Bridget grabbed hold of her before they sat back down. 'Now listen to me, Maisie Miles: a problem shared is a problem halved. You should have told me about all this before.'

Maisie chewed her bottom lip as she looked down at her

shoes. 'I should 'ave done.' She breathed a huge sigh of relief. 'New year, new life by the looks of it.'

'And your old friends are still with you,' said Bridget, giving her a little shake of assurance along with her smile. 'Remember what we said? The Three Ms. All for one and one for all, though there's only two of us now. Still, who knows what might happen in the future.'

'I must get round to reading that book. What did you say it was called?'

'The Three Musketeers,' said Bridget with a beaming smile.

'She'll be all right with me,' Aggie whispered to Bridget out of Maisie's earshot. 'I reckon I can 'andle 'er old man if 'e do come calling.'

Bridget grinned. 'I don't doubt it, Aggie. I don't doubt it at all.'

* * *

Before Christmas a card had arrived from Phyllis to Bridget's home. Besides the usual greetings, there was an added note to say she was expecting a baby.

As if we didn't know, thought Bridget.

Without Phyllis needing to write another word, Bridget knew she was unhappy. She could feel it in what was not said. It occurred to her that a girl needed her mother in such a situation, so why didn't Phyllis move back in with her mother? Knowing both mother and daughter, she guessed neither of them had broached the subject. They were very different in temperament, one's sparkly exterior hiding what some might describe as a mouse or even a shrinking wallflower. Mrs Mason, on the other hand, was harder than her daughter and very rigid in her opinions.

An obvious thought came to Bridget. If they haven't spoken on the subject, perhaps she could?

Frost glazed the night air and the moon looked as though it was made from polished silver. The light snowfall of the day before had frozen on the pavements, so she and the others who cut past the gasometer and the new air-raid shelters had to pick their way more slowly than normal.

It was on a whim that Bridget directed her feet to the house where Phyllis used to live, thinking she'd have a talk with her mother, who must be feeling lonely living there all by herself. She knew very well that Phyllis wasn't happy living with Robert's mother – who would be! So with Robert away, Bridget thought she might suggest her moving back in with her mother.

A little voice kept telling her that it was none of her business, but she so hated to see any of her friends unhappy. Perhaps the reason she felt so strongly about it had something to do with Aggie Hill's solution to Maisie's unhappiness and her part in it – small as it was. Everyone needed a nudge, she further told herself, and determined it the right thing to do.

Thanks to the moon, it was easy to find the right house, though seeing as she'd lived in Marksbury Road all her life, she reckoned her feet knew their way there off by heart.

Up the garden path, she went and knocked.

'It's me. Bridget,' she replied when asked who it was.

The door was opened and she stepped in quickly, the door just as quickly shut behind her and the hall light switched on.

Mrs Mason looked very well and at first Bridget couldn't work out the reason why – and then it came to her. She was wearing make-up, including a lipstick of a similar colour to the one Phyllis usually wore.

'Come in, dear,' she said with gushing enthusiasm that Bridget couldn't recall ever seeing before. 'You're the second visitor today. This is my nephew, lately of Hamilton, Ontario.'

A man in the uniform of a Canadian serviceman got to his feet.

'This is ar Phyllis's friend, Bridget. She lives just along the road. This is Ted Hayward. My nephew.'

A pair of smiling eyes appraised her. He had a square jaw, clear eyes and broad shoulders.

Her hand was grasped in his and given a good shake. 'Pleased to meet you, Bridget. Is that an Irish name?'

She nodded. 'Yes. My dad's from Ireland, or was originally.'

Ted smiled and said: 'My mother was a Mason; Aunt Stella married her brother Fred when he came back here from Canada. My mother married Tom Hayward. He was of Welsh descent but three generations back which is why she stayed over there when Uncle Fred came back.'

'Oh really?' Bridget was confused. She'd never heard anything from Phyllis about her father coming back from Canada.

'It was before we were married,' said Mrs Mason with a girlish smirk. 'I've never been there meself.'

'I'm staying here on and off. Whenever I've got leave, this is where I'm gonna be,' said Ted Hayward.

'That's nice.' It was in fact a disaster. There was no point her suggesting that Phyllis should come back here rather than remaining unhappy with the Harveys.

Mrs Mason confirmed her worst fears. 'Ted is going to have Phyllis's room. I expect he'll get around to meeting her when he can. His mother lives in Hamilton, Ontario. That's where my husband lived before he was forced to come back. No work you see. Still, we wouldn't have met if the Canadian Government hadn't forced him too. And then there would be no Phyllis – and the new baby of course.'

There was something brittle about Mrs Mason's smile, like wallpapering over a crack in the wall.

'Will you stay for a cup of tea?' Mrs Mason asked.

Bridget declined, saying she had to get home but would pop in again.

In the meantime, there was nothing else she could do to help Phyllis – if indeed she wanted help.

33

A NEW YEAR DAWNS

The snow was piling up on the scullery roof, the fragile structure bending under its weight. If the house had been gloomy before it had started snowing, it was even more so now, the air itself seeming to have turned a desolate shade of grey.

Maisie's things were packed, but it would be some time before the horse and cart came to take her away from the Dings, St Philips' Marsh and down to King Street. In the meantime, she kept herself occupied, putting dishes, pans and cutlery away, sweeping the floor, dusting the mantelpiece and kicking against the skirting. The latter was purely to keep the mice at bay. They could have the run of the place once she was gone, but she'd like it to herself for now, thank you very much. Let her father deal with them.

She stopped scrubbing down the draining board. The sink was empty, but in her mind's eye she could see it full of dishes, feel his body against hers and hear his voice. *'You're not my daughter.'*

Bile rose in her throat. Continuing to scrub helped banish the thoughts and the words, the stench of him and the lust in his eyes. She glanced at her watch. She'd bought it for herself for Christmas. It really made her feel as though she'd gone up in the world. Sid had suggested in his last letter that she buy herself something nice for Christmas. She'd taken his advice, even though it had been some time since she'd seen him. His features were beginning to dim.

What with the watch, the cards she'd received and Christmas dinner at Bridget's, she conceded that it had been the best Christmas she'd ever had. Only the spectre of her father's imminent return diminished her current happiness.

The sudden knocking at the front door made her discard the scrubbing brush and question whether the horse and cart had come early.

Using her fingers, she brushed her hair behind her ears, then took off her apron and smoothed her hands down over her hips.

Pasting a smile on her face, she opened the door. The smile dropped more quickly than she'd acquired it when she saw it was Grace Wells standing there. She was dressed in a black coat with a brown fur collar. From her hat, a stiff net veil covered the top half of her face. Despite the veil, Maisie was instantly aware of her looking her up and down before she spoke.

At last, she said, 'You don't 'ave to invite me in if you don't want to, but I wanted to explain a few things.' There was sadness in her eyes and the corners of her mouth were downturned.

Without saying a word, Maisie opened the door wider and let the older woman step into the hallway.

'In here,' she said, pushing open the living-room door.

Thanks to her efforts, the room smelt of lavender wax polish, a smell that would linger only as long as she was in residence. It would disappear under layers of filth once her father was home from prison.

Grace Wells sniffed and looked round. 'I ain't never bin yer before. Yer mother lived in this?' She tutted in disapproval. 'It could do with knocking down.'

'I ain't got round to paint and wallpaper and I'm not going to. I'm moving out.' Maisie resisted looking at her watch and giving her grandmother the impression that she'd prefer her to leave. There were questions she wanted answering and Grace Wells was the only one who could answer them.

She offered her a seat, which was instantly accepted. Maisie remained standing, her arms folded and a defiant jut to her chin, not because she didn't welcome this visit, but because she was scared of what she was about to find out.

'Would you like a cup of tea?' Maisie asked.

Grace Wells shook her head and there was purpose in the eyes that seemed as dark as her own. 'You wanted to know why your mother said to tell me she was sorry.'

Her grandmother's eyes fixed her from the other side of a net veil that dripped melting snow like constant tears.

Maisie sank into a chair in case whatever she was about to hear made her faint. Not that she was one for fainting. She'd been brought up too tough for that. 'Ma didn't say what she was sorry for.'

The next look she received was bold and forthright. 'I know what she was sorry for, and sorry she should indeed have been.' Grace Wells sighed and looked towards the fire, her fingers flexing as she did so, as though she was seeking warmth or the details of half-buried memories. 'Your father was in prison when Gwen met John. She already had a kid – your brother?'

Maisie nodded and thought of Alf's hair, a totally different colour to her own. 'Yes. My brother. Excuse me. Are you saying that my mother was not your daughter?'

'My son John was your father. They fell in love and were planning to snatch the boy and run away together. Then she got pregnant with you. You were born six months before your father came out of prison.' The sadness in her eyes intensified. 'They let 'im out early before they 'ad time to get away.'

Maisie leaned forwards hands clasped between her knees. 'I found half a photograph. Me and me mum. Was my dad on the other half?'

Grace Wells nodded. 'I remember that photo. I should imagine yer mother tore that half off so it wouldn't rile her old man. Frank nearly killed 'er when 'e found out about 'er and my John.'

The face beneath the net veil paled until there was little difference between her complexion and the snow settling outside the window.

'John?' Maisie felt the word form along with the question it roused in her mind.

The dark eyebrows arched in the winter white face.

For her part, Maisie felt as though her body was creased, her thoughts confused. She thought of the photo in the tin, reached for it from where she'd left it on the table, prised off the lid, got it out and looked at it. Her finger scraped along the ragged edge where one half of the photo had been ripped from the other.

Maisie felt as though an electric shock had shot through her. It felt as though she had a terrible pain in her chest. Her brown eyes glistened and her heart lurched from one question to another. There was one question above all others.

'Where is he? Where's my father?' She appealed to Grace Wells, who was indeed her grandmother, but not on her mother's side, she was her father's mother.

It was suddenly as if Grace Wells had been weighed down with such heavy sadness that she was diminished in size, her face and body seeming to crumple. 'Frank killed 'im or got somebody to kill 'im. Would 'ave killed yer mother as well, but stayed his 'and. He should have been 'anged. Would 'ave been if I'd 'ad my way. My John was found in the river, 'e was. Death by misadventure, they said, but I knew different. So did yer mother. But there you are, a woman needs a man to survive in this world. Yer mother did a deal with Frank Miles. She'd betray my John as long as she didn't 'ave to give you up and 'e agreed. You were the last bit of 'im that she clung onto. That was what she was sorry for.'

Maisie remembered the bowl and the piece of rubber tube Grace Wells had shown her; the implements of abortion.

'I know what you're thinking,' Grace suddenly said, her look piercing. 'You're wondering why I didn't 'elp yer mother get rid of you. I could 'ave done, but you see...' Her eyes narrowed and a tear trickled wetly down her cheek. 'You were my son's child. My grandchild. Blood, as they say, is thicker than water. I couldn't do it. Not to my own.'

The room was becoming darker.

Grace Wells looked at the weather beyond the window then got to her feet. 'I 'ad to come and tell you the truth and put you in the picture. Now you know. I'll see meself out. You know where I am if you ever want to visit me again. And let me know where you are, if you're disposed to do so. Or you can move in, if you like.' The sad look returned. 'I get lonely livin' alone, and you being my granddaughter...'

She looked at Maisie with pleading in her eyes. Here, thought Maisie, is the offer I've been waiting for; a decent home away from York Street and the likes of Frank Miles.

One half of her thrilled at the prospect of living in a comfortable house where the wind whistled up the narrow streets of the houses on the hill. The other half kept thinking of that piece of tube and the enamel bowl. She imagined the visitors, girls and young women who'd got themselves in trouble. She imagined the bloodied results of her grandmother's stock in trade and couldn't do it. Aggie's offer was preferable.

When no answer was forthcoming, Grace Wells made her way out into the passageway. Maisie made no attempt to follow her but stayed where she was, staring into the fire, trying to compose her thoughts, to understand all that had happened, to come to a conclusion about her future.

The fire went out and the cold intensified, yet it was some time before Maisie really noticed it. The tears could have frozen on her face for all she knew. She didn't move until the driver of the horse and cart was banging on the front door.

'Coming,' she shouted, springing to her feet and brushing the wetness from her eyes.

Coat, scarf, gloves, and hat were all in place before she picked up her things and headed out of the house. She took one final look at the house she'd been brought up in.

All she wanted to take with her was packed into two battered suitcases. The rusty tea caddy had been discarded and the photograph was now nestling amongst her clothing in one of the cases. There were so few memories, though for the most part she didn't want to remember her dreary life here. She had not been close to her parents and she and Alf had their own lives.

She was still in shock following Grace Wells's visit. She could now understand why her mother had never shown her affection, the reason being that she dare not. Frank Miles would have killed the pair of them. It seemed he was quite capable of it.

She felt lighter in spirit as she closed the door to number five York Street behind her. The only regret she had was knowing that Alf was only her half-brother, though she doubted it would make much difference. They had shared the same lifestyle, endured the same uncompromising unkindness.

The driver gave her a hand up onto the seat at the front of the cart.

It was New Year's Eve and tomorrow would be New Year's Day. Although it was bitingly cold and the snow was crunching underfoot, Maisie didn't feel cold as she headed for Aggie's pub.

On arrival, she was helped down, the driver following on behind with her cases as she made her way across the slippery cobbles of King Street. She stopped just before the door and stood looking up at the black-and-white façade, the overhanging upper storeys. Despite the blackout, lead-paned windows glistened in the moonlight, each one like a sparkling diamond cutting through the gloom.

The old inn had been here for centuries and could tell many a story of times past: of Bristol sailors and Bristol people all the way back to the Middle Ages and even before that, to a time when the Anglo-Saxons had sailed up the river and called their settlement Brigstocke. How many sailors had supped beer in its bar, how many men had been press ganged onto Royal Navy ships? How many women had cried when their men had gone off to war or sailed across the Atlantic to found a new colony?

This ancient quayside hostelry had seen it all. It could tell stories, but to her, on this night, pushing open that solid oak door would be like entering a different life and she looked forward to it. Her new life had begun when she'd first started work at the tobacco factory. Since leaving school and starting work she'd found herself surrounded by people who were good to her, who didn't do her down, who didn't make her feel that she was less of a person than they were.

With that thought warming her mind, she stepped from the cobbles and onto the first of the two steps up to the door of the inn, twisted the wrought-iron ring that served as a handle and went in.

* * *

On the other side of the Atlantic and just before Christmas, Lyndon O'Neill's mother had finally confessed that she'd torn up his letter to Bridget, the girl who'd taken him on a guided tour of Bristol.

'It was in your best interests,' she'd whimpered, making a silly moue with her lips as though she was sweet sixteen. 'You'll thank me for it in time.'

He didn't believe he would ever thank her for it, but he was now forewarned. Due to the present circumstances in Europe and Britain, it was not a good time to visit. But at least he could write, even intermittently. It was too late to send Bridget a Christmas card, but if he wrote something now it should get to her some time after New Year. Who cares if a Christmas card didn't arrive until January? At least she would know he was thinking of her.

He realised any letter from her would be intercepted by his mother. To that end he arranged to use a friend's address.

'That should do it,' he said, and smiled to himself.

Bridget read the card again and again. After explaining that the letter he'd written her had gone astray and he'd only just found out about it, Lyndon O'Neill told her to write to him at a friend's address.

I'm sure it will get to me then. Be assured that I'm thinking of you. I was thinking of you on Christmas Day when the King's Christmas Speech was on the wireless – and I read of it in the newspapers. Be assured many of us over here are watching you over there.

Bridget smiled when she read the words. The King had got it right and so had Lyndon. What struck her as amazingly wonderful was that he'd heard it and thought of her.

She had heard the speech and remembered some of it off by heart. She closed her eyes and said them out loud.

'A New Year is at hand. If it brings us a peace, how thankful we will all be. If it brings us continued struggle, we shall remain undaunted.'

They would indeed remain undaunted and hopefully, in time, would meet again. In the meantime, she mouthed God Bless the King, and added, God Bless Lyndon O'Neill.

ACKNOWLEDGMENTS

With grateful thanks to Mrs Patricia Ogbourne for sharing her memories of wartime at Wills, Bristol.

MORE FROM LIZZIE LANE

We hope you enjoyed reading *The Tobacco Girls*. If you did, please leave a review.

If you'd like to gift a copy, this book is also available as an ebook, digital audio download and audiobook CD.

Sign up to Lizzie Lane's mailing list for news, competitions and updates on future books:

http://bit.ly/LizzieLaneNewsletter

ABOUT THE AUTHOR

Lizzie Lane is the author of over 50 books, a number of which have been bestsellers. She was born and bred in Bristol where many of her family worked in the cigarette and cigar factories. This has inspired her new saga series for Boldwood *The Tobacco Girls*.

Follow Lizzie on social media:

 facebook.com/jean.goodhind

 twitter.com/baywriterallatı

 instagram.com/baywriterallatsea

 bookbub.com/authors/lizzie-lane

ABOUT BOLDWOOD BOOKS

Boldwood Books is a fiction publishing company seeking out the best stories from around the world.

Find out more at www.boldwoodbooks.com

Sign up to the Book and Tonic newsletter for news, offers and competitions from Boldwood Books!

http://www.bit.ly/bookandtonic

We'd love to hear from you, follow us on social media:

facebook.com/BookandTonic

twitter.com/BoldwoodBooks

instagram.com/BookandTonic

Printed in Great Britain
by Amazon

15649676R00180